"This is a grave."

Carrie brushed away the dirt from the exposed skull. A sick feeling crept into her stomach.

"Are you sure?" Cash said. "We've only uncovered a small part."

"I'm sure." Her voice became low and subdued. "It's also human."

Cash sat back to watch Carrie's worried frown as she leaned over the skull. She had become very quiet as she studied their find.

Suddenly, the sound of loose rock coming from a steep ledge about fifteen feet above them interrupted the silence. Startled, Carrie looked up in surprise. What she saw sent a cold chill along her spine....

ABOUT THE AUTHOR

M. J. Rodgers writes the kind of book she likes to read: a mystery in which a clever heroine and hero are matched against an equally clever villain. She believes such excitement and danger prove a perfect backdrop for the ultimate of all thrills— meeting that special someone and experiencing the magic of falling in love.

Books by M. J. Rodgers

HARLEQUIN INTRIGUE
102–FOR LOVE OR MONEY
128–A TASTE OF DEATH
140–BLOODSTONE
157–DEAD RINGER

Don't miss any of our special offers. Write to us at the following address for information on our newest releases.

Harlequin Reader Service
P.O. Box 1397, Buffalo, NY 14240
Canadian address: P.O. Box 603,
Fort Erie, Ont. L2A 5X3

Bones of Contention

M. J. Rodgers

Harlequin Books

TORONTO • NEW YORK • LONDON
AMSTERDAM • PARIS • SYDNEY • HAMBURG
STOCKHOLM • ATHENS • TOKYO • MILAN

For my brother, Patrick,
who combines those rare qualities of sophisticated
good looks and heartbreaking tenderness

Harlequin Intrigue edition published December 1991

ISBN 0-373-22176-2

BONES OF CONTENTION

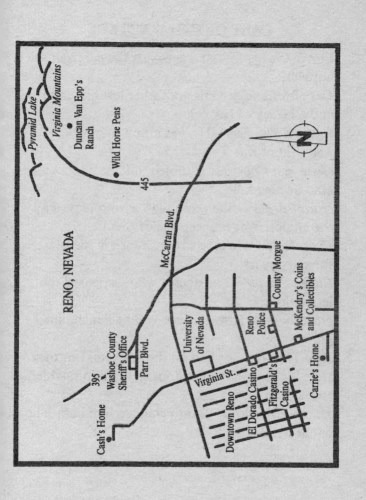

RENO, NEVADA

Pyramid Lake

Virginia Mountains

Duncan Van Epp's Ranch

Wild Horse Pens

445

McCartan Blvd.

395

Washoe County Sheriff's Office

Parr Blvd.

Cash's Home

University of Nevada

Virginia St.

Downtown Reno

El Dorado Casino

Fitzgerald's Casino

Reno Police

County Morgue

McKendry's Coins and Collectibles

Carrie's Home

N

CAST OF CHARACTERS

Carrie Chase—What tragedy of the past will she unravel?

Cash McKendry—His godfather left him land and a legacy of suspicion.

Edward Van Epp—He was about to marry wealth, but was it enough?

Gene Van Epp—He gambled, and he had a gun. Had he also killed?

Nora Burney—She was a lawyer who played all the angles. Was murder one of them?

Evan Wahl—He carried vengeance in his heart for sixty years.

Eileen Packer—The doctor who dispensed the lethal dose.

Hal Sawyer—How far had Wahl's henchman gone?

Ann Tintori—She had all the answers. But they were locked behind the door to her mind, which she couldn't open up.

Duncan Van Epp—Death claimed him before he could tell the truth.

Prologue

1931

Duncan Van Epp toiled all through the moonlit November night to dig the grave. He set the kerosene lamps beside the large, gray rock and pried the crusted top layer of high Nevada desert soil loose with the sharp steel of his shovel. When he reached the deeper, closer-packed sediments, he switched to the pickax. Slowly, painfully, he hacked the inches from the hard, ungiving desert ground, shivering as the freezing night air seeped through his clothing to ice his bones.

Somewhere inside, a disbelieving voice told him he must be in a nightmare. He couldn't be a murderer. But as recent memory flooded back, he realized he hadn't been given a choice.

His smooth hands burned from the ubiquitous cuts and chafing meted out by the pickax's rough, wooden handle. He uncurled his hands from its long shaft, taking a quick look at his shaking palms, ghostlike in the moonlit night, and sticky with blood, not all his own.

A sudden neigh from Duncan's mare fettered a few feet away brought his dark head up and his hand reaching for the rifle. Cold fear tightened the tendons in his neck as he looked around warily for signs of an intruder to his grisly night's errand.

A taut, quiet moment passed. Then the mare whinnied again and he realized she was protesting only because she wanted to be inside a warm barn on such a cold night. He put the rifle down in relief, took out and unwrapped a couple of blankets from his saddlebags, throwing one over the mare's broad back. He cloaked a second blanket over the back of the unprotesting burro huddling beside her. Then he tore up an old cotton shirt, circling the strips around his sore and bleeding palms.

It didn't help much. He felt like a thousand sharp knives stabbed into his hands when once again he raised the pickax. A hot poker of pain burned deep between his shoulder blades as the hours crawled by. And as he raised a hand to brush away the cold sweat from his eyes, he found hot tears spilling onto his cheeks.

Duncan fought against this other pain, the one that constricted his heart. Time could not be spent in mourning the dead while the living fought to survive. They were in this together now. For better, for worse, forever. So on he pounded until the tentative beams of first light stretched into a yawning haze across the purple hills of the desert horizon.

His arms were barely able to hold the pickax handle any more as he staggered around the hole, the labored wheeze of his exertions roaring in his ears. Was the grave deep enough?

It had to be deep enough. Time had run out. The sleepy, little town of Contention would be awake soon, and he, one of its leading citizens, must be back in his house, tonight's business a secret shame he would have to live with for the rest of his life.

He dropped the shovel and pickax onto the rim of the grave and lifted himself out. The two dark bundles lay where he had placed them on the ground beside the burro. He grabbed the arm of the largest and dragged it over to the hard-won hole.

Stopping at the edge, he looked at the dead body and shivered as an icy drop of sweat streaked down his spine. His mind groped for the words he should say, for the remorse he should feel, but he could find neither so he just rolled the body over into the hole.

It dropped with a shuddering thud in the still night. Stone-faced, Duncan stared at it lying at the bottom of the grave before turning away to get the second body.

This smaller body he cradled in his arms before he lowered it gently next to the larger one. There was no time to dig a separate grave for it or he would have. He tossed the gun in after the bodies without pause or ceremony. Then he grasped the shovel with his battered and bleeding hands and thrust it into the large earth mound surrounding the grave. Within half an hour, he had re-covered the hole that had taken him all night to dig.

He scattered brush over the barren top of the newly dug grave. This was an isolated spot; still one had to be cautious. He gathered his kerosene lamps from in front of the gray rock and smothered the wicks to kill the flames. Then he carefully placed them on the back of the burro and hid the shovel and ax in two burlap bags should early morning eyes greet him on his return. As he mounted the mare, his eyes rose to the east where dawn stretched out its silver strokes to paint the desert sagebrush.

A fresh, clean new day, he thought, exhaling a long, exhausted breath. He felt bone tired and sick in his soul, but it was done.

As he rode toward the dawn, the mare's quickened pace matched his own desire to be in the warmth and the light. Yet he could feel the cold darkness clutching at him from behind, dragging him emotionally back to that ledge in the foothills.

His thick, dark eyebrows met in a heavy frown as his head slowly turned backward. Would he ever really be free of the terror of tonight? Or would what he had buried in the high Nevada desert above the small, sleepy town of Contention travel with him the rest of his days?

Chapter One

Present Day

Duncan Van Epp's sun- and age-wrinkled hands carefully grasped the arms of his chair as his thin, ancient body sank into the oversize cushions. Resting back with a sigh, he squinted contentedly into the last rays of a golden desert sunset shimmering through the slatted window blinds.

The years had replaced his thick, black hair with a thin tuft of white fringe extending from ear to ear. His once heavy, dark eyebrows now resembled the wispy remnants of white cotton balls that had gotten stuck in some spilled glue. But beneath them shone two lively and intelligent eyes, evidence of a clear and fast-moving underground spring in the otherwise parched and caking landscape of his face.

Those eyes sparkled now as he watched this special day come to a close, knowing more than its light had reached an end. The years of silence were finally over. He had contacted them all, except for the sheriff's office. He'd do that tomorrow.

Tonight he was giving them a chance to come by to try to talk him out of it. They wouldn't. He had only agreed to see them so he could try again to make them understand.

Even the hawk tries impossible flights in order to find the reach of its wings. Now where had he heard that? Oh yes, it was an old Indian saying his father and grandfather had told him when he was just a boy as they sat together in this very room.

Duncan looked around his rough desert home, as though trying to see his grandparents at work building it after their long trip from Europe a hundred and thirty years before. Insulation, plumbing, electricity had all been added, but the original sturdy timber was still standing up to the test of time. He could almost see his grandfather's hands nailing each board into place with care and hope as he built a new future for them all. Had it been worth the sacrifice? Would his grandfather be proud of him today?

Almost ninety and I'm still worried about what my grandfather would think of the wrongs I'm trying to right, he mused. But he smiled as he felt the perceptible lifting of a sixty-year-old weight.

He had just one wish left. More than anything else he wanted to be able to convince them he was doing the right thing. That's why he had warned them. But it was only his old friend, Ann Tintori, who could have changed his mind.

She hadn't. Not that she didn't try when he had called her that afternoon. "Leave well enough alone," she had pleaded just as she had those many years before except this time Duncan could tell there had been no conviction in her voice. Her recent stroke had taken its toll, or perhaps she, too, was seeking relief from their long silence.

Duncan felt a bump against his leg at the same time he heard the hefty knock at the door. He looked down into the bright, curious eyes of Bonanza, his wire-haired fox terrier, as he dropped a hand to pat the little white head reassuringly. Then he slowly raised himself out of his chair and limped to the door.

They were here. The time had come.

ONE OF Duncan Van Epp's visitors stood listening to another's entreaties knowing now, after nearly two hours, that such pleas were useless.

What was to be done? The question brought a growing panic to eat at the insides of the visitor until suddenly a solution, the only solution, came to mind. Duncan Van Epp would have to die. Tonight. His insistence on telling all these dangerous things from the past had just succeeded in digging the old fool's grave. And this visitor would be happy to shove him into it.

CASH MCKENDRY WORE a worried frown as he watched his elderly grandmother, Ann Tintori, muttering to herself as she shuffled through her old files at the University of Nevada at Reno. She'd been so insistent when she called that morning, he'd rushed right over to her place. He'd let himself hope that her immediate memories were improving. But the only thing he'd been able to piece together from her disjointed answers was that his godfather, Duncan Van Epp, had called the afternoon before and triggered some need in her to dig into some old records.

"My missing journals," was all she would answer to his questions on what she hoped to find in her old office files at the university. Still it was an improvement. Except now, as Cash stood watching her frantically leafing through the stacks of old anthropology lesson plans and student reports, he felt the familiar pain in his heart for the loss of the sharp mind that had once dwelt beneath the beloved, snow-white curls.

There was nothing he could do but wait and hope. A frustrated tear escaped onto her cheek as her wrinkled liver-spotted hands tore at the records. Cash knew he could bear to watch no longer.

He turned and left the room. If things ran their normal course, she'd soon forget why she had come. He shoved his hands into his pockets and walked down the polished hallway, trying to choke down the frustration that lumped in his throat.

Purposely he buried his thoughts deep into memories of happier times with his grandmother, before her stroke had so devastatingly changed their lives. Then suddenly he found all his attention abruptly excavated as his casual glance into an open classroom door revealed the incongruous sight of a lovely woman holding a skull. Her words rang clear and ominous into the hallway where he stood.

"This man was murdered."

CARRIE CHASE carefully lifted the human skull up into the light so that the gaping bullet hole could be clearly seen. She waited for the moment when all eyes had focused on the deadly circle of light penetrating the top, right frontal skull plate. Then she quickly pulled a hand away, letting the skull's loose bottom jaw drop on its squeaky hinge, as though the long-dead man had opened his mouth in screaming torment.

The nerve-jarring squeaks of the swinging jawbone brought many nervous coughs and shuffling feet throughout the classroom. But although her students' unease made her smile internally, Carrie's expression remained grave as she continued with her dramatic opening lecture.

Her eyes traveled soberly around the room, eventually drawn to those of a very handsome student who had just stepped inside and was sitting down right before her in the front row. He had a lion's mane mixture of light brown and golden blond hair and his eyes reflected those same pleasing colors. She judged him to be around thirty-five, quite a bit older than the students sitting around him. When her eyes paused to gaze into his, he smiled in open invitation.

Disconcerted, she looked away to concentrate on her story of the skull she held. "This skeleton was found last year when new mining operations in the ghost town of Contention unearthed his bones in the basement of an old boardinghouse. Despite the unorthodox site of his resting place, there was a cross over the grave. Such a marker was curious considering the method of his demise and interment, but it tells us that at least someone had feelings for this man."

Carrie explored the skull with her fingertips as though trying to understand what those feelings might have been, before she continued, "The police couldn't identify him. I've named him Ernie because, well, anthropologists always feel compelled to personalize the human bones they find. Maybe it's because we don't want to forget that once they were part of a living person."

Carrie took a moment to listen to the hushed quiet of her students as she continued to stare at the skull in her hand. She could still feel the handsome student's eyes watching her and made a mental note to purposely avoid looking in his direction.

"Ernie was only about twenty-five when he was shot. His left-handed murderer made Ernie clasp his hands behind his head and kneel before he pulled the trigger. The position was painful because Ernie had just suffered a bad leg injury."

Carrie paused, waiting for the inevitable question that came at this time during her opening lecture. Curiously, it was the handsome student sitting directly in front of her who asked it.

His voice was pleasantly deep. It brought the eyes of many of the women students in his direction, and once there, Carrie noticed they stayed to enjoy the view. She understood why.

"I thought you said this skeleton was never identified."

Carrie nodded. "That's right."

The handsome student crossed his powerfully built tanned arms over his broad chest in a clear body-language challenge. "Well, then how can you possibly know what happened?"

Carrie looked back to the skull she still held in her hand as though she saw something in the dark, hollow eye sockets.

"Ernie told me," she said. She looked back at her students, making eye contact with several around the room, finally resting on the gold-brown eyes of the handsome student in the front row. "And after this course on physical anthropology, you will find that the bones of the dead will also speak to you."

The next silence was a contemplative one that Carrie had also been expecting. She knew most students were considering the possibilities in her statement, a little excited by them and a little doubtful that they would really ever be able to read bones.

As she gave them time to think over her words, she could see from the corner of her eye that the handsome student's gaze never left her face. A small, knowing grin remained on his lips, as though he, too, had a secret he'd be willing to share. Despite her resolve to remain aloof, she felt a very unprofessional curiosity about him.

She distracted her thoughts by acknowledging a raised hand from a squeaky-voiced young woman in the back row.

"How can you be sure it was murder? Couldn't that wound have been self-inflicted?"

Carrie shook her head. "Suicide isn't a logical conclusion from the skeletal evidence. Notice that the bullet entered the top right edge of the frontal bone and headed down into the skull. Could you shoot yourself with a rifle that way?"

Carrie watched as most members of the class made a rifle barrel out of their arms trying to find a likely position. She noticed the handsome student just sat watching her. Finally a female student on the end of the front row who was obviously left-handed spoke up. "This is impossible."

The gold-brown mane of the man in the front row nodded. "Just about the only way you could shoot yourself with a rifle would be if you pointed the barrel under your chin and were able to extend your arms to reach the trigger."

Carrie nodded at him in approval as she tucked some long strands of warm brown hair behind her right ear. "Yes, discharging a rifle so that the bullet entered your right frontal bone is virtually impossible. Therefore logic tells us that this man couldn't have committed suicide."

A male voice in the back called out. "Was the part about Ernie kneeling because of the angle of the bullet entry?"

Carrie smiled. "Yes. Very good."

The left-handed female student wasn't convinced. "Couldn't the shooter have just been taller?"

Carrie walked over to stand beside the skeleton for comparison. "I'm five-eleven, tall for a woman, over the average height for a man. Compare my size to this skeleton's and tell me what you think."

The handsome student in the front row spoke up again. "I think I see what you're getting at. With added muscle and flesh, Ernie would probably have been as tall as you. A shooter, holding a rifle at shoulder's height, would have had to be extraordinarily tall to have shot down at him."

Carrie nodded, encouraged by the accuracy of his words.

"Right. The bullet entered the frontal bone, traveled through the brain and came out at the top left of the occipital bone, or bottom back of the head. Here you can see the exit hole."

Carrie turned the skull around to point out the bullet's ragged exit point. "It was retrieved, and judging from its .45-70 caliber, the police believe it to have been fired from an 1880 Springfield .45-70 trapdoor loader, for those of you who are gun fanciers."

The male student from the middle row interrupted. "You mean this guy could have been killed in the 1800s?"

"No, not that long ago or there would have been more petrifaction of Ernie's bones from the alkaline soil in which the skeletal remains were found."

"But the gun..." the student began.

The handsome man in the front row spoke up again. "Rifles like the 1880 Springfield were still quite popular forty to fifty years after they were initially introduced."

Carrie nodded, pleased at his offered information, as she continued with the thought. "That's right. And whereas it would be difficult to accurately date a bullet from such a gun, the petrifaction of Ernie's bones makes it quite clear that he died about sixty years ago."

"What is 'petrifaction'?" a student in the back asked.

"It's a derivative of the word, 'petrify,'" she explained, "which means to convert into stone or a stony substance. Like petrified wood, after a time, bones can become rigid or inert. Ernie's bones underwent petrifaction."

Carrie watched the forward position of most of her students. Their interest had been caught in the subject. When her look inadvertently strayed to the handsome student's face, she could also tell his interest had been caught, but not just for physical anthropology. Experiencing mixed reactions, she hurried on.

"But getting back to what I was saying. The fire power and resultant skull damage indicate the shooter was about six feet away. The distance from the target, the needed height and the angle of entry required meet the geometrical probability that Ernie was kneeling and this shooter was standing in front of him aiming his rifle at Ernie's head.''

"You said the murderer was left-handed. Is that from the bullet path, too?'' the squeaky-voiced student asked.

"Yes. The bullet entered Ernie's right frontal bone here and exited in a slightly left position here. Although not conclusive, the sheriff tells me that's common when the shooter is left-handed.''

For the first time, a plump young woman in the first row, sitting next to the handsome student, raised her hand timidly. Carrie nodded to encourage her question.

"How did you get possession of the skeleton?''

"My brother is a detective with the Washoe County Sheriff's Department,'' Carrie said. "When the skeleton was found, I was called in on the case to date the bones. Since there was no recorded murder having taken place sixty years ago in the ghost town of Contention and since no records existed that would help to identify Ernie, my brother arranged for the sheriff's office to donate the remains to the University of Nevada so that I might have a visual aid in my discussions. He's an interesting one, isn't he?''

Most heads around the room nodded, but Carrie could feel the handsome student's admiring eyes watching her every movement as she patted Ernie's skull. His deep voice spoke up again.

"You keep saying 'he.' How do you even know that's a man's skeleton? I thought bones were sexless.''

Carrie tried to forget how very attractive he was so she could keep her thoughts clear. "That's almost true. Let me put Ernie's skull back on top of his spinal column and together we'll take a closer look at him.''

She stepped back and repositioned the skull on the skeletal pedestal. Then she stepped away so as not to block her students' view of the skeleton and faced her class once again.

"Ernie is basically tall and big boned and—''

"What do you mean by 'basically tall'?'' another student asked.

"My qualification is because of two things. First, sixty years ago people were shorter in stature on the average because of poorer nutrition. We've decided Ernie was probably five-eleven. That would have been considered tall in those days. However, Ernie suffered from an untreated congenital left hip dislocation, which caused his left leg bone to grow shorter and no doubt made him limp."

"How can you tell about the hip dislocation?" the handsome student asked.

Carrie pointed to the skeleton. "You can see it when you compare the ball-like head of the femur, or thigh bone, of the two legs. The right one fits into the cuplike socket in the pelvis to form a joint, but the left one won't fit. That's because it lay outside at birth. And notice these osteophytes or abnormal outgrowths of new bone are quite noticeable at the margins of the joint surfaces of Ernie's left femur and indicate he suffered from premature osteoarthritis because of the abnormality."

"And he looked shorter because he limped," a student offered.

"Yes, from the congenital hip dislocation, which, by the way, affects many more females than males. But even so, Ernie isn't female. He's tall with big bones and those physical aspects generally mean the skeleton is that of a male."

"But you're as tall as Ernie," another student protested.

"True, but today a woman of five-eleven, although certainly above average, occurs much more frequently in our population. In 1930, a female of that height would have been quite rare. Interpretation of anthropological finds relies heavily on deductive reasoning. An anthropologist makes quantifiable observations and then carefully evaluates them in the light of known data."

"What are some other quantifiable differences between you and Ernie?" Although facing away from him, Carrie recognized the handsome student's deep voice. She turned toward him, attempting to keep her voice even.

"Well, were you to see my bones you would notice they are not nearly as thick as Ernie's. That's because bones get bigger and thicker in response to heavier muscle and weight.

In a mixed population of men and women, most men would be taller, more muscular than most women, although admittedly there would be some women taller and more muscular than some men.''

His gold-brown eyes gleamed as they did a quick survey of her frame. "So how can you be sure you don't have an extraordinarily tall, muscular woman from the 1930s there?"

A packet of warmth started up Carrie's spine as his eyes traveled over her body. He wasn't just a handsome man. He was intelligent, too, and she was finding both his physical draw and the intellectual challenge in his questions very stimulating.

"I can see you're not going to believe without indisputable proof," she said. "That's good. It's what being an anthropologist or any scientist is all about. Fortunately for me, Ernie can give you such proof because there's one absolutely sure way to decide if you're dealing with a male skeleton as opposed to a female's, and that's to look at the pelvis."

Carrie shifted her position. "Now, Ernie's pelvis as you can see is tall and narrow. If the skeleton was female, the pelvis would be broad and flat. That's because a female has a pelvic cavity that is larger and designed to make room for the passage of a baby."

His eyes, just for a moment, seemed to dart from Ernie's pelvis to hers. Carrie felt the heat packet from her spine begin to climb into the back of her neck. Relaxing under those eyes was a trick that might take the whole term to master.

Another student on the end of the front row spoke up. "How did you decide that Ernie was in pain while he was kneeling?"

Carrie picked up the skeleton's right leg, thankful for the change of subject. "You see this deep crack? That's in the tibia, the larger of the two bones that extend from the knee to the ankle. Ernie couldn't have been comfortable in any position, but kneeling must have been excruciating."

The squeaky-voiced woman in the back row spoke up again. "You said earlier that he had his hands clasped behind his head when he was shot. How could you possibly know that?''

Carrie smiled as she grasped Ernie's bony wrists and raised them for all to see. She entwined the finger bones together, mimicking the position of clasped hands.

"Look closely. What do you see?''

The students' eyes were squinting at Ernie's bony hands.

The left-handed female student in the front row spoke up first. "The middle finger bones! They've been splintered. The bullet passed through them!''

Carrie smiled at her. "Very good. Actually the bullet was found still embedded in the proximal phalanx of the right middle finger. That's the first extended finger bone out of the hand. Considering the exit wound in the skull, the fingers had to be clasped behind the head in order for the bullet to be found there.''

The deep voice from her handsome student in the front row didn't sound satisfied. "Couldn't the injury to the fingers have occurred long before Ernie was killed?''

Carrie shook her head as she cautiously looked in his direction. "No. Bones are living tissue, containing cells, blood vessels and nerves. If living bone is cut, it bleeds. If it's broken, it heals. As we learn more about reading bones, you'll be able to recognize that this deep crack in the tibia and the splintering of the proximal phalanxes show no evidence of healing so they had to have occurred at the time of death.''

His gold-brown mane nodded in understanding as his eyes held hers until the next question came from somewhere to her left.

"How did you know he was about twenty-five?''

Carrie tore her eyes away from the handsome student's face. "It all has to do with bone aging signs or lack of them. And for that we need to discuss osteophytosis...''

She went on to explain the process of bone aging, keeping her eyes on Ernie until the bell rang signaling the end to the hour. She was satisfied to see that her students were as surprised as she was at the quick passage of time. Being able to catch their interest on the first day was half the battle.

While her students gathered up their notes and books, Carrie concentrated on rolling Ernie's stand out the doorway and down the hall to the office where she could lock him up for safekeeping until the next class. Just as she approached the office door, however, she was startled as it was suddenly sprung open from the other side, and Carrie found herself looking into the dark, sardonic, good looks of Edward Van Epp III.

He took his time stepping aside for her to pass. Edward had always displayed a proud, arrogant air, far too superior for Carrie to find enjoyment in the company of the thirtyish, black-haired, black-eyed associate professor of business. She knew most women in the department envied her shared office space with Edward and couldn't understand her lack of interest in one of the few attractive, single faculty men. But she had found on their only date that being around Edward's special brand of macho maleness was a real turnoff.

Now, as she rolled Ernie through the open doorway, she could see the perceptible straightening of Edward's carriage as he tried to emphasize the two inches he had on her. She smiled in secret amusement until she entered the room. Then the smile faded as she realized they were not alone. A small, frail, elderly lady was sitting at a rectangular table that was heaped with old records. Carrie halted in her tracks. It wasn't like Edward to let in outsiders and it definitely wasn't like Edward to let outsiders go through university records as this woman appeared to be doing.

Apparently Carrie's expression was transparent because Edward immediately grabbed her arm in his typically overbearing manner that had long ago caused her to forget every one of his good looks.

"Don't recognize her, do you, toots?"

"Please don't call me toots, Edward," Carrie said for the thousandth time as she extricated her arm from his clutches.

Edward shrugged indifferently. "I suppose it's up to me to introduce you. Come on."

Curiosity concerning their visitor overrode Carrie's distaste for Edward's manner as she followed him across the room.

"Carrie Chase, assistant professor of anthropology, this is Ann Tintori, professor emeritus of anthropology and the founder of your department."

Carrie's face broke into a surprised and delighted smile when she realized she was face-to-face with the celebrated woman whose anthropological discoveries and meticulous interpretations had long ago become legend to her. She extended her hand eagerly.

"Dr. Tintori! I can't tell you what a pleasure it is to meet you."

Ann Tintori's pale, colorless eyes looked up at Carrie and blinked as through she was trying to bring her face into focus. "Chase? Do I know you?"

Carrie stepped around the table, her hand still outstretched. "No reason you should, Dr. Tintori. I've yet to publish one book, much less the forty or so you've produced in your career."

Ann seemed to notice Carrie's outstretched hand for the first time and gave it a limp shake. "I have written books, haven't I?"

Uncomfortably, Carrie became aware that the initial confusion she had seen in Ann's eyes had still not lifted. Indeed, the more she stared at Carrie the greater it became. As it deepened, the woman's lips tightened as though determined to hang on to something, and she bent her head again to the folders on the desk.

"I've got to find something. It's very important. I wonder what it was."

A sick little knot tied itself in Carrie's stomach. She began to remember the gossip that had floated around the department, hinting that the brilliant and celebrated anthropologist had resigned her position because of a failing mind. Carrie had dismissed the gossip. But she couldn't dismiss Ann's behavior. Feeling incredibly sad at the deterioration of such a scholar, Carrie watched Ann's unsteady hands as they hesitantly shuffled through the dog-eared reports.

Suddenly, a deep, familiar voice coming from the open door behind her had Carrie instantly pivoting toward the newcomer.

"Grandmother, is everything all right?"

Carrie blinked in new surprise as she recognized the handsome student from her lecture standing at the door, and the import of his words sunk in. He was Ann Tintori's grandson?

Cash came forward quickly and rested a hand on his grandmother's shoulder. Although he was pleased to find his lovely instructor here, at the moment his thoughts were for Ann. Meeting strangers always distressed her and brought on more confusion. He chastised himself for leaving her alone. Her head had turned up at his words. He could see the tears in her eyes. "I came here looking for something, didn't I?" her frail little voice asked.

He squatted beside her chair and put his arm more securely about her in a comforting hug. "It's okay. We'll probably find your missing journals at home. Let's go see."

Ann nodded and Cash gently helped her to her feet. But he stopped when he came face-to-face with Carrie and he smiled. She watched his previous look of worry give way to one of interest.

"Well, Edward, aren't you going to introduce us?" Cash asked, not taking his eyes from Carrie's face.

Edward's voice sounded irritated as he complied. "Cash McKendry, Carrie Chase."

As Cash's hand closed over hers, Carrie could feel her own suddenly dwarfed by its considerable warmth and bulk. But his touch was not the rough attempt to establish an unspoken domination like the handshake she had experienced of so many men. It was more like a warm invitation that extended down her spine and made her legs feel deliciously weak.

Her own hand wrapped around his as she looked up into his gold-brown eyes, taking in his height and the expanse of his chest and feeling once again that disturbing excitement he had brought to her early morning class. She judged him to be at least six-four, a marvel in itself to a tall woman of five-eleven, who, even when she wore flats, always seemed to be looking down at men.

With conscious effort, she found her voice. "You're not really a student here, are you?"

His grin slowly broadened. "Just passing some time while I waited for my grandmother. You managed to make the wait interesting and...stimulating."

Carrie felt his look like a caress across her cheeks. She withdrew her hand from the lingering hold of his and fought down the color she knew was rapidly rising up her neck as she purposely looked away and cleared her throat for the next question.

"What do you do when you're not crashing lectures?"

"Cash is a numismatist," Edward's sour voice cut in. "Has an office just south of the downtown casinos on Virginia Street."

Carrie looked questioningly at Cash.

"Numismatist is a fancy name for coin collector," he explained, smiling. "Edward is just being scholarly about the terminology. Have you met my grandmother?"

Carrie nodded. "Just a moment before you came in, although I feel I've known her all my life. I've read all her books and most of her articles in the scientific journals. Meeting a legend in the flesh is a bit of a thrill."

Cash's smile grew as he heard the sincerity in Carrie's voice. But he read a slight shadow in her blue-gray eyes and realized she must understand Ann was not altogether well.

He hated to see the disappointment. He decided then to take a chance of showing Carrie a better side of his grandmother—her still intact and sharp analytical abilities that had fortunately come through unscathed from the stroke's memory deprivation.

He leaned over to gather Ann's tiny form within one of his long arms. "Perhaps you'd like to take a look at Ernie, Grandmother? He's an interesting set of bones Ms. Chase uses in her lecture."

To Carrie's surprise, Ann Tintori nodded. Encouraged at the response, Carrie wasted no time in retrieving Ernie from where she had left him just inside the door. She rolled him into the middle of the room for the elderly anthropologist's appraisal.

Carrie couldn't be sure, but Ann's pale eyes looked less confused, more alert as she became lost in the study of the skeleton. It took only a couple of minutes for her to finger the bones and make her proclamation. "Male, under thirty, injuries to right tibia and proximal phalanx, shot to death between fifty and seventy years ago."

The quick analysis startled Carrie and underlined everything she had heard or read about the famous anthropologist. Despite whatever confusion dwelt beneath those white curls, a sharp analytical ability still remained. Carrie found it immensely heartening as she reached for Ann's frail hand and shook it warmly. "That was wonderful."

Ann's face lit up, all at once looking younger and more at ease with a sharper focus in her pale eyes.

Delighted to see it, Carrie went on. "It took me over an hour to reach similar conclusions and that was aided by instruments, a soil sample and knowing precisely where and how deep Ernie had been buried beneath that old boardinghouse in Contention. For you to be able to just walk up to him and—"

Carrie stopped in midsentence as she saw a look of blunt horror contorting the fine features of Ann Tintori's face. Then Carrie's stunned surprise vaulted into absolutely raw and stupefying shock as the elderly woman collapsed against her grandson, shrieking loud enough to wake the dead.

Chapter Two

Carrie was too shocked to speak in the intervening moments when Cash cradled his distraught grandmother in his arms, working frantically to quiet her with his touch and assurances. Gradually her screams disintegrated into incoherent muttering, which in turn finally subsided into recurring head-to-toe shudders.

And all the time Carrie just stood before them watching, dumb and immobile and feeling wretchedly responsible although she had no idea what it was she had done wrong. When the old woman had quieted, Carrie found herself shivering anew as she watched the vacant, glassy look that fixated in Ann's pale eyes. Somehow that look was even worse than her earlier screaming.

When Carrie finally found her voice, it was barely a croak. "I'm so sorry."

As Cash looked up at her, Carrie read a deep worry and concern in both his eyes and voice. "You've nothing to be sorry about. You did nothing wrong. I don't know what has caused this unusual behavior in my grandmother. But I think that now she's quieted down, I'd best take her home."

Carrie nodded. She watched feeling quite helpless and sad for them both as Cash all but carried Ann Tintori out the door. When they had left, Carrie sank into the nearest chair feeling as limp and wrung-out as a dishrag.

"Now there's a woman whose old belfry is full of nothing but bats," Edward's voice said behind her. Carrie had forgotten he was even in the room. She bristled at the callousness in his tone.

"Edward, that's not a very charitable thing to say. It's obvious the woman's behavior is not something she can control."

Edward gave her his sardonic half smile. "Isn't that precisely what I said? Come on, toots, don't let the old bag rattle your brain cells. Just be glad it's McKendry and not you who has to deal with Lady Loony-Toons."

Carrie frowned in profound irritation at the disrespect in Edward's voice and words, but knowing him as she did, she also knew nothing she could say would have any effect. She refocused her thoughts to other things. "Have you known Cash McKendry long?"

"Long but not well. His grandmother and my great-uncle, Duncan, used to be tight. Duncan is McKendry's godfather so my brother, Gene, and I used to see McKendry when we were growing up."

Carrie's eyebrows lifted. "Duncan is Cash's godfather?"

Edward nodded. "Yeah, like I said, Duncan and Ann Tintori were tight for a lot of years. We all grew apart though. I think Gene and McKendry have crossed paths on occasion. But frankly I hadn't even seen McKendry or his grandmother in years until this morning."

"You didn't know Ann Tintori when she taught here?"

Edward shook his head. "She was a little before my time. Naturally, I heard all the stories about how she was losing it so bad the board of trustees put their foot down a couple of years ago and convinced her to resign. After seeing this morning's little display, all I can say is it's a good thing."

Carrie shook her head sadly. "It must have been hard on her to have to resign her academic position that way."

Edward shrugged as he pressed his palms together, flexing his biceps in complete unconcern. "Old should make way for the young. Look, I've got to get going. I'm meeting Margaret for brunch."

Carrie drew a blank for a second until she remembered that Margaret was Edward's fiancée. Part of the reason she knew she had forgotten was because she was still surprised that the obnoxious business professor had somehow managed six months before to meet and sweep the sophisticated and very eligible Reno heiress, Margaret Preston, right off her feet.

Of course, objectively Carrie admitted Edward was smart and good-looking, in a macho, insolent way. But she couldn't imagine a woman falling for a man with his particular brand of arrogance. Still, she knew she was hardly a barometer of the vagaries of love, and Reno's most sought-after heiress must have found something there to quicken the heartbeat.

She tried a polite inquiry. "How is Margaret?"

Edward's tone assumed its unflinchingly superior air. "Typical woman. Falling apart with nervousness that the wedding won't be well attended. Her family comes from old wealth so appearances are very important. Invitations have gone out to the mayor and governor."

Carrie raised an eyebrow, not because she was impressed at the possible wedding guests, but she was beginning to see from a sudden gleam in Edward's eye how much he was, despite the flippant disdain that laced his words.

"I'm visiting Duncan today, Edward. Why don't you bring Margaret by, too, so he can finally meet her?"

Edward wrinkled his nose and hurried toward the door like the room had suddenly developed an unpleasant odor. "Get real, toots. Duncan's old desert ranch isn't anything I'd want to take my woman to see. I'll catch you later."

Carrie shook her head. Edward had introduced Carrie to Duncan on their first and only date, nearly a year before. Indeed, she suspected Edward had brought her along to see his great-uncle as an excuse to not stay long at the elderly man's desert ranch.

But Edward had miscalculated. It proved intellectual love at first sight between Duncan, the eighty-nine-year-old retired lawyer, and Carrie, the thirty-year-old college instructor. She and Edward had ended up spending the whole day with the old gentleman at Carrie's insistence.

Carrie had started visiting Duncan on her own after that, bringing him provisions that she knew must be difficult for him to get since he lived so far from town and no longer drove. Over the past year, Carrie knew he had come to depend on her visits—not just for the provisions but for their talks. And she wouldn't have missed his stories of early Nevada for the world.

Which was why she couldn't understand Edward or his brother, Gene. Although Duncan's only relatives, they pointedly ignored him. If Duncan had been a disagreeable old man, she might have understood their avoidance even if she couldn't condone it. But he was a delightful personality with a sharp mind and the ability to make the most beautiful figurines out of the hard, obsidian rock he found in the desert earth surrounding his home.

It was this ever-expanding collection that added particular spice to Carrie's visits. With patience and care he had carved the glassy, vitreous volcanic stone into beautiful works of art, using the obsidian's subtle tonal gradations to help form the desert images he knew best: curled rattlesnakes, delicate sagebrush or quirky piñon trees.

Just thinking about the small works of art made Carrie wonder what he might have for her today. She checked her watch and found that it was already nine-thirty and knew she'd best be on her way. It would take her about forty-five minutes to drive from the center of Reno to the small northwestern ghost town that had once been the thriving silver town of Contention. On its barren desert outskirts was the ranch that belonged to Duncan Van Epp.

The day was already hot and dry as the Jeep buzzed along the two-lane highway. Under the engine's pleasant drone, Carrie's thoughts began to wander to Cash McKendry and she wondered why Duncan had never talked about his godson. Or had he? Now that she thought about it, Carrie did seem to remember Duncan mentioning a godson.

Well, today she would quiz Duncan more closely about Cash. And since Edward had said his great-uncle and Ann Tintori were close, perhaps Duncan would also know what was wrong with the elderly anthropologist, which could then explain the odd behavior she had witnessed.

Carrie stomped on the gas pedal, impatient now for what she anticipated would be a lively talk with her old friend.

When she was two-thirds of the way to Duncan's place, she passed by the pens to the right of Highway 445, where the wild mustangs were herded and put up for adoption. For Carrie they always brought to mind Duncan's story of the dappled-gray stallion who escaped from the roundup years before, taking several mares with him. Duncan had told Carrie he had seen the wild stallion and his herd roaming the hills of his property and was glad they had found a place to be free.

Now, as she looked at the horses crowded into the pens, she wished they could all escape. No doubt it was an impractical and purely romantic wish, but she couldn't help thinking a world growing so populated that it crowded out its remaining wildlife seemed to be cheating those of future generations from enriching contacts with the other fascinating species inhabiting the earth.

As she turned up the dirt road leading to Duncan's house, in her mind's eye she could see him waiting on the white, wooden front porch, ready to wave a curled, ancient hand as his wire fox terrier and constant companion, Bonanza, barked his greeting. It was a comforting image as she battled the desert dust being whipped up by the Jeep's tires.

But as she approached Duncan's entry gate, she couldn't see any figure on the front porch of his sturdy and well-kept, wooden house. The hands on the analog clock on the dashboard of her old, gray Jeep angled at ten-fifteen. She turned off the motor and then wondered whether she should have called first.

No. Duncan knew she came this time every week. The only reason she'd call was if she couldn't make it.

Bonanza's immediate barking and appearance from beneath the overhang on the front porch reassured Carrie. She reached for her shoulder bag on the passenger seat and got out to approach the front door. Bonanza immediately ran up to her and kept up a steady yapping at her heels. His appearance separate from Duncan's began to concern Carrie. In all the time she had known the man and dog, she had never seen one without the other.

She leaned down to stroke his one dark ear in his otherwise white coat. "Is Duncan around back? Is that why you're outside?"

Bonanza kept yapping and jumping around her excitedly as Carrie walked quickly around the back of the house to see if Duncan had missed the sound of her Jeep. As she passed the small dog cemetery to the side of Duncan's home where all his previous Bonanzas had been laid to rest, she noticed a new cross had been added over a freshly dug grave. It confused her, but at the moment her concern over finding Duncan claimed all her attention.

It was then an awful uneasiness began to play upon her mind. Had Duncan been out for an early morning walk and fallen?

She put her hand up to shade her eyes and concentrated on looking out in the distance. It was no use. Waves of heat radiated across the expanse, causing weird distortions around the copious sagebrush. Then she suddenly dropped her hand as the full import of Bonanza's presence on the front porch finally registered. If Duncan had fallen out in the desert, Bonanza would not have left his side. So he couldn't be out there.

But if he had fallen inside the house? She raced back to the front porch, Bonanza following her hurrying footsteps. She took the four front steps two at a time and grabbed for the doorknob.

She pushed the door open and rushed in, Bonanza almost tripping her as he scurried ahead between her feet. Slits of light filtered through the drawn shades and there was a small lamp on in the corner. Its faint light and the bright rays streaming in from the open door behind her caught the white tuft of Duncan's hair like a halo around his head. Her elderly friend was sprawled in his favorite rocking chair, Bonanza now whimpering at his feet.

Carrie slowly stepped toward the silent figure and inch by inch dropped down to her knees in front of him as though she had gotten caught in some slow-motion camera. She placed her hands on his as they rested on his lap. The cold flesh beneath her fingertips sent a chill to her heart. It was as she feared. Duncan Van Epp was not sleeping. He was dead.

She continued to kneel in front of him, holding on to his hands as though her touch could warm them. The tears ran unchecked down her cheeks. So many memories of their past year together flooded her thoughts. She saw again the excitement in his pale eyes as he held up one of his obsidian figurines for her to examine. She heard again the pride in his voice as they walked his land amidst the beautiful sagebrush.

An incredible sadness gripped at her heart as she realized that they would share no more such memories. The wonderful, old gentleman she had come to know and love was gone forever.

Bonanza whimpered as his front paws kneaded his dead master's pant leg. Recognizing his pain and wanting to offer comfort, Carrie raised a hand to stroke the dog's head.

It was then she saw the huge shadow that descended on them both and in a fraction of a second, her heart soared into her throat in unreasoning panic. She jumped uncontrollably and whirled around to stare back at the open doorway.

Blinded by the sunlight, she blinked frantically to the echo of the deafening heartbeat in her ears until she could make out a man's tall silhouette, standing stock-still in the entry. She sucked in her breath until finally her eyes adjusted and she recognized the color and shape of the gold-brown head of hair and the outline of a familiar face.

"Cash." She exhaled in relief as she sank back to her knees.

She could now see from the sad expression on his face that he understood what had happened. He walked over to her and dropped down on one knee, putting his arm around her in a comforting gesture.

They knelt together in front of their dead friend for a minute before Cash spoke. "He lived a full life, I suppose.

Still I feel cheated, like I didn't have nearly enough time with him."

Carrie was surprised at his words mirroring her own thoughts so closely. When she looked over at his face, she saw the tears that had wet his cheeks. It was at that precise moment she decided she liked Cash McKendry very much.

They got to their feet and she took a seat in the chair opposite Duncan, sitting across from him just as they had sat together talking so many times during the last year. She could hear Cash's voice in the background, reporting the death to the Washoe County Sheriff's Department over Duncan's old black candlestick-shaped phone.

Her eyes touched the familiar room once more as a stubborn part of her refused to let the spirit of Duncan Van Epp slip so quickly away. On his workbench by the window, the new outline of a small, horse-shaped obsidian figurine caught her attention. She was just about to get up to take a closer look at it when for the first time she noticed the empty drinking glass and whiskey bottle on the table before Duncan.

Her forehead puckered into a frown. In all her visits to Duncan's home she had never once seen him drink liquor, nor had she even noticed a bottle in his kitchen cabinets.

Then she saw something else that struck her as strange. The glass he had poured the liquor in was crystal, one from a set she knew Duncan didn't use except on special occasions. The last time he had asked her to bring down the crystal from the top shelf they had toasted sparkling apple cider together on Christmas Eve. A touch of unease flicked up her spine.

Cash's voice came from just behind her. "Now I understand why I've been unable to reach him by telephone all morning. At least it looks like he went quietly. The sheriff will contact the coroner."

When Carrie didn't immediately respond, Cash circled her chair and bent to his knees so their eyes would be level. "A coroner's examination is required when someone isn't under the care of a doctor, even someone like Duncan who passes away naturally."

Carrie shook her head. "The idea of the coroner isn't what is bothering me, Cash. Look at that whiskey bottle. I would have sworn Duncan didn't drink."

Cash straightened up and leaned over the table, turning the neck of the whiskey bottle around to get a better look at it.

"Well I admit the whiskey surprises me, but Duncan did have a drink occasionally, Carrie. I shared some sparkling champagne with him myself last New Year's."

Still, Carrie felt uneasy about the scene before her. "I guess I could understand a little celebration champagne with company on occasion. But I don't see Duncan opening up a bottle of whiskey for himself to drink alone at night out of some of his fine crystal."

"The circumstances do seem a bit unusual...."

Carrie didn't like the way Cash's voice had just faded away. She watched him bend down to sniff at the rim of Duncan's empty glass. Then he straightened up, frowning.

"It smells like whiskey all right. But it's a strong-smelling whiskey. If the smell was strong enough, it might—"

Cash glanced down at her then, looking even sadder than he had at the sight of Duncan's death. His full lips had drawn into a tight line. "Maybe this wasn't... He was in pain, Carrie. He never said anything, but sometimes I could see it on his face. Maybe it was too much pain."

Carrie jumped to her feet. "No, Cash! Not suicide! No matter how bad the pain, Duncan never would have killed himself."

Cash stepped forward to extend his arm around her shoulder, but Carrie retreated. She didn't want to be comforted by someone who thought her friend could commit suicide. She felt if she accepted such comfort, she would also be accepting that the possibility was true.

She heard a new distant note in Cash's voice with his next question. "Why did you say that Duncan drank this at night?"

Carrie didn't turn to look at him when she answered. She was still upset at the implication in his earlier words. "Well, look around. The lamp is on in the corner. He wouldn't have turned it on during the day. This is just how I found the house when I walked in the front door a few minutes ago."

She had no sooner gotten the words out than Cash came to stand in front of her as though needing her full attention. "How did you get in?"

She shrugged. "I turned the knob and walked in."

Cash shook his head. "Duncan always locked his doors at night, a habit going back to a time when outlaws were known to steal a settler's horses and burn down his home. A locked door gave the family time to get into the dirt cellars. He would have locked the door, unless..."

Cash's voice had faded again, irritating Carrie. She turned to him. "Unless what?"

Cash sighed. "Unless he thought—"

Carrie shook her head, her voice breaking with the pain of having to fight when all she really wanted to do was cry. "No. You're implying he knew he wasn't going to live throughout the night because he planned to commit suicide. I thought you knew him."

"Yes, Carrie. I knew him."

She turned away from the sadness in Cash's eyes then, knowing his thoughts were as painful to him as they had been to her.

But she wouldn't let herself believe the possibility he presented. There must be other explanations that would make sense. Besides, she found herself being mentally poked by something that finally got her attention. She turned back toward Cash as the thought cleared.

"When I drove up, Bonanza was outside and the door was closed. Doesn't that sound strange? Everywhere Duncan went, that dog was with him. Why wasn't he with Duncan on the night of Duncan's death?"

Cash's sad look changed into a more contemplative one as Carrie watched him considering her question. He stood in the middle of Duncan's living room and looked around as though he might be seeing it for the first time. Then without hesitation he moved over to the kitchen counter where a white envelope lay. He gave it a cursory glance and immediately brought it to her.

As she took the envelope from Cash's hand, she looked down at her name scrawled across the outside in Duncan's familiar handwriting. She turned the envelope over. It was sealed. Her barely acknowledged, momentary dread that this might be a suicide note vanished. Duncan always put his check in an envelope for the groceries she brought him. She purposely tore open the flap in front of Cash's watching eyes and took out the contents.

The envelope contained a short note and three one-hundred-dollar bills. Carrie barely looked at the money as she read aloud the words Duncan had written.

"This is last month's grocery money I owe you, Carrie.

Sorry for the cash but my new checks haven't come in the mail yet. And thank you again for understanding I need to pay my own way. A man who stands on his own two feet is a man who walks in dignity."

The last words caught in her throat as she folded up the paper and shoved it back into the envelope and into her purse. She gulped, trying to dislodge the new lump of pain. "That's the Duncan I knew, Cash. That man would never take his own life."

Cash reached out to touch Carrie's arm, but she stepped back. He dropped his hand.

"I think we'd both best wait outside for the deputies so that we don't disturb anything else in the room. I'll get Bonanza."

Carrie nodded, stepping through the doorway and onto the porch into the bright sunlight. Her eyes burned with pain until her irises adjusted to the radical difference in light. She moved over to the porch railing as though needing it for support. That was when she once again saw the new cross over the recently turned ground in Duncan's small dog cemetery. Its meaning still confused her as did so many other things, but her grief pushed speculation aside.

A moment later Cash came through the doorway, gently holding a barking and protesting Bonanza in his arms. He leaned over and tried to close the door with a couple of fingers, but the latch didn't catch. Finally he had to put Bonanza down in order to properly close the door. The dog immediately began to jump against the closed door, scraping at it with his front paws and whining.

"Look at that," Carrie said, as she pointed to the very extensive splintering at the bottom half of Duncan's front door. "Bonanza must have been out here all night to have done such damage with his toenails. Something's wrong. Duncan would never have shut him outside."

Cash was frowning as he watched the dog. He didn't say anything.

Finally Carrie turned away to look out at the quiet and serene landscape, willing it to ease the emotional turmoil flowing through her. As the shock of Duncan's death was beginning to subside, she found other thoughts returning.

"I must telephone Edward. I must tell him about Duncan." She began to walk toward the door until Cash stepped in front of her.

"After we talk to the authorities," he said. "There's plenty of time. We shouldn't disturb anything else inside."

Her head was shaking. "It's not suicide," she said. "Duncan respected life too much to take his own."

Cash didn't say anything as he looked over at her, but the haze in his eyes told Carrie he wasn't seeing her. Another disturbing sight was playing through his mind. She suspected it was an old man in pain sitting all alone at night and drinking despondently from a bottle of whiskey.

Chapter Three

Cash answered the Washoe County deputies' questions, but his mind churned with another he couldn't answer: Why was Bonanza left outside? In all the years Cash had known his godfather, Duncan had always kept a "Bonanza" at his side.

As the deputies turned to take Carrie's statement, Cash mulled over different scenarios. Could Duncan have staggered into the house when he started feeling bad? Could a strong wind have blown the door closed behind him, inadvertently trapping Bonanza outside? Could Duncan have been too weak to get up to let the dog in?

No, that didn't make sense. Cash had needed his full grip to pull the door closed, so he very much doubted it could be blown shut. Besides, there had been no wind last night. The explanation just didn't fit. But what did?

Cash's hand rubbed the back of his neck as his forehead furrowed. He had hoped Duncan could explain why his call to Ann the afternoon before had unleashed such odd behavior in her. But now that his godfather was dead, all that remained was more unanswered questions.

He looked over at Carrie as she gave her statement to the deputies and found his frown lifting. As soon as they had been introduced that morning, he knew she was the college teacher who had brought so much pleasure to his godfather this past year.

Cash felt himself strongly drawn to Carrie because of her concern and kindness toward his godfather. His own weaknesses had taught him the value and incomparable strength of human compassion.

Of course, he admitted her looks weren't hard to take, either. With her luscious, long brown hair, her large, ethereal blue-gray eyes and her considerable height and slimness, she could have easily been a popular showgirl in a major Reno casino.

But he liked the fact that she didn't rely on her physical appearance to get her through life. Her lack of makeup or jewelry seemed to say she was even rather ambivalent about how beautiful she was. And now as he watched her standing on Duncan's front porch in nondescript white cotton slacks and overblouse with her thick hair draped casually behind her ears, he found himself enormously attracted to an unadorned allure that was all her own.

Natural. That was the word for her. Such naturalness and compassion must have been a potent twosome for Duncan. No wonder his friend had enjoyed her company so much. Cash was finding he was enjoying it very much himself.

The two deputies were just closing their notebooks when the coroner wheeled Duncan's body past. Cash watched Carrie turn from the sight of the gurney to look north toward the Virginia Mountains. He could also see new tears swimming through her eyes.

Before he knew it, he had walked over to her and his arm had found its way around her shoulders. "I'm afraid I'm not carrying a handkerchief," he said.

Her right hand fumbled inside her shoulder bag and brought out a tissue. She determinedly wiped away the tears.

Cash's arm tightened. "Did Duncan ever tell you about the Indian legend concerning the wild mustangs?"

Carrie's voice was husky. "That when a life kindred to the wild is released from its earthly body, the mustangs dash through the canyons, trying to keep up with the racing soul as it makes its way into the next world, for if they can catch and join with it, both will become immortal. The greater the soul, the louder the pounding of the hooves as they echo through the canyon walls.''

Cash smiled, pleased that Carrie could relate the legend so well. Without conscious intent he drew her more closely to him, enjoying the warm softness of her body and catching an elusive scent, something familiar that he couldn't immediately place.

Carrie turned, the soft look in her eyes telling him her mind still raced with the wild mustangs in the northern canyons. Then he watched her expression change as she became aware of the featherlike strokes of his fingertips traveling along the sleeve of her cotton blouse. She looked surprised as she stepped out of his arms.

Her voice was a little unsteady. ''I didn't have a chance earlier to ask you about your grandmother. Is she all right?''

Cash felt disappointed at Carrie's physical withdrawal but was beginning to see she wasn't the type of person to become easily involved. He liked that. He also liked the concern he now heard for his grandmother coming through in her words.

''Ann had a small stroke a few years ago, Carrie. She's regained the physical movement that was originally impaired, but she has difficulty with some of her memory skills. Some of the past is crystal clear, some is cloudy. Her moment-to-moment concentration seems to suffer most. Until this morning, as devastating as such a memory impairment can be, I would have said that was the extent of her debility. Her emotional outburst was... Well I can't offer you any explanation for it.''

Carrie's tone was reassuring. ''I don't expect one, Cash. I feel so sad for her. What a dreadful day this has been for you.''

The openness and sincerity shining out of her lovely face had him closing the few steps that separated them. He had an overwhelming urge to touch her once again. But as he raised his hand to her smooth cheek, she stepped back, an understanding of his intent deepening the gray in her eyes.

She spoke rapidly, her voice a smidgen too high. ''I told the deputies I would drive to Edward's house to tell him about Duncan. If I knew his brother, Gene, well enough, I'd approach him.''

Cash dropped his hand but resolved not to let her get away so easily. "We'll go together. Then get a late lunch?''

Carrie shook her head. "No, I have an afternoon class.''

Cash took a step toward her. "You're still upset. No one could expect you to work today. Call them and explain.''

Carrie started down the porch steps in the direction of her Jeep. "Thank you for your concern, but the university can't get a substitute on such short notice. The students are counting on my being there. Besides it's not my way to drop out when I receive a blow. The discipline of work will help me to get through the pain.''

Cash heard the conviction in her voice. She was stronger than he had originally thought. That didn't disappoint him.

"Let me drive you. We can come back for your Jeep later.''

She shook her head. "I appreciate what you're trying to do, but I can take care of myself. I'm worried about Bonanza, though. I haven't seen him in over an hour.''

"He's okay, Carrie. A deputy locked him in the back of his patrol car so the coroner's personnel could perform their tasks.''

"What will they do with Bonanza?''

Cash shrugged. "I offered to take him, but they wouldn't let me because I'm not officially 'family.' They'll drop him at an animal shelter until family members are contacted.''

Carrie frowned as she slipped into the driver's seat of the Jeep. "I don't like it. To lock Bonanza up, among strangers, right after he's lost Duncan...''

Her voice faded; the worried look remained on her face.

"Don't worry,'' Cash said. "I'll make sure he's okay.''

She watched him intently for a moment. Then she smiled, looking satisfied at what she saw. She started up the engine.

Her smile felt nice. Cash watched her drive away, recognizing she was stirring the sparks of some warm feelings out of the cold ashes of his past. He resolved to see her again— very soon.

CARRIE PULLED IN FRONT of Edward's modest home on the outskirts of Reno. His red Corvette was parked in the driveway. She approached the front and pushed on the doorbell.

Edward came to the door with his shirtsleeves rolled up, exposing large forearms covered in black hair. He was frowning.

"What on earth brings you here?"

"Can I come in?"

Edward shrugged and turned aside so she could pass. "The cleaning woman just left so there's coffee. Come along."

Carrie stepped inside and closed the door behind her. She followed him into the kitchen, gathering her thoughts before she spoke. She had decided on the drive over that the best way to tell anyone such tragic news was straight out without a lot of preliminaries. She took a deep breath in preparation.

"Edward, I found Duncan dead this morning. I'm very sorry."

Edward walked over to the kitchen table and sat down in a nearby chair. When he finally spoke, his tone was flat. "It had to happen someday."

He said nothing else for several moments, just stared blankly at the refrigerator, as though he was expecting the door to open. Carrie remained where she was at the edge of the kitchen, wondering what he was feeling. From some dark memory her father's blank and uncommunicative face flashed before her. And then she knew why. Her father had worn precisely the same expression when he had been told of her mother's death those many years before.

Carrie shifted uncomfortably on her feet. Her father had been one of those men who never expressed themselves emotionally except with anger or contempt. She believed the expression of positive emotions was the important way a person gave of him or herself to other people. The lack of expression of such positive emotion from both her father and Edward made both men appear small and selfish, judges of, rather than participants in, humanity.

Finally Edward turned to her. "Sit down. I'll call Gene and let him know in a minute. Pour yourself some coffee."

Carrie took the offered seat but declined the coffee.

"A heart attack, I suppose?"

Carrie exhaled. "I'm not sure. He was sitting in his favorite chair in the living room. I think he went quietly."

Edward nodded. "Best way, of course. No lingering illness. He wouldn't have wanted to be a burden."

Carrie suspected it was Edward who had been most concerned about Duncan possibly becoming ill and being a burden. She tried to find more charitable thoughts.

"Is there anything I can do for you?"

Edward waved his hand in irritation. "I'm no invalid. I'll contact Duncan's lawyer about the will."

Carrie felt annoyed that the first thing Edward thought of was a will. Prudently, she kept her reaction to herself.

"What about the funeral arrangements?" she asked.

"I'll discuss it with Gene. Do you know where they took him?"

"The Washoe County Coroner has him now. I'm sure as soon as the autopsy is completed, you'll be able to have the body picked up by whatever funeral home you decide to use."

Edward stared at her, surprise in his eyes. "Autopsy?"

Carrie leaned forward in her chair. "It's routine. Duncan had neither been ill nor under a particular doctor's care."

Edward sneered. "Stupid to perform an autopsy on a man that old. Waste of taxpayers' money."

He got to his feet and Carrie took it as her cue to rise. "Will you be taking your classes today?" he asked, as he headed in the general direction of the front door.

She nodded as she followed. "Do you want me to contact anyone at the university for you?"

Edward shook his head as he paused at the front door and methodically cracked the knuckles on each hand. "You know Duncan and I weren't close. When my parents died in that car accident, Duncan brought Gene and me up like an old army drill sergeant. That's why we both split as soon as we completed college.''

His tone and words were harsh, but Carrie judged that at least Edward was being honest about the matter. She began to wonder for the first time what it was like for him and Gene being brought up by an ancient uncle. Had Duncan really been that hard on the boys?

No, the unfeeling disciplinarian image wouldn't jell in her mind. Nothing could convince her that the gentle, loving man she knew could be anything else.

Then Carrie remembered the dog. She took a step forward. "The deputies took Bonanza to an animal shelter. Do you want him, Edward?''

Edward seemed to consider the question as he opened the front door. "Not now. I'll think about it.''

Carrie turned and left, not knowing what else to say. As she got into the Jeep, she looked back to see Edward still standing at the door watching her, a half frown on his face. She waved and he responded with a half wave back.

A half wave, a half smile, a half frown. Edward's stunted emotions always seemed to do things by halves. Carrie found it particularly irritating that Duncan's passing had not even merited a tear from his great-nephew.

And then she remembered Cash's warm, genuine, full-hearted tears, shed unashamedly. She had felt very close to Cash as they shared the sorrow of Duncan's death. His arms had felt so natural around her. She had been shocked to see how easily she had permitted them. Still, sharing strong emotion with someone was a great binder.

And Cash was a very attractive man with whom the idea of sharing strong emotion was anything but displeasing.

Carrie shook her head, reminding herself that Cash believed Duncan had taken his own life. As she drove to the university, she steadfastly refused to think about the whiskey bottle. There was a logical reason for it. Somewhere.

CASH KNEW GENE VAN EPP better than Gene's older brother, Edward. And although Cash considered himself in remission from his earlier gambling sickness, he knew Gene was still actively infected. Which was why he also knew he would find Gene at the El Dorado's blackjack tables rather than across the street in the Van Epp geological consultant firm that Gene owned courtesy of his great-uncle.

Because despite Gene's expensive education and the sign on his office door that said he was a geologist, Cash knew Gene was much more at home among the card tables than in any rock quarry. He quickened his pace.

Cash picked Gene out right away. His dark hair was shoulder length in the back. He wore a gold earring through his left ear, and his clothes were baggy to the point of sloppiness.

Cash clapped the younger man on the back as he took the stool beside him. "So, Gene, how's the luck running?"

"It's going to change. Any minute now," Gene said. He looked wary that Cash had singled him out. Cash knew why. The two men had never hit it off.

Cash could see Gene's face wore that unmistakable sweaty expression of a fighting fish on a hook—the compulsive gambler. Cash winced as he remembered it wasn't too long ago that that same anxious, sweating look had been his. From the corner of his eye, Cash saw Kurt Mofatt, a local loan shark who fed on the weakness of gamblers, watching Gene. Cash was pretty sure why. Gene must have borrowed money from him.

Cash waited until the hand was over and the dealer had scooped up Gene's chips. Then he laid a restraining hand on Gene's arm before he could place new chips into play.

"I need to talk with you, Gene. It will only take a minute."

Gene's mouth screwed like a twisted pretzel. "So talk. I can listen right here."

Cash wasn't surprised. The ceiling would have to fall in on a compulsive gambler with money before he left the table. With one powerful arm he lifted Gene out of his seat and with the other he dumped the remaining chips in Gene's shirt pocket.

"I thought we'd try the bar," he said.

Gene protested all the way. But when Cash finally planted him on a bar stool, Gene ordered a whiskey and soda just as though coming there had been his idea. "Well I'm here. Talk."

Cash looked Gene in the eye. "Duncan's dead."

A flash of something swung through Gene's dark eyes. He downed his drink and signaled the bartender for another. "When?"

"Looks like it was last night."

Gene shrugged. "What the hell. He was overdue."

Cash's jaw clenched, imprisoning the angry words that had sprung to his throat. If it hadn't been for the dog, Cash knew he would have let someone else break the news of Duncan's death.

"Bonanza needs care, Gene. The authorities have put him in a shelter, but you know the kind of freedom Duncan always gave the dog. He won't survive caged up. I'm willing to take him."

The second whiskey and soda arrived with a plate of dip and chips. Cash didn't like the cagey look on Gene's face as his eyes assessed him. "How much is it worth to you?"

Cash's stomach turned at Gene's insinuation. "I'm not offering to buy your great-uncle's pet, just give him a good home. If you'd prefer to take Bonanza out of the shelter—"

Gene laughed as though Cash had said something extremely funny. He downed his second drink. "I wouldn't have that mutt on a bet, and I'll lay you odds Edward feels the same way. By the way, does he know Duncan's dead?"

Cash was continuing to control his anger, but it was getting harder by the minute. "Carrie Chase went to tell him."

Gene looked at Cash quizzically. "Chase? Oh yeah, Edward's friend, the tall college teacher. Only saw her a couple of times. Looks weren't bad, but she sucked up to old Uncle like a leech. Probably thought the old geezer had a buck or two."

Cash's anger escaped his control. Having had the pleasure of meeting Carrie, he found Gene's suggestions intolerable. He wanted to hit him so bad his hand ached.

Fortunately for Gene, Cash's eyes spied the bowl of dip just in time and he substituted pounding it into Gene's nose instead of his fist. He dropped some money on the counter to cover the drinks and left the obnoxious man sputtering for air with brown bean dip plastered all over his snout.

Anger still burned through Cash as he reached his Seville parked in the lot. He yanked the driver's door open then realized he was foolish to be taking out his emotions on his car. After a moment he felt more like himself and sat down in the driver's seat to think.

First and foremost, he had to get Bonanza out of the shelter. It was obvious he couldn't expect any help from Gene and he didn't know Edward well enough to even approach him so he'd have to just take matters into his own hands. That was all right by him. He had lived in Reno all his life and had a lot of friends who he could call on for favors.

Second and more difficult, he had to tell his grandmother about Duncan's death. Despite the closeness of Ann to Duncan, he had purposely put off telling her. She had become so unpredictable. Would she begin screaming again as she had that morning at the university? Or would she be too confused to even comprehend? He wasn't sure which reaction would be worse to face.

Yes he was. Anything was preferable to the confusion. His mouth turned down in sadness as he started the Seville.

CARRIE FELT a growing impatience for her afternoon class to end. In her shock at Duncan's death that morning, she had forgotten about her brother, Tom, working for the Washoe County Sheriff's Department. Now his connection was all she could think about. With the hour's ending bell, she hurried to her office and reached for the phone, dialing his number from memory.

"Homicide, Sergeant Chase."

"Tom, it's Carrie. Can I come over to talk with you this afternoon?"

Tom's voice immediately warmed. "Well sure, Carrie. You know I always consider a visit from you special. What's up?"

"You remember my telling you about my friend, Duncan Van Epp? The one I've been visiting and bringing food to?"

"Yeah, I remember."

No matter how many times she would say it, Carrie knew the words were always going to bring her pain. "Duncan's dead, Tom."

There was a small pause on the other end of the phone before Tom responded to Carrie's news.

"I'm sorry. You must be feeling rotten. What can I do?"

Carrie exhaled, relieved and thankful for her brother's concern. "The coroner's office is doing an autopsy. Could you check on what they've found? I'd like to be certain about the cause of death."

"Sure, but didn't you tell me the guy was almost ninety? Was his death that unexpected?"

She sighed. "Maybe it shouldn't have been, but it was."

Tom's voice had begun to sound concerned. "You mean we might not be talking about natural causes?"

Carrie spoke up quickly. "No, I didn't mean that. I'm sure it had to have been natural causes. It's just that the last time I saw him he seemed so full of life—"

Carrie stopped as her throat tightened. Tom exhaled. "It's okay. I think I understand. If they've finished the autopsy, I'll have the results in about ten minutes. Shall I call or do you want to come by?"

"I'll come by, and thanks, Tom."

Carrie hung up the phone wondering at the unsettled feeling pushing against the walls of her stomach. She was just turning to leave the office when she literally ran into Cash. Her heart skipped a beat, not all due to surprise.

Warm fingers circled her arms to steady her as she stepped hurriedly backward. "You startled me," she said.

His eyes lit up as that special grin circled his lips. "Sorry. Didn't mean to. Where are you off to in such a hurry?"

"To the sheriff's office. My brother, Tom, works there. He's getting the results of Duncan's autopsy."

Cash nodded. "Yes, in class you mentioned you had a brother at the Sheriff's Department. May I tag along?"

Carrie's arms tingled where his hands were slowly retreating from their steadying hold. His showing up at her office continued to emphasize the personal interest he had first shown in her as he sat in her class. A feeling of distinct pleasure drew her lips into a smile as she tried to keep her voice nonchalant. "Sure."

He took her arm and guided her through the door in a somewhat proprietary fashion. Carrie winced. She vehemently disliked a man assuming a "take-charge" attitude with her. Still, Cash's manner wasn't arrogant or presumptuous. Or at least she didn't think so until she heard his next suggestion. "My car's right out here."

Deliberately she extricated her arm from his. "It's not necessary. I have my own."

He stood smiling at her, showing no offense. "If you'd prefer. It's just a warm day and I happened to notice this morning that your Jeep doesn't have air conditioning. I thought perhaps my car might be more comfortable."

Carrie found herself considering the logic in his words. No doubt the Jeep was already like an oven after sitting in the hot sun.

"I could drive you back to your vehicle later."

There was no hint of pressure in his tone. Carrie found herself persuaded and nodded her acceptance. As she settled into the passenger's seat of the Seville, she didn't regret her decision. The cool air bathed her face as the butter-soft leather seat surrounded her like a cushiony cloud. "Why did you stop by to see me?"

He glanced over at her briefly. "I couldn't reach you on the phone. A very helpful registration clerk named Betsy gave me your schedule. I took a chance you'd stop by your office after class."

Carrie listened to Cash's explanation, knowing Betsy was the university's *National Enquirer* and had probably supplied him with everything she knew about Carrie. She also realized that he hadn't answered the question she had meant to ask.

She tried again. "I mean, why did you want to see me?"

Cash smiled as he concentrated on the roadway ahead of them. "I thought you might like to see Bonanza."

Carrie turned toward him. "You found where they took him?"

He nodded. "And after he's been fixed up, I'll take him home."

Carrie frowned. "Fixed up? I don't understand."

"Little guy's very sore around his middle, Carrie. This morning he was so concerned about getting to Duncan, he apparently ignored the pain. But when I went to the animal shelter, I could see he hadn't eaten. Then I picked him up and he gave a yelp."

Carrie's voice carried her distress. "Where is he now?"

"Don't worry. I took him to a vet friend of mine. He'll find out what's wrong. Want to come with me when I pick him up?"

"Yes, thank you, Cash. I'd hate to think what would have happened to Bonanza if he had been left in the animal shelter injured and without attention. You said you'd help. I'm glad you're a man of your word."

He didn't say anything in response but he looked at her warmly and Carrie found her heart skipping erratically.

She concentrated on watching the road as she asked her next question. "I understand your grandmother and Duncan were friends. Has the news been very hard for her to take?"

Cash exhaled an unhappy breath. "She cried. I went to get her some tea, but by the time I got back, she'd forgotten why she was crying or why I had even come by."

Carrie's heart went out to him as she laid a hand on his arm. "Cash, is there any chance she'll get better?"

Cash felt the warmth of her touch and words mellowing the pain. "The doctors have recently put her on nimodipine, a drug that's used to improve the brain's blood flow. Despite her forgetfulness about the news of Duncan's death, I've noticed an improvement in her ability to recall recent events. As they've explained it, the memories are there, she just needs a sturdier bridge to get to them."

Carrie bit her lip. "I think losing my memory would be like losing my self-identity, everything I call life."

Cash nodded. "Lately, I've come to realize that, too. But her memory loss is selective as you saw when she evaluated the skeleton. Most things from her past are still as sharp and clear to her as ever. It's her limited memory span that's given her the most trouble. She can tell me who was at a convention thirty years ago, but she can't tell me who visited her for breakfast this morning."

Cash's voice just faded away in a quiet sadness. Carrie turned in her seat to face him. "I'm so sorry."

Cash flashed her a smile. She wore her compassion so openly he was finding it irresistible. She presented an interesting dichotomy. Whereas she gave her compassion easily, physical intimacy she held carefully in check. He wondered why. In anticipation of solving the personal mystery his lovely companion represented, he pulled into the sheriff's office parking lot.

They got out of the Seville together and walked side by side toward the large white building with the red trim. As they took the elevator to the third floor, Carrie was thinking how good it felt to stand up straight next to a man without fear of towering over him.

But as she approached the detective unit where her brother waited, one look at his expression and all thoughts of Cash were put aside.

Tom was four years older than Carrie, and three inches taller. He had the same warm brown hair color, but his blue eyes lacked the cool touch of gray that dwelt in hers. Right now she could see they were worried at the news he was about to relate. Before he got to what he obviously considered his unpleasant duty, she performed the introductions.

The two men shook hands and Carrie and Cash took a seat in front of Tom's desk. Tom seemed distracted by Cash's presence, a look of curiosity in his eyes.

"What's wrong, Tom?" Carrie asked, refocusing his attention.

Tom's dark look returned. "Duncan Van Epp died of congestive heart failure brought on by a mixture of two drugs—carbamazepine and metoprolol."

Carrie felt herself staring at her brother's face as she tried to make sense out of his words. "Duncan died from drugs?"

Tom looked back at the medical examiner's sheet. "The carbamazepine is a pain reliever. The metoprolol is an antihypertensive. Either one together or with alcohol could be lethal. Both together with alcohol in the concentrations found in Van Epp's body was, well, asking for it."

Asking for it. Tom's words swirled in to fog Carrie's thoughts. "You can't mean—"

Tom said the words she was having such a hard time forming. "Detectives have spoken with Van Epp's great-nephews and his doctor. They all agree that given the facts, the man committed suicide. Frankly that looks like the more probable explanation to me."

Carrie shook her head emphatically. "No, Tom. Not suicide."

Tom got up from behind his desk and came over to sit on its edge before Carrie. "I know Duncan was your friend, but you've got to face the facts. An accidental overdose of these drugs in the concentrations found just isn't likely. You see that, don't you?"

Carrie looked up at her brother, her back straightening, her lips tightening. "What I see, Tom, is that you've made up your mind without exploring all the possibilities."

Tom slipped off the edge of the desk, shoved his hands in his pockets and slowly returned to his chair. "Talk to her, Cash. It's obvious she's ready to discount anything I say."

Carrie's forehead creased as she waited for Cash's support of the suicide theory. But on hearing his words, her brow cleared in welcome surprise.

"Carrie's right, Tom. Duncan didn't commit suicide."

Tom's astonished look raked Cash. Then he looked from Cash to Carrie and a new expression descended on his face. "I see. What can you offer to support an accident theory?"

Cash read Tom's look and understood the thoughts behind it. He could feel Carrie watching him expectantly, but he said nothing. She looked back at her brother. "Where did Duncan get these drugs you found in his body?"

Tom shook his head. "I've already told you more than I should have because of your friendship with the deceased. From now on, Carrie, I'm afraid I'm going to have to go by the book. I'll listen to any information you have to support your accidental death theory, but the information flow is to be in one direction—from you to me."

Tom's boss came into his office then and called him out for a quick conference leaving Carrie and Cash alone. Carrie turned toward Cash, hope and curiosity shining out of her eyes.

"You've changed your mind. Why?"

Cash shrugged. "In a word, Bonanza. Let's go for a drive and I'll tell you about it."

She nodded eagerly. "I'll just write a quick note and leave it on Tom's desk letting him know I'll call later."

Carrie left her note and they went back to Cash's car.

As soon as they got underway, she asked her question. "What was it about Bonanza that convinced you Duncan didn't commit suicide?"

Cash kept his eyes on the road. "Ever since you told me Bonanza had been left outside, I knew something was wrong. Duncan loved that dog too much to just leave it outside to fend for itself while he took his own life. I know he would have provided a new home for Bonanza first. And since he didn't, I can't accept the suicide theory."

Carrie nodded. "Well I'm happy that's your conclusion. But I have to admit, I don't see how it could have been an accident, either. You agree Duncan was in full possession of his mental faculties, don't you?"

"Absolutely."

She sighed. "Well, then, there is no way I can picture him accidentally dumping too different types of pills down his throat in the quantities Tom said they found in his body. Someone would have to be an imbecile to be that careless and Duncan was exceptionally bright. How could such an accident have happened?"

Cash shook his head. "Carrie, I never said I thought Duncan's death was an accident."

Carrie jerked in her seat toward him. "But if Duncan didn't die accidentally or commit suicide then you think—"

Cash nodded, his jaw set. "Yes, Carrie. I think Duncan was murdered."

Chapter Four

Cash looked over at Carrie's unhappy expression and heard her deep sigh as she slumped in her seat. "I haven't wanted to face it, but I think part of me has realized it had to be murder, too, ever since Tom mentioned the drugs. Suicide was unthinkable. An accident unlikely. Murder is the only thing left. Still, how could someone have wanted to murder Duncan? He was the sweetest, most gentle man."

Cash nodded, hearing the sadness in her voice and feeling sad himself over what he had come to believe. "I know. But people don't just kill because someone is disagreeable."

Carrie straightened in her seat, her voice picking up volume. "But why then? What possible reason could there be for someone to kill Duncan?"

Cash exhaled heavily. "I don't know."

"Why didn't you tell Tom you thought Duncan had been murdered?"

Cash shrugged. "Tom wouldn't have listened. Your brother thinks I was agreeing with you because of a personal interest I have in staying on your good side."

He watched the words register in some surprise on her face. "You mean he thought we were—"

Cash nodded.

Carrie swallowed uncomfortably and shook her head in denial. "Turn the car around. I'll go back and straighten him out."

Cash shook his head as he smiled at her indignation, secretly amused. Tom's assumption about them was something he hoped to make true, even if the idea had not yet occurred to her.

"No point to it," he said aloud. "As you told him, your brother has made up his mind. I don't think anything I would say could sway him, not that I particularly blame him."

Carrie's voice rose. "You don't? Why not?"

"He's a law enforcer, trained to look for the simplest explanation. He has no real evidence of foul play. His natural conclusion would be suicide. He can't possibly make the same informed behavior judgments we can since he neither knew Duncan nor understood his relationship with Bonanza."

"What if we explained about Bonanza?"

Cash was quiet for a moment as he considered her suggestion. "I'm not sure our word would be convincing enough for Tom to reconsider the conclusion he wants to reach. I think we need to provide him with more in the way of concrete proof before he'd look closer at the circumstances surrounding Duncan's death."

Carrie studied his profile. "Can we do that?"

He looked over at her and smiled. "We can try."

Hope entered Carrie's eyes. Cash was glad to see it there. "Where do we start?" she asked.

"Perhaps the first thing we should consider is the method used. Since we don't believe Duncan took those drugs voluntarily, then we have to face the fact that someone else tricked or in some way forced Duncan to take them."

Carrie shivered. Cash knew it wasn't from the car's air conditioning. Her eyes looked sad, unfocused. "I didn't even know he had such medicines. Duncan must not have felt close enough to me to share the physical problems he was experiencing. All I was ever aware of was his limp and the occasional tic."

Cash found the unhappiness in her voice hard to take. He very much wanted to soothe it away. "Physical ailments were embarrassing for him to acknowledge, Carrie. I didn't know what specific medications he might be taking, but I did know that Duncan was seeing a doctor.''

Carrie's interest was immediately peaked. "He was?"

Cash nodded. "I drove Duncan to the office of a Dr. Packer last Friday. He wouldn't let me come in. But when he came out, he was carrying a small, white bag. It might have been the prescription bottles. This Dr. Packer practices out of the Desert Medical Associates Group on Mill Road. I worried about Duncan being so far away from medical help. I made a mental note of Dr. Packer and the clinic just in case.''

Carrie pursed her lips in thought. "Cash, you say you saw Duncan with a bag, but you're not sure what was in it?"

"Yes. Why?"

"Well I was just thinking how do we know for certain what medicine Duncan may have had? Wouldn't it be a good idea to go see this Dr. Packer and ask some questions about Duncan's care?"

Cash nodded. "Except that I doubt he'd even talk to us. Medical records are generally confidential.''

She smiled. "Don't worry. I got a Sheriff's Department temporary identification badge from my brother last year when I was working with him to try to identify Ernie's remains. It should come in handy."

"Handy?" Cash asked.

"Yes. I still have the ID in my purse. I'll just flash it. No one ever looks closely at them. The doctor will think we're official. All we have to do is call first to set up an appointment. Look. There's a telephone.''

Cash pulled over to the curb and waited in the car while Carrie checked the phone book for the number of the Desert Medical Associates Group. She found it quickly and made her call. He sat back in the driver's seat and watched her involved in animated conversation.

He couldn't help but notice she had perked up considerably since he had lent his support opposing Duncan's suicide. And pursuing the lead of the doctor was keeping her occupied. But he could see that she hadn't really taken in the import of Duncan having been murdered. When she did, he was sure other very unpleasant facts would begin to make themselves felt. They were already occupying most of his thoughts.

She came back to the Seville smiling. "Dr. Eileen Packer, obviously a 'she,' will see us as soon as we get to her office on Mill Road, Suite 205. She was just on her way out, but she'll wait. I spoke to her personally by the way, and left her with the impression we're sheriff's detectives."

Cash smiled as he heard the pride in her voice. "Nice work. Ever have a desire to join law enforcement?"

She shook her head. "Absolutely not. Having to deal with criminals all day is not exactly what I call a living."

"So instead you devote your time to the examination of old, dead bones," Cash said.

Carrie grinned as she heard the tease behind his words. "Actually, the bones may be dead, but their stories aren't. Every time I pick up the bone of a man or woman who lived hundreds, maybe thousands of years ago, I think about what it must have been like for them. Often I'm able to see evidence of their life struggles mapped into the shape and development of their skeleton. It's like a piece of scientific history, quantifiable in ways the words of a history book can only approximate."

Cash was smiling. "Yes, watching and listening to you lecture, I could see and hear the interest and energy you have for your work. Strange that while I was growing up I never was that curious about my grandmother's profession. But I admit I found your lecture this morning rather...exciting."

She was pleased at the sincerity in his tone. "Does that mean you're thinking of signing into the class as a real student?"

He smiled. "Might not be a bad idea unless you have some rule about not seeing your students socially." He glanced over at her trying to read her response to the subtlety of his unspoken question.

Carrie felt excited by the gentle probe of his words but didn't feel comfortable in offering an encouraging response. She couldn't deny she was attracted to him in many ways, but she wasn't one to rush things.

As he looked back at the road and she could study him in some leisure, she found herself admiring the clean lines of his face. Perhaps because of her profession, bone structure was one of the first things Carrie noticed about a man. Cash had a remarkably symmetrical chin and very strong jaw angle that came from a perfectly shaped mandible, or lower jawbone. It gave his whole face a look of added character and determination.

When he looked over at her again, he saw her studying him and smiled. Carrie felt embarrassed to be caught watching him.

"Do you have a notepad?" she asked, hoping to camouflage the reason for her blatant staring as her hand dived into her shoulder bag and came out with a pen.

He didn't seem fooled by her change of subject. "Yes, I think you'll find one in the glove compartment. Why do you need it?"

Carrie retrieved the notepad and clipped her pen to it. "If I'm a sheriff's detective asking questions, I'd better have a pad ready to jot down the answers. Isn't that the building?" she asked, pointing to the right. "Dr. Packer said it had a tacky yellow sign in front."

Cash nodded, parked the car around back and they headed for the entrance. He noticed that Carrie opted to take the flight of stairs rather than wait for the elevator. He wasn't sure whether that was a sign of impatience or the desire to keep physically fit. He suspected it might be both.

Dr. Eileen Packer was in her late fifties, with the type of solid, square shape and deep voice that Carrie judged probably gave patients confidence. Carrie identified herself as the woman who had just called from the sheriff's office and flashed her identification. As she had predicted, Dr. Packer didn't give it a second look but waved them to take a chair.

"How can I help you?" she asked as she carefully folded her hands before her on the desk.

Carrie spoke up. "When did you last see Mr. Van Epp?"

"First and last time was Friday."

"First and last? You weren't his regular doctor?"

"No. Duncan Van Epp didn't have a regular doctor, or at least that's what he told me. Still, from my brief examination, I found him in amazingly good health considering his age."

"You didn't give him a complete examination?" Cash asked.

Dr. Packer shook her head, an action that hardly stirred her short gray-brown hair.

"He refused lab tests. I was lucky he let me check his blood pressure. Mr. Van Epp told me his longevity could be attributed to the fact that he avoided doctors on every possible occasion."

Cash smiled as he could just hear Duncan saying those very words. "Why did he come to see you?" Carrie asked.

Dr. Packer shifted in her chair as though suddenly uncomfortable and her dark eyes squinted into a slight frown. Carrie saw a glimpse of something flash through them but it was too fleeting to identify. "He was in considerable pain."

Carrie fought through a sudden sadness. "From what?"

"Trigeminal neuralgia."

Carrie shook her head. "What does that mean?"

Dr. Packer shrugged. "It's an intense pain along some very special cranial nerves that contain motor and sensory fibers into the face. People with it often develop a tic. Mr. Van Epp had the tic and the pain."

Carrie remembered the tic very well. She hadn't realized it caused Duncan pain. She tried to swallow down the sadness that surfaced again at the loss of her friend.

Cash recognized Carrie's sudden withdrawal and suspected the reason for it. He tried to camouflage her obvious pain from Dr. Packer's watching eyes by directing the doctor's attention to him. "How were you able to diagnose his illness without tests?" he asked.

Eileen Packer looked at Cash, but he had the feeling she was still watching Carrie out of the corner of her eye.

"His symptoms were most specific and the tic was quite visible. There was no doubt in my mind."

"What medications did you prescribe for Duncan Van Epp?" Carrie asked.

Dr. Packer frowned in the first sign of irritation, the prominent age wrinkles deepening around her eyes. "You know I did give all of this information to another detective early this afternoon."

Carrie ran her wet palms as unobtrusively as possible across her slacks as she attempted to keep her voice steady. "Yes, Dr. Packer, and I realize that having to repeat it is no doubt tedious, but investigative personnel are often required to re-ask questions to insure all ground has been covered."

Cash could tell from the look on Dr. Packer's face that she wasn't exactly buying the explanation, but she seemed to resign herself as she got up and made her way to the corner file.

Carrie looked at the neat stack of recently typed envelopes with the Desert Medical Associates embossed return address lying on Eileen Packer's desk. She decided they must be the monthly bills prepared and waiting to be mailed.

After only a moment's search in the file, Dr. Packer pulled out the new, thin folder with the name of Duncan Van Epp typed neatly across the top. She returned to her desk and opened the file. Carrie had her pen and notepad ready.

Dr. Packer was looking down at the information as she read. "Carbamazepine in tablets of 200 milligrams each. His dose was initially 200 milligrams every twelve hours."

"Initially?"

Dr. Packer nodded. "It was a starting dose. Continual use on a regular schedule for three months is necessary in order to determine the drug's effectiveness in relieving the pain of trigeminal neuralgia. I gave him the three-month supply. Mr. Van Epp was to call me and let me know if the dosage worked."

"Did he contact you, Doctor?" Cash asked.

Eileen Packer leaned back in her chair, her voice laced with irritation. "I told you. It takes three months before the effectiveness of carbamazepine can be determined. The drug has to gradually build up in the system before it can be felt. I only gave it to Mr. Van Epp last Friday."

"And you instructed him carefully as to how much to take?"

"Of course. Although frankly, I didn't even think he planned on taking the pills. He was looking for some procedure that would eliminate the problem, not mask it with a pain pill. As a matter of fact he used those very words."

"Did his attitude irritate you?" Cash asked.

She shrugged and watched the folder on her dead patient as though she was seeing him again. "He was reared during a time when pain was just a fact of life. The dislocation of his hip must have given him considerable pain for many years. I think he felt he should have been able to get rid of the other 'annoyance' or live with its pain, too."

The doctor's words surprised Carrie. She leaned forward in her chair. "Duncan Van Epp suffered from a dislocated hip?"

Dr. Packer nodded at Carrie. "Not a treatable one, at least not at his age. Today when a baby is born with the problem there are splints that can be—"

"Doctor, are you saying Duncan was *born* with a dislocated hip?"

Dr. Packer nodded at the visible rise in Carrie's voice.

"And it was painful?" Cash asked.

Dr. Packer ran a hand over her unmussed hair. "Very. And the trigeminal neuralgia. I don't know how he stood it as long as he did. Of course, that must be why he..."

Dr. Packer's voice trailed off, but it was obvious she was accepting the suicide theory for Duncan's death.

Cash spoke up. "Earlier you mentioned you *gave* Mr. Van Epp a three-month supply of carbamazepine. You didn't write a prescription for it?"

Dr. Packer squared her shoulders uneasily. "I had recently received a supply of free samples from a large pharmaceutical firm. I gave a portion of those samples to Mr. Van Epp to try."

"So you didn't write a prescription?" Cash re-asked.

"No. I put enough samples for three months in a bag and Mr. Van Epp took it with him. They're not habit forming. Properly taken, there shouldn't have been any danger."

"Do you normally hand out medication that way?" Cash asked.

"Occasionally. As I said, I had this supply—"

"Why did you select Mr. Van Epp to be the recipient?"

Cash watched Dr. Packer's tongue flick across her teeth, as though something had built up there she was trying to scrap away.

"Look, the truth is I thought Mr. Van Epp might hesitate to have a prescription filled. He seemed disappointed that pain pills were all I could offer him. He wanted a cure. I wanted to provide him with some relief. I thought if he had the pain pills on hand, he might be more inclined to take them."

"So you gave him the pills because you didn't think Mr. Van Epp would have had a prescription filled?"

Dr. Packer nodded, looking resigned. While Cash was handling the conversation, Carrie was straining her neck trying to read the doctor's notes in Duncan's file. Unfortunately, it looked just like gibberish to her. She redirected her attention to Dr. Packer.

"Another drug was found in Mr. Van Epp's system, Doctor," she said. "Did you prescribe that one for him?"

"You mean the metoprolol," Dr. Packer said. "No, as I told the other detective, I gave him no such prescription. Mr. Van Epp's blood pressure was excellent, one-twenty over eighty. No such medication was indicated."

"This metoprolol is for high blood pressure?" Carrie asked.

The doctor nodded. "Yes. It's a relatively well-tolerated antihypertensive. Mr. Van Epp didn't need it, and even if he had, its combination with carbamazepine is always contraindicated."

"Contraindicated?" Cash repeated.

"To be avoided," Dr. Packer interpreted.

"Why is that, Doctor?" Carrie asked.

"Both drugs block actions of the sympathetic nervous system. Together in sufficient dosage they could block enough to cause heart failure, as apparently they did in Mr. Van Epp's case. But your coroner knows all this just as well as I, and he was the one who determined the cause of death. I must say that neither of you has asked questions very different from the other detective."

Cash leaned forward in his seat. "Is there something else we should be asking?"

Dr. Packer frowned, looking suddenly a decade older than her fifty-five plus years. Then she sighed heavily. "Look, it's been a long day. Is there anything else?"

"Just one more question," Carrie said. "Why did Duncan Van Epp select you out of all the physicians in Reno?"

Dr. Eileen Packer turned her head abruptly from Carrie. Cash thought he saw something hidden surface for a moment and then resubmerge itself in her dark eyes, but he couldn't be sure. When she spoke, her deep voice seemed carefully controlled.

"I was surprised to see him. Older men generally don't select women doctors—cultural bias, you know. Of course it may be he didn't know I was a woman until he walked into the office. Now, if you'll excuse me, I'd like to get home to my family."

Dr. Packer rose and Carrie and Cash took it as their cue to do likewise. They left her office and walked slowly back to his Seville in the parking lot.

"Did she seem a little tense to you?" Carrie asked.

Cash nodded. "Yes, like she was nervous or afraid but was trying not to show it. Might be natural, though. She's lost a patient and it was a drug she personally packaged and insisted Duncan take with him that helped to kill him."

"Duncan knew she was a woman before he went to see her," Carrie said.

Cash turned to catch a glimpse of the frown on her face. "How do you know?"

Carrie looked up at him, the gray in her eyes deepening. "Because Dr. Eileen Packer is listed on the directory with her first name prominently displayed. Duncan had to have known and he selected her personally. I wonder why.''

Cash shrugged. ''Well whatever the reason at least we know now that Duncan *didn't* have a prescription for the high blood pressure drug. Where did it come from?''

Carrie was still frowning as she opened the passenger's door. ''What is it?'' Cash asked as he watched her.

She paused next to the car, holding on to the rim of the door. ''He might have been taking the antihypertensive medicine already. It would explain why his blood pressure appeared normal.''

''I didn't drive him to another doctor,'' Cash said. ''Did you?''

Carrie shook her head. ''No. But he may have found a way to go without either of our help.''

Cash thought about the logic in her words. ''Yes, you've made a good point. He refused blood tests. I guess the only way to really know would be to canvass every other doctor in Reno to see if Duncan Van Epp had been their patient.''

Carrie shrugged. ''If I know Tom, he's already in the process. He's pigheaded at times, but he's thorough in his investigative techniques. Maybe I can get a peek at his files in a day or so when his detectives have received their answers.''

''And maybe we can do other things in the interim,'' Cash said.

She looked up at him. ''What did you have in mind?''

She was standing close to him, leaning on the car door, her large, blue-gray eyes full of curiosity. Cash again detected her light sweet scent that seemed somehow familiar, but which he still couldn't place. He fought to concentrate on her question as other more pleasant thoughts started to invade his mind.

''I'd like to go back to Duncan's house and have another look around,'' he said.

''What do you hope to find?''

''Think about the scene this morning when you found Duncan. He was sitting at the table with the bottle of whiskey and the one glass. Did you see any pills or pill containers on the table?''

Carrie shook her head. "No, that's right. Where were the pill containers?''

''My guess would be someone put the pills in Duncan's drink and hid the bottles from him. And that means he or she waited for the pills to take effect and probably had a drink with him.''

"I don't follow," Carrie said.

"Well, Duncan wouldn't have sat there and ignored Bonanza's barking if he was outside. Bonanza must have been in the room.''

"Oh, I see," she said. "That means the person who put the pills in Duncan's drink had to wait until they took effect because he or she was the same person who put Bonanza outside. And since it's unlikely Duncan would have drunk alone, you think this person must have had a glass of whiskey with him?''

Cash nodded at her reasoning but did not have a chance to respond further as a noise distracted them both. They turned as the back door to the medical center opened and Dr. Eileen Packer came out. She looked at them quizzically as though something was bothering her as she made her way to her car.

Cash immediately realized that Cadillac Sevilles were hardly included in the unmarked cars owned by the Sheriff's Department. He pointed to the passenger seat of the Seville and Carrie slipped in. He circled around the car to the driver's side. "She's becoming suspicious of us," he said when he was behind the wheel.

"Because of the car?" Carrie asked.

He nodded, not surprised Carrie had also read the doctor's uneasy look and had come to the same conclusion. "Oh, well, it can't be helped now.''

He started the engine. "It's almost six o'clock. Time for me to pick up Bonanza. Still want to come along?''

"Yes, definitely. Do you have a yard where he can roam?''

Cash nodded. "I think he'll be satisfied, but I'll take you by to see it so you can judge firsthand."

Carrie realized she was presuming too much to be questioning the facilities he was providing for Bonanza. "That isn't necessary. If you say it's satisfactory, I'm sure it is."

He looked over at her then, a steady look that began to warm the palms of her hands. "Your confidence is nice, Carrie. I'd like you to see my yard, nonetheless. Won't you come?"

She nodded, thinking she was far from immune to his obvious interest and natural warmth as they rode to the animal hospital.

Cash introduced her to his veterinarian friend, a small, thin, average-looking middle-aged man with a big nose and bad teeth. She forget his six-syllable name immediately after hearing it, but she'd never forget his words.

"X rays show two of this little guy's ribs are cracked. Cash, I've seen this kind of injury before, I'm afraid. In my opinion, this dog's received a vicious kick. Now I've taped him so he can heal properly, but keep him warm, make sure he gets light exercise and get these pills down his throat twice a day."

Cash nodded solemnly at the vet and carefully picked Bonanza up. The dog whimpered softly. Cash continued to look grim and didn't speak to Carrie until they were outside. When he did, Carrie could hear the fierce sadness in his voice.

"I thought he hurt himself trying to get into the house. It never occurred to me he'd been deliberately kicked."

Carrie petted Bonanza's head and a pale little tongue came out to lick her wrist. She hardly recognized her own voice.

"It was the murderer, wasn't it?"

She could see Cash's eyes flash with anger as he gently held the little dog to him. She felt her own rising anger and indignation like an expanding balloon choking off the air to her throat.

For the first time since Cash had mentioned the probability that Duncan had been murdered, the truth and total horror of his statement was beginning to sink in. Some cold-blooded fiend had viciously kicked a little dog and poured poison down the gentle throat of a kind and wonderful old man. A furious frustration engulfed her, spilling hot, burning tears down her cheeks.

Cash watched Carrie's face and realized what was happening. He laid Bonanza on the seat of the car and put his arms around her.

She resisted, angrily flipping the backs of her hands against her cheeks to rub away the tears. "I'm all right. It's just that...damn, how could anyone do anything so cruel!"

He thought he had come to terms with the manner of Duncan's death, but her pain and anger made him realize his own had just been smoldering beneath the surface. Now it flared up to join with hers. It was a moment before he could speak. When he did, his voice was thick and strained.

"I'll find out who did it, Carrie. If it's the last thing I do."

Chapter Five

She straightened at his words. Cash could see that despite the tears still squirting from their corners, her eyes glowed with a fierce resolve. "You mean *we'll* find him."

He knew then she was not one to sit idly by while others took care of things. He admired the determined fire that flashed out at him and wondered what other passions lurked there in the deceptively cool, blue-gray of her eyes.

Carrie read the subtle change of expression in Cash's eyes. She sensed his body closing the distance between them and she felt the push of her own body toward him. A second more and she knew she would be folded in his arms, responding to something much more than a comforting embrace.

Quickly she stepped back, feeling uncertain and off balance. She was not a woman easily drawn into a romantic affair. And with every racing corpuscle in her blood she knew that this was not a man to be easily kissed or embraced.

Cash watched both her initial excitement and subsequent withdrawal. With an effort he remained at arm's length.

"Let's take Bonanza home."

They were there within fifteen minutes. Carrie found Cash's home to be a rambling ranch-style, white with a brown shake roof and surrounded by several acres of brown, water-starved grass, a by-product of Reno's frequent droughts.

He drove directly into the garage and they entered the house through the connecting door into the kitchen. Everything was clean but cluttered. As Carrie stepped into the living room, her attention was drawn immediately up where open skylights between wood beams made it seem like outdoors. A profusion of healthy plants suspended from the wood beams were bathing in the late-afternoon sunlight.

"This is lovely," she said, still looking up.

"The openness and sunlight appealed to me, too," Cash said as he gently laid Bonanza on an ottoman. "Up is about the only place there's still room in here as you can no doubt see."

Now that Carrie had stopped looking up and started to look around, she could indeed see. The large living room was furnished wall-to-wall with an assortment of couches, tables and chairs. Its walls were full of paintings except for one, which backed an enormous, six-foot-by-three-foot tropical fish aquarium.

"You must have lived here a long time."

He smiled a little sheepishly. "Escrow closed three years ago."

"You moved a lot of stuff from your old place?"

"I had just gone through a divorce. The furniture and the old house stayed with my ex-wife."

Carrie heard no bitterness in his tone. She wondered why he had divorced his wife and at the same time decided he must be a collector indeed to have accumulated so much in such a short period of time.

"Can't resist a sale?" she suggested.

He smiled. "I've been known to show up at one or two."

She liked him for admitting it.

"The very helpful Betsy in the administration office at the university tells me you've never been married. Is she right?"

Carrie nodded nonchalantly, pleased at his interest. But she became a little self-conscious as he continued to watch her. Duncan's death had assaulted some of her deepest feelings. Whatever she was beginning to feel for Cash was too new to be examined. She turned and walked over to the aquarium to gaze at the fish.

"Peaceful, aren't they?" Cash asked, suddenly by her side. "I remember reading once that watching fish is a very effective way of lowering blood pressure. Interesting thought, isn't it?"

Carrie's senses reached out to gather in his impressive height, the expanse of his shoulders, the drawing warmth of his body. Her right arm tingled where it brushed against his.

"Yes," she said, not removing her eyes from a large angel fish and yet sure her blood pressure was perversely on the rise.

"Do you have an aquarium?"

"No," she said, trying to concentrate on his question and ignore the warming signals her body was sending. "Pets require concerted effort and care. I've promised myself I won't get one unless I'm ready to make such a commitment."

"And you've felt hesitant to commit?"

Carrie suddenly knew Cash's question was a personal one that extended beyond pet care. Before she could respond, she felt something bump her lower left leg. She looked down to see Bonanza rubbing his bandaged rib cage against her calf.

"I think he wants company, Cash," she said as she knelt down to pat his head. "He's feeling lonely without Duncan and at least we smell familiar. Do you suppose he's hungry, too?"

"He might be. I've got some dog food in the car. I've also got three stray cats who adopted me this last year and will be needing some attention soon."

He had no sooner gotten the words out when a meowing chorus began at the sliding glass doors that led out to the backyard. Cash took a moment to fill the cats' dishes and to stroke their backs. Fortunately, Bonanza didn't show any immediate interest in cat chasing and lay complacent in Carrie's arms.

Carrie smiled as she watched Cash petting his menagerie. Another image, nearly forgotten, of her mother's large, gentle hands caressing the ears of a lost kitten came suddenly to mind and then scooted away just as quickly.

"Might as well fix something for us, too," Cash said getting to his feet and sliding open the door to reenter the house. "I'm a pretty plain cook. Tonight's menu is broiled steak, microwaved baked potatoes and canned corn. Hungry?"

Carrie was about to decline when her stomach growled loudly. It was so on cue that she and Cash laughed. "I guess that's your answer."

He smiled as much more than social politeness warmed his tone. "I'll be back in a minute to feed you both."

She was glad to stay. Still, despite the pleasant company, Carrie found unpleasant thoughts occupying her mind as they prepared the meal and sat down to eat. Between bites of dinner, she shared a few thoughts with Cash.

"The more I think about it, the more I realize that whoever killed Duncan had to have been somebody he knew."

Cash speared some potato. "Why do you say that, Carrie?"

"Well, I very much doubt a casual robber would take the time to make the murder look like a suicide."

Cash chewed on her words for a minute. "You're right. Someone did that, didn't they?"

"Yes. I think the bottle of whiskey was brought by the murderer so the poison could be put in the drink."

Cash nodded. "Could be. Duncan would have been polite enough to have shared a drink with someone who coaxed him. Which again brings up the question, where is the missing glass?"

"Yes. Did the murderer take it or put it back on the shelf?"

Cash rose, taking his dishes with him. He ignored the dishwasher and began to fill up the sink with sudsy water. "Come with me tomorrow and we'll have a look through Duncan's house."

She got up to place her dishes on the counter where Cash could wash them. He immediately became aware of her sweet, light scent. He inhaled deeply as she reached across him for a towel.

"Duncan's place is bound to be locked."

Cash reordered his thoughts as he handed her a washed plate. "Duncan gave me a key. We'll have no problem getting in. What time will you be free?"

She was drying the plate he had handed her. She went over it twice as she thought about her answer. "My morning class will be over at nine. I could leave soon after."

Cash nodded. "How about if I pick you up at the university? No reason to drive two cars out."

Cash knew any other woman he had spent time with would have automatically assumed he would drive. But Carrie exuded a definite independence. Her reluctance to let him drive the first time had shown it to him. Since then, he noticed it in the way she opened her own doors. Still, if he went slow and easy, he should still be able to convince her. He smiled as he handed her another dish to dry.

She smiled back. "No. I'd rather drive my Jeep to Duncan's. I'll meet you there at ten."

He took her words quite graciously, considering the disappointment they were causing him. He could have sworn she was neither oblivious nor indifferent to his interest. Later, as he drove her to her Jeep, he found himself snatching looks at her quiet profile in the subdued light of the car's interior.

He began to wonder what had kept her single and his wondering expanded as he thought of other questions he'd like to ask. It was too soon. He would wait. And in the meantime, there was much to keep his attentions occupied.

Topping the list was the very pertinent question of Duncan's murder. Someone his godfather knew had done it, which meant it was probably someone Cash knew, too. But who?

AFTER CASH HAD DROPPED her at her vehicle, Carrie made a detour to the grocery store on her way home. When she got to the check-out register and realized she didn't have enough cash in her billfold, she pulled out the white envelope with the money Duncan had given her and handed one of the hundred-dollar notes to the grocery clerk.

"Lady, this money don't look right," the young checker said as he turned the hundred-dollar bill over in his hands.

Carrie frowned at him. "What do you mean, it doesn't look right?" she asked, automatically correcting his English.

The checker leaned across the counter, shoving the back of the note in her face. "It don't have no 'In God We Trust' across the top. See there? Somebody has done passed you some funny money, lady. You got some *good* money to pay for these groceries?"

Carrie was dumbfounded. She reached into her wallet to hand the clerk another hundred-dollar bill.

The clerk looked at it and his head began to shake. "This one ain't no good, neither. Look, don't try to dump this queer on me. Last month some dude stuck me with two funny twenties and my boss mouthed off about firing me. Now, how you gonna pay for this food?"

Embarrassed, Carrie wrote a check to cover her groceries and waited while the suspicious checker verified that she matched the picture on her driver's license and demanded to see two more credit cards before clearing her to go. She was relieved to finally pick up her bags of groceries and head for the Jeep.

But once home, her temporary embarrassment faded into concern over the implications in the grocery clerk's words. As soon as she put her groceries away, she got out the three one-hundred-dollar notes and examined them more closely.

She remembered hearing once that counterfeit money had the same serial number. Would her three one-hundred-dollar bills have the same number? She read off the first. "E-0-0-0-4-3-7-A." Then she went to the second. "E-0-0-0-4-3-8-A." She breathed a sigh of relief. They were different. Then the closeness of the two numbers began to cause her concern. She read off the third bill. "E-0-0-0-4-3-9-A."

The bills were in sequence! 437. 438. 439. Did that happen often? She looked at them again, noticing for the first time that they were crisp to the touch, as though freshly printed. Yet the paper looked faded, as though from age.

Age? She looked at the issue date of one of the notes and received another shock. To the right of the picture of Benjamin Franklin in small print was the inscription Series of 1930. Quickly she looked at the other two notes and found they also had a series date of 1930. These crisp bills had been printed over sixty years before! Did that account for their unusual appearance? Or were they really counterfeit as the grocery checker had claimed?

She knew she needed the benefit of an expert's opinion and then remembered Cash was a coin collector. A glance at her watch told her it was too late to contact him tonight. She tucked the notes back into their envelope, slipped it into her shoulder bag and headed for bed. But it was hours before sleep would override the question churning in her mind: Where had Duncan gotten such strange money?

CARRIE WAS STILL THINKING about the unusual money as she drove to Duncan's place the next morning after class. She felt an excited anticipation at seeing Cash again and discussing the notes with him. She knew her decision to drive herself had obviously disappointed him. She smiled. It felt rather nice that he wanted to be with her.

Still she was used to driving herself places and she liked it. It gave her a sense of control. Without the small diligences, life could get out of hand so easily. A few extra bites of food every day and one day one woke up overweight. A few skipped exercises and one day one woke up no longer fit. It was the casual inattention to such small details that often caused the most profound changes in life.

Vividly she remembered her father's angry words droning away on the subject as her overweight mother sat with head bent, in her kitchen, which, like her life, was hopelessly out of order.

"It's a mess! You're a mess!" her father shouted, his voice reaching clearly into the hallway where a young Carrie watched.

Remembered scenes of her father's yelling and her mother's cowering were always painful—the worst from her childhood. Carrie was so busy fighting to shove them back into some dark recess of her mind that she found herself looking up in surprise to see the trip was over and Duncan's house sitting before her.

Neither Cash nor his car was in sight. She turned off the Jeep's engine. Rather than sit in her hot vehicle she decided to make for the shaded porch. She walked up the front steps and headed for Duncan's old wooden rocker. She settled back in it and closed her eyes against the bright sunlight.

She could almost feel her old friend's presence as the sway of his chair gently rocked against the porch slats. He had told her often of how he had sat here and looked out on his beloved desert. It was from this very chair where only a couple of years before he had seen the wild, dappled-gray mustang stallion gallop past, his hoofs kicking up the desert dust as his silver mane and tail flew in the freedom of flight.

Carrie was so engrossed in the quiet of her cherished memories that she was totally unprepared when suddenly the quiet was rudely shattered by a horrible roar, mushrooming up from the porch's floorboards as though it had just escaped from hell, shaking the foundation in a deafening frenzy of some demonic dance.

Her eyes flew open as the adrenaline shot her to her feet and had her leaping from the seemingly possessed porch. As her body cleared the vibrating structure, Carrie's wits returned and she knew this was no supernatural demon at work. Her ears strained to locate the source of the hellish noise and ground shaking. It seemed to be coming from the back of the house. Carrie quickly turned the corner.

She couldn't believe her eyes. A giant, ugly orange Caterpillar tractor, its sharp metal jaws scooping up the desert dust, was shaking and roaring on its two endless belts like some ravenous beast. The racket was so deafening, she pressed her palms to her ears so she could hear her own thoughts.

Just about the time she was wondering how she might be able to get the driver's attention, his head turned in her direction and he suddenly shoved the tractor into park and switched off the engine. In relief at the sudden quiet, she dropped her hands. A burly figure jumped from the cab and started toward her.

He looked in his thirties and wore a frown of ill will across his dark-bearded face. He was over six feet and heavyset, with large arms bulging out of his soiled, sleeveless T-shirt. His chest and belly were enormous and reminded Carrie of the shape of a beer keg. One whiff of his breath when he stopped in front of her and she was sure he had been drinking.

"Did the old man think some sweetie could persuade me to stop?"

An angry indignation rose up in Carrie at the man's words. "Who are you? Why are you running your machinery on Duncan's land?"

An ugly sneer curled the pink strip of his lips within the curly mass of his dark beard. "That ain't the old man's land, sweetie. Don't play innocent with me. I told Van Epp last week. He don't sign, we don't stop. It's just that simple."

Carrie's fists balled. "You've been harassing Duncan with your noise? You've been trying to get him to sign something?"

The man's dark eyes narrowed as he frowned. "I'm in no mood for twenty questions, sweetie. Now, where's the old man?"

Carrie didn't really want to answer this obnoxious man, but she decided that might be the best way to get him to respond to her questions. She tried to keep her voice even. "Mr. Van Epp is dead. He died sometime Sunday night."

Carrie wasn't sure what response she expected from the man, but his immediate and loud denial certainly wasn't it.

"The hell he is! I saw him in that shack last night just as I have for the past week when I've dug my ditches. You think Hal Sawyer is some dummy?"

Carrie tried to make sense out of the man's words. "Your name is Hal Sawyer?"

"It ain't Goldilocks and the three bears. Now where is he?"

Then to Carrie's immediate terror, one of Hal Sawyer's large, grimy hands grabbed at her arm.

Immediately she wrenched her arm away, incensed that he dared to touch her. When he grabbed for her again, she swerved and angrily kicked him as hard as she could in the ankle. He let out a howl and a string of filthy curses. Carrie turned and ran. She heard his labored wheezing behind her as she sprinted back to the Jeep. As soon as she jumped in, she locked the door and rolled up the window as quickly as she could.

It wasn't quick enough. At the last instant, Sawyer shoved a grimy hand through the window. Carrie yanked on the window crank and just managed to imprison his forearm against the windowpane.

He let out an ugly oath as the sharp edge of the pane bit into his hairy flesh. Then his angry words wheezed out at her. "You just wait til I get a hold of ya!"

Carrie ducked the straining hand extended on her side of the windowpane. She kept the steady pressure on its pinned arm caught in the window as Hal Sawyer yelled foul, guttural threats. The unbearded upper half of his face was rapidly turning red.

She couldn't have cared less. An indignant fury gripped her. "Look, Sawyer, if you want to walk away with your right arm intact, you'd better walk away now!"

He ignored her threat. Maybe because of the liquor that fogged his brain or the anger that chained his emotions. His response was a slew of almost unintelligible cursing.

Carrie's knuckles were white from the tension in her hands as she clutched the window crank. Her muscles were shaking under the strain. Suddenly she realized she didn't know how much longer she could hold the foul-mouthed man at bay.

Her initial anger turned to fear as she stared at his fingers still spread inches from her face, wiggling like octopus tentacles, stretching closer and closer.

Her heartbeats lumped together as a sick, hard pit of terror grew in her stomach. Desperately, she fought to keep the window in its position. She closed her eyes and tried to close her ears against the dreadful obscenities spewing from Sawyer's sewer mouth.

Then suddenly the awful cursing just stopped. For a moment, she kept her eyes shut, not believing it could be true. When no cursing resumed, she opened her eyes and raised her head to see a powerful arm around Hal Sawyer's thick neck. Sawyer's dark eyes were bulging from the pressure against his windpipe. Then, with extreme relief she heard the words of a deep, familiar voice from behind him.

"This is the way it's going to be, chum," Cash said. "The lady is going to roll down her window and you're going to remove your arm. Then you're going to put that arm around your back. Otherwise, I'm going to break your neck. You got the picture?"

When Hal Sawyer did not immediately respond, Carrie watched the muscles flex in the powerful arm around his neck. The next second she saw new fear slash through Sawyer's dark eyes as his head bobbed up and down.

"It's all right, Carrie," Cash said. "Lower the window."

With shaking hands she slowly cranked the lever, releasing the pressure on Sawyer's forearm, but leaving a deep red mark. He yanked his arm free and immediately lurched back and swung his fist into Cash's face. Cash swerved out of harm's way, but the movement caused him to lose his hold on Sawyer's thick neck. The man twisted out of Cash's arms, shoved him to the ground and took off at a run back toward the Caterpillar.

Cash raced after him, but Sawyer had circled the Caterpillar and jumped into his waiting Ford Bronco before Cash could catch up. The man gunned the truck and drove away in a cloud of dust.

Cash angrily brushed the desert dust clinging to his shirt and jeans, disappointed he hadn't been able to hold the man. He circled back to where he had left Carrie. She got out of her Jeep as soon as she saw him, a small frown of worry on her face.

"Are you all right?"

He grinned. "Just a little dusty. How about you?"

She nodded and smiled, but he could see the white patch of fear still radiating around her mouth. His hand lightly clasped her shoulder. "You sure?"

Her answering nod took on more depth as her smile expanded.

"What was that all about?" Cash asked, dropping his hand.

A deep sigh escaped from her lips. "I'm not sure, but I intend to find out. That was Hal Sawyer. Ever heard of him?"

Cash nodded. "Yes, I recognized him. He's hung around the casinos for years, prone to drinking and fighting. He's a mean one. When he's not playing bully, he's Wahl's chief mining engineer."

Carrie didn't mask her surprise. "Evan Wahl? You mean Reno's mining magnate?"

"Yes," Cash said. "Several years ago Duncan lost a fight against Wahl's attempt to secure mining rights in the ghost town of Contention, which borders his land. It was Wahl's mining people who dug up Ernie, the skeleton in your lectures. Didn't you know?"

Carrie shook her head. "Not about the fight between the men."

Cash shrugged. "Doesn't really matter. Their disagreement is ancient history. What was Sawyer doing here today?"

Carrie's lips drew tight. "He was deliberately making noise by driving a heavy piece of machinery on Duncan's land."

She watched Cash rub the back of his neck, looking uneasy as he considered her words. "Carrie, I can understand your thinking so, but actually where the Caterpillar is parked back there is not Duncan's land. It's the outskirts of Contention."

Carrie protested. "But the ghost town is miles from here."

"What's left of it, yes. But the town's official boundaries extend pretty close to Duncan's house. I'm confused by what you said just a moment ago, though. What did you mean Hal Sawyer was *deliberately* running the machinery?''

Carrie licked her dry lips as she tried to make sense out of Sawyer's behavior and words. "He implied he was harassing Duncan for a week to try to get him to sign something. Do you know what?''

Cash's previous frown deepened. "Duncan didn't mention any noise harassment to me. Damn it, I wish he had. I'd have taken care of Sawyer and Wahl, too, if necessary. That old mining magnate is obviously too imbued with his own self-importance if he thinks he can get away with such tactics. Still, I'm not surprised Duncan tried to handle the business by himself.''

Carrie's lips tightened as she thought of the gentle old man having to listen to the terrible racket she had been subjected to and insisting on enduring it alone. A fierce anger rose up within her.

"Let's get inside, Cash. I want to call Evan Wahl. I've got a bone or two to pick with that man.''

Cash heard the anger in her voice and understood its provocation. He was feeling particularly provoked himself. He started up the stairs to Duncan's home with Carrie at his side.

Cash put the key in the lock and pushed the door open at the same time he leaned inside to flip on the light switch. Before he had time to turn back toward the room he heard Carrie's sudden sharp intake of breath. He whirled around to face into the room. What he saw made his blood boil.

The once-neat home of his friend was a shambles. Even Duncan's beautiful obsidian figurines from his worktable and display shelves had been thrown onto the wooden floor.

He heard Carrie on the phone calling the Sheriff's Department as he walked through the rubble in every room, clenching his fists.

Then he righted a living room chair and sank into it, telling himself that nothing anyone did to Duncan's property could possibly hurt Duncan anymore. He had been responding as though his friend was still alive. He put his head in his hands trying to find some peace of mind.

It was a few moments later when he looked up to see Carrie kneeling beside his chair, watching his face with some concern. He tried to smile. "Foolish to be incensed about this, huh?"

She leaned over and picked up a beautiful, hand-size obsidian mustang stallion, dappled gray with a silver mane and tail, just like the one Duncan had told her ran loose in his northern land of hills and canyons. It was a figurine she had only briefly glimpsed on his worktable yesterday, no doubt the last figurine Duncan had ever made. She fingered it lovingly.

"This was his work, Cash. These were his things. It makes me incensed, too. Who could wreak such wanton destruction?"

Cash exhaled. "It's not just wanton destruction. Look around closely. Things weren't just ripped and broken. They were taken apart and searched, like someone was trying to find something."

Carrie stood up, slipped the mustang figurine into the oversize pocket of her tunic blouse and looked around again, finding truth in Cash's words.

"Cash, could it have been the murderer?"

Cash came to his feet. "You took the thoughts right out of my head. Before the Sheriff's Department gets here, I'd like to check for those pill containers and the second good crystal glass."

She stepped forward, looking doubtfully into the kitchen at empty cupboards and broken glass strewn on the floor. "We don't have a chance of finding that glass now."

"That leaves the pill containers," Cash said. "Shall we try the bathroom?"

Carrie nodded. But once in the bathroom, they found the medicine cabinet empty and its contents also scattered on the floor. Carrie's eyes searched through the white, round pills.

"Bayer," she read. "Just aspirin."

"Whatever was in there wasn't aspirin," Cash said, pointing to the empty shells beside a rectangular-shaped box that looked like the kind Contac came in. "See the sticker on the outside?"

Carrie had bent down to get a better look.

"Carbamazepine," she read aloud. "That's it, all right. The name of the medicine Dr. Packer told us she had given to Duncan for his pain. But the only pills I see on this floor are aspirin. That means the carbamazepine container was already empty when whoever ransacked the place knocked it to the floor."

Carrie's voice turned triumphant. "And it's the only one here, so Duncan didn't have the hypertensive medicine. And if the hypertensive medicine wasn't his, someone else brought it here. Cash, we've got to point this out to Tom."

Cash got to his feet as she straightened beside him. But as he did so, he brushed up against the shower curtain and another empty pill container came rolling out from under it. "Wait a minute."

He squatted next to it and read the label, a frown digging into his forehead. "Look at this."

Carrie was down beside him reading the new label before he got the words out. The prescription was written by a Dr. Haskell for Mr. Van Epp. Carrie's hopes sank. "Metoprolol," she read aloud. "The high blood pressure medicine they found in Duncan's body. Damn."

They both straightened up and walked into the living room feeling subdued. Carrie's mind was fighting for an explanation.

"Okay, so Duncan did have the two medications. That still doesn't mean he took the pills knowingly."

Cash was nodding. "Actually, since we found the empty pill containers in the bathroom, I'd say it supports our belief that Duncan didn't intentionally take the overdose."

She raised hopeful eyes to his. "It does?"

"Well, yes. If Duncan deliberately overdosed on pills, it doesn't make much sense that he'd return the empty containers to a bathroom shelf after he was finished swallowing the contents."

Carrie nodded. "Yes, that's a bit too neat, isn't it? It seems more likely that the murderer returned the pill containers to the shelf in the medicine cabinet so that Duncan would not have suspected they had been emptied into the whiskey."

"Yes, much more likely," Cash said. "I wonder if Tom—"

Whatever Cash was wondering, Carrie wasn't to know because before he had a chance to finish his statement, he was interrupted by an angry voice booming at them from the doorway.

"What the hell have you done to my great-uncle's place?"

They whirled around to see Gene Van Epp stride into the room, a shotgun held tightly in his right hand and pointed in their direction. His face was contorted in anger. Carrie heard the intake of her own startled breath.

Cash's voice sounded irritated next to her. "Put the damn gun down, Gene. We found Duncan's place this way."

Gene Van Epp advanced farther into the room, the gun still pointing at them, a wild look in his dark eyes. "So you say. Well, I don't believe you. I can shoot you two, you know. You've trespassed, broken in and are going through my great-uncle's stuff. I've caught you in the act. No law in the land will convict me for protecting what is mine. Yeah, I can shoot you right now and get away with it."

Carrie stared at the gun and the wild look in Gene Van Epp's eyes and firmly believed the man was crazy enough to carry out his threat. Her lungs seemed to collapse within her chest as she tried to inhale through a constriction of immobilizing fear.

Chapter Six

"You'll shoot no one, Van Epp," a familiar voice said from the doorway. "Put the gun down. Now."

In immense relief Carrie turned to see her brother and a uniformed deputy standing there with guns drawn. Gene squinted at them, looking decidedly annoyed.

"All right. All right. I was just trying to scare them, is all. I'm putting the gun down. See?"

Gene eased the gun onto the wooden plank floor and straightened up again. The deputy closed the ground between them, stretched Gene up against a wall and proceeded to search him for other weapons while Gene heaped verbal abuse on him and kept demanding that Carrie and Cash be arrested.

As Cash stood by watching the procedure calmly, Carrie went over to her brother. "I'm sure glad to see you, Tom. As they say, you arrived in the nick of time."

Tom gave her shoulder a quick, obligatory pat before putting his weapon away and frowning into her eyes. "I was close by so I took the call of the break-in. What are you doing here?"

Carrie read her brother's look and knew she was in for trouble. She stood her ground. "I'm looking for evidence. The last time we spoke, you told Cash and me that it was up to us to supply you with information to prove Duncan didn't kill himself."

Tom shook his head. "Not by breaking and entering you don't."

Carrie shook her head. "We didn't force our way in. Duncan gave Cash a key. He was Cash's godfather, after all."

Tom was still shaking his head as he pulled her aside to be sure Gene and the deputy were out of hearing range. "Carrie, you have no legal right to be here. This house and all that's in it now probably belong to that bad-tempered lout over there who is just looking for an excuse to have you and Cash arrested."

"What have we done to him?" Carrie asked.

Tom shrugged. "You personally, nothing. But he and your friend, Cash, had a mild altercation yesterday that ended up in wounding Gene's pride. He's out for revenge. This morning he tried to file an assault charge against McKendry. When that failed, he did file a dognapping charge against your friend."

Carrie hurried to explain. "The dog was injured, Tom. Cash took him to a vet to have him treated. Gene had no right. How did he even know the dog was gone?"

Tom held up his hands at Carrie's angry tone. "Keep your voice down, Carrie. Look, considering the circumstances, I don't think the dognapping charge will hold water. In truth, Gene had gone to the animal shelter with the intent of having Bonanza put to sleep."

"He was going to kill Bonanza? For God's sake, Tom, he's the one you should be arresting!"

Tom gestured Carrie outside, obviously realizing he couldn't count on her unemotional response. Once down the porch steps, his blue eyes squinted at her through the bright sunlight.

"Look, Carrie, if I'm lucky today I won't be arresting anybody. I'll tell Gene that you and Cash came to Duncan's place at my direction. It's not the straight truth, but since I did ask you both for evidence to support your theory on Duncan's death, I'll make a generous interpretation of how that might have influenced your subsequent actions. However..."

Carrie hated Tom's "howevers." Ever since they were children she had come to learn that the "howevers" were generally followed by the dire consequences of her previous actions. She waited stone-faced while inwardly she cringed.

"If I do arrest somebody today it will probably be you for impersonating a Sheriff's Department detective. Dr. Packer called the office this morning curious to know more about the 'woman detective' who came to see her yesterday afternoon."

Carrie knew the news wasn't going to be good, but those words made her heart sink. With difficulty she held her ground. "I was trying to find out how Duncan got the medication that killed him."

Tom shook his head. "Damn it, Carrie, that's my job. Just because I brought you in as an anthropology expert when we found that old skeleton a year ago, you can't go around acting like you're part of a Sheriff's Department investigation anytime you feel like it. Now I know Duncan was your friend, and I'm trying to make every allowance for your grief in this matter, however—"

Carrie didn't feel ready for whatever might follow. She spoke up quickly.

"Yes, Tom, I was out of line. But Duncan neither committed suicide nor was his death an accident. He was murdered."

Tom blinked at her, the look on his face giving her the impression she had just spilled hot coffee all over his brain cells.

"What did you say?" he finally asked.

"I said murder, Tom. Someone poisoned Duncan Van Epp by putting those two drugs in that whiskey and tricking him into drinking it. That same person kicked Bonanza, breaking two of his ribs, and shut him outside the house, something Duncan never would do. And now the murderer has torn Duncan's house apart, searching for something."

Tom watched Carrie's face, a contemplative frown rippling his brow. "What was this murderer supposed to be searching for?"

She bit her lip. "I don't know."

Tom's hands found his hips. "Your guesswork on this is very unlikely. If someone murdered Duncan Van Epp to steal something from him, why did this person wait until a full day later to search the premises?"

Carrie stood in front of her brother, her hands on her hips mimicking his stance. "Perhaps it was necessary in order for the killer to murder without having it look like murder. By waiting until the next day, he could make the break-in look like an act of vandalism, something not associated with Duncan's death."

Tom shook his head. "You're giving your fictitious criminal the benefit of too much logic. It's much more likely this was a simple suicide and an unassociated break-in."

Carrie's anger stretched her vocal cords. "A *simple* suicide? Is that the operant word here, Tom, the one that's driving your investigation? Look for the simple solution? Forget about whether it's the right one?"

Tom's look became dark. "I don't deserve that."

Carrie kept her chin up, despite the fact that she knew she was sticking it out. "No, most of the time you don't, Tom. Most of the time you are the best detective sergeant in the Washoe County Sheriff's Department since Dad was there. Most of the time your investigative work is flawless. Most of the time."

"But not now, huh?" Tom's voice turned sarcastic. "And you know all about investigative techniques, don't you, Carrie? You took scores of units in criminology while you were getting your doctorate in physical anthropology."

He knew of course she had no formal training in criminology and his sarcastic remarks were an attempt to bring that fact as painfully as possible to her attention. It was an uncomfortable reminder, considering the importance she placed on formal education. But it wasn't uncomfortable enough to get Carrie to back down from her stand on Duncan's death.

Her back straightened into a board. Her voice sounded as hard and unyielding. "Duncan was murdered. I'll prove it."

Then she turned from her brother and walked quickly away toward her Jeep, ignoring his calls after her to stop. Cash was waiting beside the Jeep when she reached it.

"I picked up Duncan's mail. It was stuffed with the usual junk mail advertisements and this box of new bank checks. This envelope doesn't have a return address."

Carrie was still feeling the anger of her exchange with her brother. She barely glanced at the white envelope with Duncan's name and address scribbled across the front in almost illegible markings. There was something familiar about the handwriting, but at the moment her anger held all her concentration.

"Better put it all back in the mailbox, Cash. I don't want my brother accusing us of stealing anything."

Cash heard the hurt and anger in her voice and gave her an understanding nod. "Follow me back into Reno and I'll buy you lunch. I know a place with an excellent buffet."

Carrie nodded as she got into the Jeep, not trusting her voice to sound normal. As she backed the vehicle out, she saw Tom watching her, an exasperated look on his face. She hated leaving with these bad feelings between them, but to give in to Tom would be to accept Duncan's death as a suicide. She couldn't do it.

As she followed Cash toward Reno, she shifted uneasily on the warm seat. That was when she felt the bulge in her pocket and remembered the mustang figurine she had placed there earlier.

Carrie realized she shouldn't have removed it from Duncan's home, but turning around and going back now was out of the question. She'd just have to call Tom later after she'd calmed down to let him know she had it. She also realized that in her disagreement with her brother, she had forgotten to mention her earlier run-in with Hal Sawyer. As it had many times in the past, her anger had robbed her of all other thoughts.

Once back in Reno, Cash led Carrie to Fitzgerald's Casino. She followed him through the buffet line on the third floor, but returned to their table to just pick over her food.

Cash asked for no explanation, just ate quietly across from her. It was because he didn't pry that Carrie finally told him about the bitter words she had shared with her brother. He listened quietly through it all; then she felt his hand gently encircling one of hers as it lay on the table.

"I think not being believed is the most frustrating thing we human beings can experience," he said. "When someone refuses to believe us, they're saying that either we're lying or that we're not capable of perceiving the truth. Either message is a heavy blow because it strikes at the very core of who and what we are."

Carrie sighed. "Trouble is, Cash, no matter how sure I am that Duncan was murdered, I really have no idea how to go about proving it. Tom is right. I have no training."

Cash considered her words. "Well, neither do I, of course, but I'm a great believer in basic intellect and good common sense. I think we both possess those."

She smiled over at him, thankful for his support and very drawn to the kind of man he was proving to be. She raised her cup for a sip of coffee and found her hand a bit unsteady as the warmth of his touch slowly withdrew.

"I know you'll be happy to hear Bonanza is doing fine this morning," Cash said. "He's much perkier and doesn't seem nearly so sore. I thought I'd pick him up from the house and bring him down to the office this afternoon to keep me company."

"With all this activity we've been involved in because of Duncan's death, how are you managing to keep your business going?"

Cash scratched an ear in an unconcerned way. "I've been closed since yesterday. I'll open up this afternoon for a few hours for some regular customers and then I'll adjust my hours through the rest of the week as necessary. I'm my own boss."

Carrie smiled. "Must be nice. I used to think becoming a teacher would allow me to control my own time and material, but I soon learned restrictions and structures come with it just as with most any other job. Still it has its compensations."

"The interaction with the students?"

She smiled and nodded, pleased he had understood without her having to tell him.

"You're very good at getting the students involved, Carrie. But I thought anthropologists preferred to be in the field unearthing ancient bones and making startling discoveries?"

She shook her head. "It sounds far more glamorous than it is. I spent six months in the burning sun in Africa at an archaeological dig while I was working on my doctorate. I found the flies bite, there was never enough water for a bath and I was becoming perpetually bent over from the unending hours of scraping away at the earth, trowel and brush in hand."

"Did you find anything?" Cash asked.

"Not exactly what you'd call earth-shattering fossils," she said. "Two teeth of some ancient pig, nothing of ancient man whom I had gone to study. Do you enjoy what you do?"

Cash nodded. "Very much. I've always been a history buff, and numismatists have to know a lot of history. Actually, Carrie, now that I think about it, I believe we're both just different types of historians. You learn about people from their bones. I learn about them from their means of monetary exchange."

Monetary exchange. The words shot like an arrow through Carrie's head, piercing the clog of intervening events to strike a bull's-eye at an item that had been foremost in her mind just that morning.

"Cash, I almost forgot," she said as she reached into her bag to retrieve the envelope, and handed it to him. "There's something strange about this money Duncan left for me."

Cash leaned forward in his chair, taking the notes out of the envelope and studying them intently for several minutes. His voice was laced with interest and growing excitement. "Yes, I see. They were distributed in 1930, yet they look crisp and new, in uncirculated condition. And the serial numbers are in sequence."

"They're real, aren't they?"

"Oh, yes. Not only is this money genuine U.S. currency, but it's worth considerably more than its face value."

Carrie frowned. "Considerably more? I don't understand. How can paper money increase beyond its stated face value?"

"Actually, in the last thirty-five years or so, the collection of paper currency has increased to such an extent that notes that were once plentiful are now rare. Collectors are competing with one another for the acquisition of choice notes. More and more, paper currency collecting is becoming an adjunct of coin collecting and almost all us numismatists collect both."

Carrie felt intrigued. "How much more than face value would one of these notes bring?"

Cash shrugged. "I can't say for certain without checking with the current *Paper Money of the United States* guide back at the office. Let's go there as soon as we finish lunch."

He leaned his elbow on the table as he stirred some cream into his coffee. Carrie felt the new tension in him. She knew something else was on his mind, but his next words gave her a jolt. "Carrie, have you considered that this old money might have something to do with Duncan's murder?"

Her eyes became bright and she sat up straighter in her chair. "You mean if these bills are valuable and Duncan had more of them, someone might have killed him for them?"

"Somebody ransacked his house looking for something."

Carrie's eyebrows met in a frown. "But the envelope addressed to me was left. Doesn't it seem logical that would have been taken, just in case?"

Cash sipped his coffee. "Maybe the person never thought Duncan would put any money inside. You said he normally paid by check."

Carrie bit her lip. "Even if we were able to go back and search Duncan's place, it wouldn't tell us much. If we didn't find any money, it could be either because there wasn't any to begin with or that the murderer already found it and took it."

Cash watched the dejected look on her face and leaned toward her, trying to imbue his voice with confidence. "That doesn't mean we can't do anything. We've got these three notes."

"What can they tell us?"

"Well, there has to be a reason that money wasn't in circulation. The 1930 issue was distributed through the middle of the '30s. Remember what else took place during that time frame?"

Carrie chewed the side of her cheek in thought. "All I can think of is the Great Depression."

Cash smiled. "Bingo, the Great Depression, a time of little money and what little money people had, they needed for food, clothing and shelter. I can't see them hoarding any of the stuff."

"Yes, people needed life staples right then, didn't they?"

Cash nodded. "And add to that the fact that paper currency wasn't even considered collectible in those days and you have a further reason for not holding on to it. Why was this money an exception? Why wasn't it in circulation?"

Carrie's eyebrows rose as she picked up one of the three notes and gently turned it over in her hand. "It's intriguing, isn't it? Do you really think we can discover the history of these bills?"

"We can try, Carrie. Are you game?"

Carrie nodded as she got to her feet, lacing the strap of her shoulder bag over her arm in preparation to leave. She felt good in Cash's company. Part of it was because he was handsome and charming, of course. But he was also intelligent, dependable and caring—qualities she found even more attractive.

"Well, hello, Cash!" a feminine voice said suddenly from behind Carrie, startling her. She turned in surprise to see a stunning redhead in formfitting jeans and sweater.

Cash immediately extended his hand and smiled. "Hi, Tiffany. Good to see you. I'd like you to meet Carrie Chase. Carrie, this is Tiffany Raven, a performer here at the casino."

Carrie took Tiffany's extended hand and felt the woman give hers a good solid shake. The smile beneath the woman's heavy makeup was also good and solid. Carrie found herself liking the openness she found in the woman, despite a note of jealousy that had uncharacteristically begun to play beneath her outward calm.

"Won't you join us?" Carrie asked, surprised to find her invitation nearly ninety percent sincere.

Tiffany waved her hand negatively. "No, I can see you've finished. Besides I've got rehearsals for the late show. Just caught a glimpse of you, Cash, and thought I'd come by to ask if you'll be there tonight."

Cash nodded. "You know I never miss."

Tiffany nodded at his assurance and turned back to Carrie. "Nice to meet you. I've got to run if I'm to be on time. Bye."

Carrie watched her retreating back, realizing that the note of jealousy she initially felt at Tiffany's appearance was rapidly composing into a symphony. It seemed pretty obvious that Cash and the very attractive redhead were quite "close" for him not to miss any of her performances.

Carrie felt the glow of only a moment before fading in the perfumed wake of the pretty showgirl. It came as a distinct shock to her to realize she had begun to accept Cash's displayed interest in her as an exclusive right and resented it being bestowed elsewhere.

She knew it was naive of her to think that someone as attractive as Cash would be walking around both unattached and uninvolved. Still, she had made just such an assumption. Well, now she knew better. Apparently he was a collector in all parts of his life.

Cash recognized a new formality in Carrie's body language as she strode toward her Jeep. Just a few moments before he could have sworn she had given him a much warmer message. As he drove the short distance to his shop on Virginia Street, he kept trying to figure out what could be bothering her.

Then in a flash it came to him. Tiffany. Should he have explained Tiffany was married to a friend of his and that they met every Tuesday night at a Gamblers Anonymous meeting?

Maybe the former explanation, but not the latter. While you were trying to initially engage the attentions of a woman, you didn't immediately blurt out that you had spent years as a compulsive gambler and were only now considering it under control. That was hardly the way to win the interest of someone special like Carrie.

But he should have explained about Tiffany. Carrie Chase was not the type of woman who would like feeling his intent was to make her one of a number of women he had on a string and Tiffany's remarks could very well have left that impression. He didn't sleep around. He didn't like Carrie believing he did.

When he thought about it, however, he realized there was a bright spot. If she hadn't been interested in him, Tiffany's reference to their meeting later wouldn't have bothered Carrie. Still, he didn't want to make these kinds of mistakes with the attractive anthropologist. He had already found out the hard way that thoughtlessness could rapidly ruin a relationship.

He had the shop door open about the same time Carrie had parked her Jeep and joined him. They entered the store together and Cash flipped on all the lights, hoping for an opening that would let him remove the palatable wall of stiffness he could feel coming from his companion.

Carrie's disappointment about what she imagined to be Cash's extensive love life was temporarily forgotten, however, as she looked around in pure delight at the vast array of coins and other collectibles that lined the spotlessly clean shelves of the small shop's walls. Shiny, glistening objects caught her eye at every turn. The antiquity of so many of the coins were remarkable and she was thinking she could spend a whole day here just enjoying looking at all the different treasures on display.

Cash watched her as she moved from shelf to shelf, fingering the objects of his profession, looking as though she didn't want to miss a single one. He was enormously pleased at her interest and said nothing for several minutes, not wanting to interrupt her obvious enjoyment. When she finally seemed to become conscious of him again, she grinned a little sheepishly.

"Sorry. Didn't mean to get sidetracked. Do you really know the history of all this?" she asked as her hand swept across the shop encompassing the thousands of items lining the shelves.

He smiled. "I've had a lot of years to devote to their study. I'm not much for nightlife and partying, Carrie."

Carrie wasn't sure how to read the message in his words or even if there was one. She felt the intensity of his look, but found Tiffany's image interfering with her ability to return the interest reflected there. She purposely turned away.

"I'd like to call Evan Wahl now," she said. "Events sidetracked me from getting to him this morning."

Disappointed at her pointed withdrawal, Cash just nodded toward the phone on the desk. "I'll check on the money. The telephone directory's underneath the set."

Carrie found a number for Wahl Mining. When she punched it in, a man's voice answered.

"This is Carrie Chase. I was a friend of Duncan Van Epp. I need to speak with Evan Wahl right away."

"Mr. Wahl is unavailable."

"When may I speak with him?"

"Speaking with Mr. Wahl is not possible, Ms. Chase."

Carrie felt her blood pressure rise. "I need to talk with Mr. Wahl about a very serious legal matter and—"

"Then contact Mr. Wahl's attorney. Goodbye, Ms. Chase."

Carrie sat back in astonishment at the loud dial tone buzzing in her ear. The man had hung up on her! In irritation and anger she dropped the telephone receiver back onto its base.

Cash was returning to his desk with a large red-and-white covered book taken from his shelf of many similar volumes. One look at Carrie's expression and he knew the conversation had not gone well. "What did he say?"

"He wouldn't even take my call."

Cash shrugged. "Frankly, that doesn't surprise me. Men like Wahl are rarely accessible. Don't worry. We'll find a way to get to him. Let's concentrate on trying to trace the notes Duncan gave you. Yes. Here they are. Design 208, number 1804-2 issued from 1929 to 1935 in sheets of six. Since your three notes are in uncirculated condition, they are each worth about four hundred dollars."

Carrie stared at Cash. "Did you say they are *each* worth four hundred dollars?"

He watched her, enjoying the excitement in her voice. "Yes. A total of twelve hundred dollars. Looks like our initial thoughts of robbery being behind Duncan's murder might not be too far off base."

Carrie licked her lips. "Cash, how can we find out where this money has been all these years?"

"It may not be possible to learn all the answers, but looking at these notes can help to point the way at least to some. For example, notice that in addition to being in numerical sequence, these notes have all been overprinted with the seal of the First National Bank of Nevada and the charter number 8424 is in the middle of the vertical axis on either side."

Carrie leaned over to look where Cash's finger was pointing. "What does that mean?"

"The Treasury Department now distributes Federal Reserve notes without regard to the districts imprinted on their face. But back in the thirties when these notes were printed and issued, the Treasury Department would have forwarded these notes to the nationally chartered bank of Nevada for the overprinting process and only that bank would have distributed the money."

Carrie thought she might be catching on. "So the notes were distributed in Nevada back in the early 1930s. Since they're in uncirculated condition and still in Nevada, you think that could mean they've been held locally since their issuance?"

Cash nodded. "That seems the logical explanation."

"How can we know how Duncan got hold of them?"

"Logically, I would say there are only two ways. Either they were recently passed to Duncan by someone releasing them into circulation without knowledge of their true value, or it was Duncan who has been holding on to them, also probably without knowledge of their true value."

"How can we find out which is the case?"

Cash exhaled. "Well since the person releasing them didn't know their true value, let's toss out the possibility that the money came from a collector. Frankly, Carrie, it seems much more likely that it was Duncan who's held this money all these years."

Carrie shook her head. "But why? He obviously didn't recognize its increased value."

Cash shook his head. "Stumps me. But if I remember correctly, the First National Bank of Nevada is now part of First Interstate Bank. If that's the case, we might be in luck. I've got a friend from college working at First Interstate. Maybe he can find a record of some kind. They must have made some notation when they overprinted these notes from the Treasury in those days."

Carrie nodded eagerly. "Can you call your friend?"

Cash reached for the phone and dialed. He renewed his acquaintance with his friend for several minutes before he gave him the description and numbers on the notes.

"Issued in 1930? Cash, that was a hell of a long time ago. You realize we've probably got nothing," his college friend said.

"Yes, but you'll look?" Cash asked.

"It'll take some time. I'll call you back tomorrow."

As soon as Cash put down the phone, he could tell from the look on Carrie's face that she understood they were fighting some pretty incredible odds. All the more reason it surprised him when her next words were said with real determination.

"Never mind, Cash. We'll find the answers we need to clear Duncan's good name. We've got to. We're the only ones who care."

Her eyes had deepened into a mysterious steel-blue as they gazed up into his. Cash felt their strength of purpose and something else. He searched deeper for that elusive quality, and just for the briefest of moments, glimpsed something incredibly sweet and infinitely fragile. Then it was gone.

"Carrie, I—"

Cash wasn't sure what he was about to say but in any case he didn't get a chance to say it as the ringing telephone interrupted him. Reluctantly, he answered, stating his name.

"Mr. McKendry, this is Nora Burney, the late Duncan Van Epp's attorney. You are named in his will. Please be in my office at ten o'clock sharp tomorrow morning for its reading."

Cash agreed as he made a note of the attorney's address. Then on a sudden impulse he asked, "Can you tell me who else will be present for the reading?"

As Nora Burney read off the list to him, Cash was jolted by the mention of one particular name. "I'll tell Ms. Chase and my grandmother, Mrs. Burney. You don't need to call them. Thank you."

"You'll tell me what?" Carrie asked as soon as Cash hung up.

Cash turned to her. "Duncan's will is to be read at ten o'clock tomorrow morning. You're to be there along with all his other beneficiaries. And you'll never guess who one of them is."

Carrie couldn't mistake the look of disbelief on Cash's face. She found herself leaning so far forward in her chair that she was at its edge. "Who?"

Cash let out a long breath. "The very man who harassed Duncan up to and probably including his final day on this earth—Reno's mining magnate, Evan Wahl."

Carrie slumped back in her chair as though she had been hit. "I don't believe it. Duncan barely had enough money to support himself in his final years. What bequest could he possibly be leaving a multimillionaire like Wahl?"

Cash's eyebrows rose. "What, indeed? And considering their fight over the mining rights to Contention, why would Duncan even have wanted to leave Evan Wahl a dime? Something is very strange here, Carrie. Very strange."

Chapter Seven

Despite Carrie's eagerness to go to the will reading Wednesday morning, she forced herself to call Tom before leaving for Nora Burney's office. As soon as he answered the phone, she took a deep breath and launched into her apology.

"I'm sorry, Tom. You bent over backward for me yesterday, and I showed my gratitude by acting like an imbecile. I'd like to think I'm adult enough to disagree with your conclusions and still act reasonably. Just walking away like that was childish."

Tom's voice sounded relieved. "It's okay, Carrie, I understand. You've always run in to champion the cause of those you've perceived as weak or mistreated. A reincarnated Joan of Arc, that's you. That's why you refuse to accept Duncan Van Epp's suicide. You won't let him be that weak—not even in death."

Her brother's words surprised Carrie. "Tom, what are you talking about? You can't really see me as some medieval warrior or crusader."

"No, but in a way I see you as a modern-day one. Think back to your relationships, Carrie. Remember that guy, Bob, whose company was trying to ax him on some trumped-up charge because he wanted to start a union? You didn't even like the guy until his trouble started. Then all of a sudden you two became an item."

"I wasn't in love with him, Tom. I was just—"

"I know—helping him out. Just like you 'helped out' that guy, Gordon, who couldn't handle money. You lost interest in him when he opened a savings account and proved he could balance a checkbook."

Carrie's tone picked up protest. "Tom, my feelings for those men aren't something you have the right to dissect or pass judgment on. I resent—"

"I know, Carrie, and were I in your shoes, I would be resenting me, too, about now. I've only brought up your relationships to Bob and Gordon because I think you're drawn to people who need help. You've got a soft spot for the weakness in others. It touches you somehow."

She sat quietly for a moment, just thinking about Tom's words. "Tom, I don't think—"

"Look, Carrie. I'm not trying to beat you over the head with this thing. I just want you to understand what motivates you sometimes—what is probably motivating you in your refusal to accept Duncan Van Epp's suicide. I'm not out to change you. Hell, I like you the way you are. For one thing I know if I was ever in trouble, you'd be there. Stubborn and bullheaded you may be but ... in a nice way."

Carrie exhaled in frustration. "Thank you for that anyway, Tom. You're wrong about Duncan, you're wrong about me but ... in a nice way," she said, deliberately using his own words. "And now I've got a couple of things I need to tell you. First, I removed a mustang obsidian figurine from Duncan's place yesterday. It wasn't intentional. I just slipped it into my pocket and forgot to leave it in the house when I left."

"Was it like the others that were strewn across the floor?"

"Yes."

"Where is it?"

"Sitting on the nightstand next to my bed."

"Well, leave it there for now. When you find out whose property it becomes, you can return it. What else?"

"It's about a man named Hal Sawyer."

Carrie went on to explain her confrontation with the mining engineer the previous morning behind Duncan's place. As she had anticipated, Tom wasn't too encouraging about the possibility of the district attorney bringing assault charges against Sawyer.

"It's okay though, Carrie. There are other ways to handle a bully like this Sawyer. I'll pay him a visit with a couple of big, mean-looking deputies and let him know he'd better stay away from you, or your big brother is going to come down on him hard. That's the kind of message his type of mentality understands. Are you going to the reading of the will now?"

Carrie felt surprised at Tom's question. "Well, yes. How did you know?"

"I'm a great detective, remember? Let me know if anything special happens. Talk to you later."

As Carrie replaced the receiver on the telephone base, she frowned at the covert message in her brother's words. If Tom thought Duncan committed suicide, why was he still keeping tabs on the case?

She shook her head in confusion, realizing, as she made her way to her Jeep, that she may have been reading more into his words than her brother intended. As she drove to the attorney's office she also found herself speculating on Tom's comments concerning her relationships. Yes, it was true she felt a strong desire to offer a hand when she met someone who could use some help. But it was natural, wasn't it? All decent people had those feelings, didn't they?

Still, the implication in Tom's words had begun to cause her concern. Was she drawn to weakness in others? And if so, why?

As she pulled into the parking lot of the lawyer's office, she was irritated to see she was a couple of minutes late. She took the stairs two at a time to the second-floor conference room. As she grasped the knob and swung the door open, she felt the eyes of those seated around the room's large, oblong table quickly swing her way.

She singled out Cash's face immediately. His white teeth shone against his deep golden tan as they flashed a greeting that warmed her down to her toes.

She deliberately tore her eyes from his handsome face and caught sight of Ann Tintori sitting next to him. The elderly anthropologist was wrapped protectively in a faded pink coat and seemed small and sad. The clear focus in her eyes and the set of the woman's chin gave Carrie the impression that Ann understood she was at the will reading of her dead friend. She smiled at Ann's sad face.

Then like a compass needle, Carrie's eyes swung toward the elderly man sitting to Ann's right—the man she knew must be Evan Wahl, Reno's famous mining magnate. He, like Ann, had to be in his eighties. But whereas she was small and frail, he was big and bony, with a huge beak of a nose, a gray-brown handlebar mustache, and a swab of similarly colored hair still quite thick surrounding his crown. He was dressed in a fine, dark suit with a thick gold chain of a hand-held watch swinging from his vest. Both of his large, bony hands clutched a sturdy black cane that sat midway between his prominent knees.

Carrie read his expression as that of a man used to absolute authority and irritated with the current proceedings because he was not directing them.

"Dr. Chase?" an impatient voice called.

Carrie's attention switched to a young, sleek brunette in a pin-striped business suit who was just rising from a seat at the oblong table to extend her long, red-tipped fingernails for a handshake. Carrie's hand safely ran the gauntlet and was met by soft flesh. The woman was at least four inches shorter and her dark eyes looked up at Carrie with undisguised disinterest.

"I'm Nora Burney," her slightly nasal voice said. "You're late."

It was a statement of fact with minimal rebuke. Carrie accepted it without returning comment and took a seat as the lawyer pointed toward a vacant chair on her left. As Carrie sat down, her eyes once again briefly touched Cash's face across the table. Despite the reason for the current assemblage and the recurring image of Tiffany, she couldn't help feeling warmed by the light resting within his gold-brown eyes.

"And now for the benefit of everyone, I will name each of you and at the same time insure that all beneficiaries are present as indicated in the will," Nora Burney said. She adjusted her glasses farther back on the bridge of her sharp, pointed nose.

"Is there anyone here who objects to the naming and will reading being tape-recorded?"

No one made any objection. Nora Burney turned on the tape recorder that sat next to her on the table and announced the purpose of the gathering as the reading of the will of the late Duncan Van Epp.

Carrie listened to the attorney list each of their names counterclockwise around the table. She started with Gene and Edward Van Epp III who sat immediately on her right. Then she named Cash, Ann Tintori, Evan Wahl and finally Carrie.

The tension in the suddenly quiet room felt like a physical thing as the lawyer paused ever so briefly before she began to speak the words written by the now-dead man.

"'My funeral has been both arranged and prepared for by me. My remains will be cremated and the ashes scattered into the wild horse canyon of my property in the Virginia Mountains. I have always felt a part of those mountains, at one with the wild mustangs who run free through its canyons, and of the Indian teachings of harmony with all life. It is my request that my ashes be scattered on the third evening following my death according to an ancient, Indian custom. Those who wish to attend the ceremony are welcome.'"

Carrie felt the tears collect at the back of her throat. Hearing these last words of Duncan's, even through the nasal voice of his lawyer, brought so clearly to mind the heart and spirit of her dead friend. She swallowed, trying to control her grief and her sense of loss at his passing. Then she realized that she had missed something the lawyer had said.

"Could you repeat that, please?" she asked.

Burney turned to her with the look an irritated mother might give her inattentive child. Carrie felt inwardly amused since she knew she was at least three years older than the lawyer.

Burney's tone strained out her words. "I said the sheriff's office has determined the death occurred during the early evening hours of Sunday. Therefore the ceremony of the ashes will take place this evening in the Virginia Mountains. Anyone wishing to attend may stay afterward and I will give them the name of the mortuary personnel to contact."

Carrie murmured a thank-you and the attorney continued with her reading of the will.

"'At the time of my death, my attorney was instructed to compute the exact cash value of my bank account. It is...'"

At this point Burney looked above her glasses and filled in what was obviously a blank in the line of the will. "Sixty-six thousand, two hundred and thirty-six dollars and fifty-two cents after all taxes and miscellaneous obligations."

She looked back at the paper in her hands. "'Of this amount I bequeath to Evan Wahl the sum of three thousand, one hundred and eight dollars, the final payment on an obligation long past due. I only wish my other slate of debt to him could be washed so clean.'"

Carrie looked over at Evan Wahl for some sign of recognition as to the meaning of Duncan's strange words, but Wahl's face was a stone mask.

Nora Burney continued reading.

"'I also bequeath to Ann Tintori, a lifelong friend, the sum of twenty thousand dollars, and I thank her most sincerely for her emotional support through many hard times.'"

Carrie looked over at Ann Tintori and saw tears at the corners of the woman's eyes. The elderly woman raised a thin, blue-veined hand to wipe them away. Carrie had no doubt that Ann was following these proceedings fully.

"'After these two bequests, the remaining sum in my bank account is...'"

Burney paused again, this time to check her notes. "'Is forty three thousand, one hundred and twenty-eight dollars and thirty-seven cents, an amount to be divided equally between my two great-nephews, Edward Van Epp III and

Gene Van Epp, in fond memory of their grandmother and the only woman I have ever loved, Elisabeth.'"

Once again Burney paused. Carrie was intrigued to learn that Duncan had loved the boys' grandmother. She looked to their faces to see how they were taking the news. Edward's expression was bland indifference. When her eyes traveled to Gene's face, however, she caught him biting his lip, a worried, dark look cloaking his countenance.

"'To Cash McKendry, my godson and good friend, I bequeath the deed to all the land of my desert ranch, knowing he will protect the wild mustangs who still roam its untamed hills.'"

Carrie heard an anguished gasp. At first she looked at Cash, but soon realized the exclamation had not come from him. She followed his stare to the rapidly reddening face of Gene Van Epp. Nora Burney's eyes remained on the paper before her as she read on.

"'To Carrie Chase, a lovely light who has brightened many of my recent dark days, I bequeath my desert home and all its humble contents, knowing she will treasure them simply because they come from me. Such is the genuine sweetness of her nature.'"

Carrie didn't want to cry, but the tears had begun to swallow her eyes. She looked down at her hands in her lap, fighting to keep control.

"'And finally, to Cash McKendry and Carrie Chase I give joint custody of Bonanza, my terrier and trusted companion, for six months following my death, knowing they both care for Bonanza and will enjoy his lively company. At the end of that joint custody period, I charge them to decide between themselves who will keep Bonanza as a pet, trusting that once they have had a chance to get to know Bonanza and each other well, they will find the decision an obvious one.'"

Carrie lifted her head, surprise managing to control the flow of tears still swimming in her eyes. She looked from the lawyer to Cash and found the latter watching her with a similar surprised stare.

The lawyer's thin, nasal voice whined on. "'This will was signed by me at Washoe County, Nevada, on July 1...'"

Just a little over two months ago, Carrie thought, as once again her mind wandered as it sought to put the words of Duncan's will into context. He had sat with his lawyer and made the decision to give her his beloved home and all his cherished personal possessions, even joint custody of Bonanza. He couldn't have told her more clearly how much he cared.

The lawyer's voice kept on reading through the final paragraphs of signatures and witnesses but Carrie wasn't paying attention. She was thinking again of Duncan and missing him. Then she remembered that he hadn't just died. He had been murdered. With new eyes, she looked around the table at the people sitting there. Could one of them have killed him?

"Ladies and gentlemen, that completes the reading of the will of Duncan Van Epp. Once again, should any beneficiary contest this will, he or she shall forfeit all said bequests and shall instead receive one dollar to—"

"Contest it? You bet I'm going to contest it!" Gene Van Epp yelled suddenly as he jumped out of his chair, his gold earring swinging beside his unshaven jaw. "The land was to be mine, all mine. McKendry tricked the old man into willing it to him!"

Gene Van Epp was pointing at Cash who sat composedly shaking his head. "You can't believe what you're saying, Gene."

Nora Burney turned in Gene's direction. "Mr. Van Epp, contesting your great-uncle's will would cause you to forfeit—"

Gene's color deepened to a muddy red as he turned to the lawyer. "Shut up! You're in on it, too. That's not my uncle's will. It's a fake! There's money beneath that land and you know it! I'll get my own lawyer. I'll show you. I'll show you all!"

And after that impassioned speech, Gene stormed out of the room, slamming the door behind him.

Carrie felt the residual anger still sizzling in the air, but Nora Burney's slightly nasal voice spoke up in apparent unconcern. "Are there any questions or further comments?"

The room was silent. "Then, ladies and gentlemen, this concludes this will reading." Nora Burney leaned over to switch off the tape recorder.

"If Mr. Wahl and Mr. McKendry will kindly remain, I have one further item of business I need to discuss."

"Ms. Burney," Carrie said, "you said you had the name of the mortuary where Mr. Van Epp's prearranged burial instructions were being handled?"

Burney nodded. "It's written on this card."

Carrie leaned over to take it from her hand, noticing that she had several others.

"May I have one of those, too?" Cash asked.

Burney nodded and handed him one. Edward Van Epp also reached for one. But Evan Wahl remained erect in his seat, stone-faced, clutching the curved handle of his sturdy black cane. Carrie was beginning to wonder if the man ever spoke.

She had pivoted in her chair to reach her shoulder bag in preparation to leave when out of the corner of her eye she saw the lawyer hold up a thick document. Burney leaned toward Cash and Wahl.

"Mr. McKendry, this is a signed agreement between Evan Wahl and Mr. Duncan Van Epp dated last Saturday which awards to Mr. Wahl unlimited mining rights to Mr. Van Epp's land. As this agreement was signed prior to his death, it is legally binding on—"

Shock vibrated through Carrie's frame like a physical jolt. She jerked around in her chair and shot to her feet before the attorney could get out another word. "No! It's not true! Duncan would never have signed such a document!"

Cash was also on his feet, his knuckles white as his hands gripped the table. "Where did you get that agreement? Did *he* give it to you?"

Cash's angry voice vibrated in the direction of Evan Wahl. Nora Burney's face went white beneath her rouge.

She just sat looking at them both with her mouth open. Faced with both Carrie and Cash's immediate denouncements, she was obviously at a loss for words.

Suddenly, Evan Wahl's angry, age-deepened voice boomed up from Carrie's left, causing her to jump in surprise.

"No, Burney didn't get the signed agreement from me. Hal Sawyer, my chief mining engineer, convinced Van Epp to sign, if it's any of your business."

Carrie turned to the formidable old man, totally unintimidated and unafraid as she felt the growing anger from his words warming the enamel on her teeth.

"That's not possible, Mr. Wahl. Hal Sawyer told me himself yesterday morning that he would continue to run your heavy machinery next to Duncan's house until he forced Duncan into signing. Since Duncan was already dead by then, getting his signature on this agreement would have taken nothing short of reincarnation."

Carrie watched her words bring a rush of deep color to Wahl's grayish skin. Suddenly he lurched forward. His big, bony hands snatched the document out of Nora Burney's hands. Then to Carrie's amazement, he straightened up to a towering height and ripped the thick agreement in two as though it were no bulkier than a postage stamp.

His voice growled fiercely at Cash. "Keep your stupid mining rights. The agreement and this conference are at an end."

Carrie found herself in uncensored awe as the old man turned and stalked toward the door, stabbing his cane periodically into the carpet as though to emphasize he had just wasted far too much of his precious time and would waste no more.

She was just gulping down her shock at the surprising actions of Evan Wahl when she was struck anew to hear a small, familiar voice calling out in uncharacteristic, crystal clarity. Carrie jerked around to see Ann Tintori standing straight and stiff, an amazingly coherent look in her frightened eyes.

"Duncan said past sins must be revealed! Dear God, he was right! Our silence has been wrong!"

And then to Carrie's continued amazement, Ann Tintori collapsed into her chair and sobbed. Cash immediately gathered his distraught grandmother in his arms, trying to soothe away the heartrending sobs emanating from her fragile little frame as his mind plunged headlong into new speculation generated by her amazing declaration.

Duncan had been about to tell something about past sins? His godfather and friend had been silent about something? Was this what Duncan had discussed with his grandmother on the afternoon of his death? Could this have been the news that had caused her to become so agitated? If so, what was in her "missing journals" that she had been so eager to find?

Desperately Cash worked to restore a semblance of calm to Ann's shaking frame so that he might ask the questions that burned in his thoughts.

Carrie watched Cash's ministrations, feeling confused by the words in Ann's outburst and helpless to lend a hand. She was just wondering what assistance she might be able to offer when she overheard Edward's mocking tone behind her.

"Have you ever seen such a ridiculous farce, Nora? And all over the foolish will of a foolish old man."

Carrie turned in anger to glare at Edward's sardonic smile. "Don't speak about Duncan that way, Edward."

Edward's thick, dark eyebrows raised in surprise at the vehemence in Carrie's voice. "Hey, toots, what's eating—"

"And don't call me 'toots'!" Carrie snapped.

Edward frowned as the uncompromising tone in Carrie's voice and look finally registered. He shook his head as he leaned his arm across Nora Burney's shoulders. "Obviously our anthropologist here thinks she's Dustin Hoffman in drag today. Give me a ring when the check's ready, Nora. Twenty thousand isn't much, but it should buy a small wedding trinket for my fiancée."

Nora Burney's eyes shone in obvious amusement and appreciation as they followed Edward's casual meander to the door. When the woman's eyes turned back to Carrie, however, the warmth had left them. Her nasal voice took on a distinct scold.

"He didn't mean anything by what he said about his great-uncle. Don't you understand men can't show their *real* feelings and that's why they denigrate the very things they care about?"

Irritation scratched along Carrie's nerves and found its way into her next words.

"No, Ms. Burney, what I do understand is that *real* men are whole human beings who care about the feelings of others and consequently think about what they say before they say it. Now if you'll excuse me...."

While Nora Burney's mouth continued to purse in disapproval, Carrie shoved the strap of her bag more firmly onto her shoulder and turned to Cash and his grandmother. Her irritation at Edward and the lawyer instantly dissipated as she saw Ann's sad face as she lay within Cash's supporting arms.

Carrie dropped down to her knees before them. "How is she?"

Cash shook his head. "I'm not sure."

"Duncan was right," Ann said in a small, little voice.

Cash shrugged. "It's what she keeps repeating to whatever question I ask, despite the fact that I think her memories of their conversation are clear. Maybe she'd feel better in more familiar surroundings. Would you like to go home, Grandmother?"

Ann nodded, a small tear in her eye.

Cash gave her shoulder a little squeeze. "Will you follow me as I drive her home, Carrie? I'd like you to be there when she feels like talking."

Carrie nodded, pleased to be included.

Cash helped Ann Tintori to her feet and began to escort her from the room as Carrie followed. When they had gotten into the hallway, however, he stopped and turned to Carrie. "She doesn't have her purse. She must have dropped it when she was sitting in the chair. Would you check for me?"

Carrie nodded and turned around to head back into the room. Nora Burney was bent over her briefcase. Carrie could see the lawyer's long, sharp fingernails were delaying her efforts to slip in the will and its associated papers. Carrie ignored her and headed for the chair where Ann Tintori had been sitting.

Finding it empty, she bent over to check underneath for Ann's purse, spotting it lying between the chair's back legs. She was just reaching for it when she jumped at the sudden, loud exclamation coming from the direction of Nora Burney.

Carrie jerked toward the woman at about the same time that Cash pushed open the door and lunged in. He looked quickly at Carrie and finding her all right, visibly relaxed as he realized the lawyer had been the one who yelled.

Indeed, the look on Burney's face was still full of horror. "The damn briefcase latch tore my thumbnail off! It's bleeding!"

Carrie approached the lawyer and gently clasped the woman's hand. Her nail had been torn right down to the quick. Carrie's hand dived into her shoulder bag for some Kleenex and she used it to dab at the excess blood trickling down Nora Burney's hand before wrapping several tissues around the damaged nail trying to put some pressure against the exposed and still-bleeding vessels.

"You'll need to keep some pressure on the wound for a time, Ms. Burney. Some antiseptic is also in order, I would say. Would you like to see a doctor?"

Nora Burney looked a little pale beneath her rouge, but she shook her head.

"No, of course not. It was just the suddenness of the pain and blood. I'm all right now."

Carrie nodded and turned back to resume her retrieval of Ann's purse from beneath her chair. But no sooner had she turned from the lawyer when she heard another cry. In disbelief her eyes flew back to Nora Burney's face. But the lawyer looked as surprised as Carrie. Then Carrie realized the direction of the new outburst hadn't been from where Burney stood. It was coming from out in the hallway!

She started for the doorway that Cash had already run through, her heart beating in her chest like some wild thing as a terrible foreboding gripped at her insides. Grabbing the door frame, she swung her body into the hallway. Then she halted in her tracks, her worst fears materializing in living color right before her eyes.

There was Cash racing to the bottom-stair landing where Ann Tintori lay sprawled like a broken, little rag doll.

Chapter Eight

"She's hanging in there, Mr. McKendry. The fall broke her right hip and has given her a concussion, but her vital signs are steady and we have hopes she'll recover."

Cash's initial relief at the doctor's introductory words clouded over as the medical woman's qualification sunk in. "You have hopes? You're not sure?"

The doctor's short blond curls shook. "Mrs. Tintori isn't young. We've wired her hip so it will heal, but she hasn't regained consciousness yet. Her head X rays show some swelling and clotting at the site of the concussion. We think we'll have it under control soon and if we do, she's got a good chance of making it."

The doctor's words ate like acid through Cash's hope. He took a deep, steadying breath. "When will you know?"

"It's impossible to say. She could remain this way for days. The best thing you can do is leave her in our hands. Believe me, we'll give her our best."

"May I see her?"

The doctor's hand steered Cash toward the nurses' station. "She's in intensive care. All you'd see are tubes. Leave your number with the nurses' staff and I'll call you the moment we know one way or the other."

Cash complied. He had ridden to the hospital in the ambulance with his grandmother while Carrie had followed in her Jeep. As she drove him back to his car, an uneasy quiet settled on them both.

When he finally spoke, Carrie could hear almost a desperation in his tone. "I've got to occupy my mind, Carrie. If I let myself dwell on her lying back there—"

"I understand, Cash. Tell me what you think she meant by those strange words about 'past sins.'"

"I don't know. But whatever they were, Duncan told her he wanted to reveal them." Carrie watched Cash lean forward in his seat, resting his elbows on his knees as he steepled his hands beneath his beautifully shaped chin. His voice sounded deep and contemplative. "Duncan called my grandmother Sunday afternoon. I don't know what the call was about, but Monday morning she begged me to take her to the university to look through her files. She was so insistent about finding those missing journals. I wonder."

"What is it, Cash?"

He turned to look at her. "Ann's missing journals may give us a clue as to what's going on. Will you help me try to locate them?"

She purposely turned the wheel. "Off we go."

Cash flashed an enthusiastic smile that sent tingles to the backs of her knees. "Thank you, Carrie. Your being with me through this means a lot."

ANN TINTORI'S STUDY smelled of old leather book bindings and cinnamon, an imaginative room deodorizer contributed by long brown sticks of the spice in an open jar on the desk. Carrie found it a pleasant smell.

"Ready for some history of my family's past in the old West?"

Carrie left her place at the desk to join Cash near an open file cabinet. "Is that what's in Ann's journals?"

Cash nodded as he lugged a stackful of leather-bound journals over to the couch and let them drop. He sat down and opened the top one. He was trying to focus on it, but Carrie's sudden nearness as she settled next to him on the couch was proving to be a major distraction. Her scent was warm and enticing and he could feel a heat rushing to the point where their thighs lightly brushed.

Carrie leaned over Cash's arm as she tried to get a better look at the journal he held. She was immediately struck by the clear, perfect penmanship of the printing on the yellowed paper.

"'Ann Tintori, Contention, Nevada, June 2, 1928.' Cash, I didn't realize your grandmother once lived in Contention."

Cash tried to ignore the racing of his pulse at Carrie's close proximity. With a concentrated effort, he cleared the sudden thickness in his throat as he answered her question.

"Contention is where my grandmother and her three brothers were reared. The two eldest boys took off for California to find work when the depression hit. Only her younger brother stayed to work in the Nevada silver mines. But that's in a later journal. This 1928 one is the first. My grandmother began it on the day she and my grandfather, Paul, married."

"You sound like you know these journals well."

Cash shrugged. "It's been a while since I've seen them. Grandmother came to visit me as often as she could after Mother died. On cold days we'd cuddle about the fire and she would read to me from one of the journals, but she guarded them very jealously and forbade me to read them on my own."

"But you're going to read them now?" Carrie asked.

Cash tapped the beginning page reluctantly with his fingertips. "Right now I just want to see if any are missing. But if reading them is the only way to find out what's going on, I'll do it."

Cash closed the first journal from the year 1928 and put it aside. He opened the second in the pile and they noted it began on January 1, 1929. The third one was labeled January 1, 1930.

"These are in chronological order, all right, Cash. That means this next one will be January 1, 1931."

But it wasn't. When Cash opened the fourth journal, it read January 1, 1933. Quickly he looked through the remaining pile.

Carrie heard the excited rise in his voice. "There's a journal here for every following year up to and including 1965, but there's none for the years of 1931 and 1932. Those are the missing journals, Carrie. They have to be the ones my grandmother was trying to locate. What do they contain that she was so desperate to read to help her to remember?"

Carrie knew Cash's questions were frustrated, rhetorical ones seeking no reply. "Did your grandmother ever put the journals in a place other than that file cabinet?"

Cash shook his head.

Carrie searched her mind for other answers. "Maybe the years of 1931 and 1932 are contained in the back half of the 1930 journal? Perhaps if we skimmed through it—"

Cash nodded eagerly at Carrie's suggestion and grabbed for the 1930 volume. He set it on his lap and opened it from behind, scraping back pages with his thumb. He began to read aloud.

"December 20. Another family moved out of Contention today. Ever since the stock-market crash last year, things have been getting progressively worse. The papers say an upturn is coming. I wish I could believe them."

Cash raised his eyes from the journal to look over at Carrie. "This has to be December 20, 1930, with the reference to the stock-market crash of the year before. It looks as though the years of 1931 and 1932 are definitely missing."

Carrie nodded. "Why don't you read to the end of this journal? It may refer to events that followed."

Cash nodded, quickly finding the place where he had just stopped reading. "This is the rest of that day's entries.

"Edward returned to Contention today after eloping last week with Elisabeth, Duncan's promised bride. This has been such an unhappy affair! Elisabeth is such a stupid little fool! Any woman with half a mind could see Duncan was the smarter, kinder brother. If only she had listened to me about Edward's quick-rich schemes and defect of character. But Elisabeth is blind to all but Edward's dark, handsome looks.

"Duncan will listen to nothing said against them. He loves them both too deeply and too well. And there is the real tragedy, because I fear they know his heart and will use it against him."

Cash looked up from the journal and sought Carrie's eyes. Like his, hers reflected the astonishment of what he had read.

"How awful for Duncan," Carrie said. "Your grandmother didn't read this part to you, did she?"

He shook his head. "Perhaps she thought it was too personal to Duncan. Remember the words he used in his will? He was still describing Elisabeth as the only woman he had. ever loved. I wonder what happened to her and his brother Edward."

As though of one mind, Carrie reached down to turn to the next page of the journal and Cash continued reading.

"December 24. Christmas Eve. Several days ago, my Paul and I cut down a piñon pine tree and brought it into the house to decorate. But like our Christmas spirit, the decorations remain packed away and neither of us lift a hand to bring them out. So we sit in front of the fireplace and watch our unadorned tree shed its needles like sharp, pointed tears.

"Times are so bad. Money is so difficult to make. Orders for Paul's carpentry have dropped off to nothing and we take whatever people offer to pay their debts. This morning it was a scrawny chicken and we were so happy.

"It's been six months since the financial support stopped for my anthropological excavations at Pyramid Lake. I'll go on as long as I can without it, but somehow we have to eat and buy fuel for this winter. Paul suggests we take in boarders. We have a couple of extra rooms since the children we planned on never came. Considering the times, I'm glad now they didn't.''

Cash stopped reading. From the look on his face, Carrie could tell these were other entries his grandmother had not shared with him. She could also tell he was somewhat reluctant to go on, but they both knew they had to if they hoped to find an answer to the mystery from the past.

"There's nothing about Duncan, Edward or Elisabeth in that entry," Carrie said. "Does Ann mention them again?"

Cash scanned the page. "Yes, a later entry. I'll read it.

"December 28. Edward and Elisabeth have moved in with Duncan. Poor Duncan! Elisabeth claims it's only temporary. She's heard the silver mines will be offering jobs again soon, but even if one comes through for Edward, I know him too well to think it will last. He reminds me so much of my younger brother. Immature. Irresponsible. Thinking only of today.

"Then there is Duncan. Dependable, sober, and so quietly sad! How can he stand to be around Edward and Elisabeth so much, constantly being reminded of their betrayal? With businesses and people leaving every day, there's no work for him here. He says a law school friend has written he needs help in his practice back East. I pray Duncan will go to him for a while and heal.

"That's the last entry for the year, Carrie," Cash said as he closed the journal and put it down. "What a sad business. It's a little eerie to read about family and a friend when they were young and living through a time that you've only known through the pages of a history book. Duncan never talked about such things with me. Did he ever say anything to you?"

Carrie shook her head. "He filled me with the stories of Indian legends told to him by his father and grandfather. Perhaps his own personal history was too painful for him to speak about. I'm afraid your grandmother's entries have whet my appetite for more. I wonder what the first entry for 1933 is?''

"Me, too," Cash said as he smiled at her while reaching for the 1933 journal. He opened the first page and began reading.

"January 1. My beautiful baby girl smiled at me today, bringing in the spring despite the snow still lying on the ground outside. Paul danced around the room with her, singing like a crazy man.

"I've never realized how much Paul missed our not having children until our little Grace came our way. Now, despite the awful terror of the last years and the financial hardships of these times, we know the undaunted hope of new life.

"Holding her in my arms these past difficult months has truly been the only thing that has kept me sane. Elisabeth's child has saved Duncan, too. Little Edward II has helped to focus his loss away from Elisabeth's death in childbirth. Duncan's determined to bring up the boy as his own, and with my prodding, put the sins of the past behind him. Finally, I feel certain he will keep his silence. It's a brand-new year and a brand-new future for us all."

Cash closed the journal. "Did you notice the terminology Grandmother used in this last entry?"

Carrie nodded. " 'Sins of the past.' Is it a coincidence?"

He shook his head. "She might have been referring to Edward and Elisabeth's betrayal of Duncan's trust."

Carrie nodded. "Who was Grace?"

"My mother. The other baby was Edward II, the son of Duncan's brother and Elisabeth. We know from this that Elisabeth died in childbirth. But why was Duncan the one to bring up the child? Where was Duncan's brother, Edward?"

Carrie shook her head. "Perhaps if you read your grandmother's subsequent journals, you'll find references to those lost years."

Cash took her suggestion and he and Carrie read quietly to themselves for the next couple of hours through the following years of his grandmother's neatly printed journals. But as they closed the last one, they did it no wiser.

Cash's tone was laced with frustration. "There's not even a mention of Edward. Indeed, nothing that occurred during 1931 or 1932 had ever been referred to again. It's as though Grandmother had purposely wiped those years from her mind and her writing."

Carrie nodded. "There is a lot about Edward II's upbringing, however. It's far different from what I heard."

"In what way?" Cash asked.

"Well, for one, I never knew Edward II both married an alcoholic and became one himself. Your grandmother's journals say Edward's wife had the two boys, Edward III and Gene, before she got drunk one night and stepped in front of a truck. Then Edward Van Epp II collapsed into a gutter in an alcoholic stupor and froze to death, leaving Duncan with two more boys to raise."

Cash looked questioningly at her. "Duncan told you something different?"

"Actually, Duncan never spoke of bringing up his nephew," Carrie admitted. "But Edward Van Epp III always told me his mother and father died in a car accident."

Cash shrugged. "So Edward lied. I'm not sure I blame him. We all try to clothe some naked truths in the finery of wishful thinking. That's what Duncan did about Gene and his gambling. Bailed him out so many times, Gene still doesn't know what it's like to face up to the consequences. Although now that Duncan is gone, I imagine he's about to find out."

Carrie looked around the less than tidy study. "Is there another place your grandmother could have put those missing journals?"

Cash exhaled. "She's misplaced many things since her stroke. Even her normal neatness has suffered. Unless she regains consciousness and remembers..."

Cash's voice just faded away at the painful memory of his grandmother lying helpless in the hospital. The silence that followed while each dwelt on their own thoughts was so deep that when the study's old-time grandfather clock chimed the hour, they both gave a start. Carrie jumped to her feet.

"Cash, if I don't hurry, I'm going to be late for my afternoon class. Shall I drop you by your car now?"

Cash got up and nodded. As she turned toward the door, a long, silky strand of her warm brown hair drifted just for an instant across his cheek, like an enticing caress. He knew it was time to bring up a subject he had previously rehearsed. He paused and turned to her as they reached the door.

"I saw Tiffany and her husband, Michael, last night and told them about your being a physical anthropology teacher at the university. Tiffany was most interested and asked me to invite you over for dinner so she can talk to you about the life of a teacher. She's going for her secondary education teaching degree so I know she's eager to pick up some inside information."

For Carrie, the message in Cash's words came through loud and clear. Tiffany was married; he wasn't involved with the attractive showgirl, and he wanted her to know it.

Cash had been watching Carrie's face for her reaction to the news. The smile she gave him was both happy and wise. He felt totally transparent as he stepped forward, staring at the unpowdered shine on her nose as though it was some precious jewel.

"So do you want to go to Michael and Tiffany's place tonight for dinner and a boring talk about work or would you rather accept a nice romantic, candlelight dinner invitation from me?"

She grinned then laughed in a happy, unrestrained manner that he found instantly infectious. "Romantic candlelight dinners win hands down with me every time."

He smiled into the merry blue of her eyes until he saw the sudden cloud collecting inside them. "What's the matter?"

"Tonight's the night of Duncan's funeral service and you may be called to the hospital at any time for your grandmother."

Cash nodded wondering how either situation could have slipped his mind. Then he realized his feelings for Carrie had blotted out everything else and he felt a bit awed at their strength.

"I could pick you up around seven-thirty for the service."

Carrie pursed her lips. "Why don't you let me pick you up? I like to drive. I find being a passenger is too…passive. Doing things, even simple things like driving, keeps me mentally active, aware—in control. I need to feel that way."

He read an interesting message in her words. She needed to feel in control? Was that need behind her withdrawals to his advances?

"Why don't you drive my car, Carrie? I'd love to be a passenger for a change, and you'd make a lovely chauffeur."

Her returning smile was easy. "All right, I'll leave my Jeep at your place. There's a lot to talk about. We haven't even discussed Duncan's will or how his bequests might tie into his death."

Cash was nodding as he held the door open for her. "I'm still wondering why Duncan left money to Evan Wahl and Wahl's equally strange behavior in tearing up that mineral rights agreement."

Carrie stepped past. "Maybe he realized that he couldn't get away with a forged document and decided to cut his losses?"

Cash didn't sound convinced as he followed her to the car. "But what would even make him take a chance with a forged mineral rights document? What is beneath Duncan's land that could be so valuable?"

AT TWILIGHT, THE DESERT was covered with billowy thunderclouds, streaking across the sky in the promise of a late-summer storm. The small group of people who showed up on the ridge above wild horse canyon hugged jackets and sweaters against the cold breeze that swept among the jagged rocks.

It was a steep climb and had taken Carrie and Cash twenty minutes to make it to the top. Once there, Carrie looked around to see Edward Van Epp and the funeral director silently waiting.

Carrie realized the director was of Indian descent as soon as she got a look at his long, straight black hair, tawny skin and high cheekbones. He wore a dark suit, a highly starched white shirt, a black tie and moccasins on his feet.

But it was his eyes that caused her to stare. They were truly remarkable eyes, so dark and deep that they seemed to hold eternity within them. As they briefly touched hers, she felt an unexplained quiet along her skin, like an emotional blanket had been cloaked about her.

After a moment of silently watching each, the Indian turned toward the canyon and raised his arms as though he might gather the thunderclouds into them. Carrie could have sworn the air currents had begun to swirl within the span of his outstretched hands, obedient to their call. Then his voice, like the heavy groan of the earth, rose until light enough to evaporate into the moist air.

None of the service he performed was in English; indeed, Carrie wasn't even sure the sounds he made were words from any language. But the vibrations flowed inside her as though emanating from within her very being.

Then the sounds stopped and Carrie opened her eyes, only then realizing she had shut them. She watched entranced as the Indian raised Duncan's ashes to be scattered to the wind; and as though happy to take the offered gift, a propitious gust caught the precious gray dust and carried it away in a dark swirling trail that meandered gently between the canyon walls and then finally out of sight.

An absolute silence enveloped her. Then the lightning flashed like a swinging silver sword, cutting through the sky, and the ground began to rumble as though caught up in a terrible earthquake. Unafraid, Carrie walked the few steps to the edge of the ledge where the Indian stood. She looked down knowing what she would see.

The racing herd of wild mustangs tore down the narrow canyon in single file as the thunder from the gathering clouds roared in unison to their hoofbeats and the lightning continued to cut into the rocks all around them. To Carrie, standing there watching their flight, they seemed not like earthly creatures at all but enchanted spirits racing Duncan's soul, trying to flee from the heaviness of their earthbound gravity. As they faded out of sight, she found herself wondering if one would make it.

"Carrie?"

It was Cash's voice. She turned to find him at her side. The Indian was gone. She had been so caught up in the dash of the wild mustangs that she had not noticed when he had slipped away.

"Are you ready to go?" Cash asked.

She nodded and turned to see Gene Van Epp standing at the other edge of the flat ledge, next to his brother, Edward. Hal Sawyer was helping Evan Wahl to climb down the steep slope.

"How long have the others been here?" she asked.

"Wahl and Sawyer arrived right as the service began. Gene came in close to the end. I guess they all found it hard to stay away. It was quite moving... remarkable really, I mean the way the mustangs ran, wasn't it?"

Carrie heard the wonder in Cash's voice and realized that he, too, had felt the spiritual impact of the ceremony.

"Of course the thunder and lightning from the storm could explain their stampede," he said, as though willing to offer up a rational explanation.

But Carrie knew he had been as touched by the living enactment of the old Indian legend as she had been. And what's more, she could tell he wanted to believe in it as strongly as she did.

Her logical, rational mind told her such beliefs were silly and sentimental. But she found she could suspend her disbelief on this occasion and that she liked Cash all the more for his ability to embrace the unlikely and sentimental, too.

The threatening rainstorm broke in a torrent as soon as they reached the base of the cliff. She and Cash dashed for his Cadillac, only minimally damp as they slipped onto the seats.

Carrie drove back into Reno, both she and Cash silent as they still felt the spiritual impact of Duncan's funeral service.

But Cash was aware of something else, too, from the sudden desert rainstorm. It was the sweet, heady smell of wet sagebrush, a fragrance so sensually pleasing that he had never known another like it. Until he met Carrie. For now he knew why the light, sweet scent that seemed naturally a part of her skin had been so seductively familiar. Carrie's natural fragrance was very much like that of the summer desert after a rain.

He looked over at her quiet face as she stared straight ahead at the slick highway. He almost reached out to touch her. At the last minute he held back and instead pushed the button to let the window down an inch, welcoming the cooling drops of wet rain that soon pelted his face.

"If you'll stop by my place, you can see Bonanza and then I'll take you out to dinner," he said aloud after a while.

Carrie looked up at Cash's words and was surprised to find herself already on the outskirts of Reno. She turned up a street leading to his house.

"I don't feel like going out tonight, Cash. How about a quiet dinner at my place in about an hour?"

His words warmed in pleasure. "That would be great, Carrie. Are you sure an hour will give you enough time?"

"Oh, sure. I'll just throw something together."

WHEN CASH ARRIVED at her place an hour later, he was met with the heavenly smell of homemade dinner rolls directly from the oven. Their fragrance filled the house and made Cash's mouth water. He decided to be brave and risk some candor.

"I hope you're not one of those sophisticated hostesses who dawdles over hors d'oeuvres and cocktails for an hour before getting down to the important business of eating."

Carrie laughed as she gave Bonanza's head a pat. "Well, if I was, I'd hardly admit it after that, ah, gentle hint. Come on, everything's ready. I've even set a place next to the dining room table for our furry friend here so he can feel part of the family. Did you call the hospital and leave this number with them?"

"Actually, I've had all my calls forwarded to your number. Hope you don't mind," he said, following her into the kitchen.

Carrie smiled at his freshly shaven face. "Not at all."

Together they dished out the cream-of-asparagus soup and followed it with steamed swordfish seasoned in butter and lemon sauce, accompanied by broiled, cheese-stuffed tomatoes and a lightly sautéed selection of summer squash.

Cash enjoyed the lightly seasoned, well-prepared meal very much. It was obviously anything but "thrown together." He was particularly surprised at the excellent homemade cheesecake she served for dessert and almost complimented her on her cooking. He hesitated because she might be sensitive to compliments on traditionally feminine talents.

But she was definitely all-female. He found his eyes traveling appreciatively over her gently swelling curves, hinted at in the simple, light blue dress she was now wearing. Reluctantly he switched mental and emotional gears to respond to her next statement.

"Cash, I keep thinking about the mineral rights agreement Wahl tried to push Duncan into signing and then pretended he had signed. That all implies Duncan's land is worth something, or at least the mineral rights to it are. Remember Gene Van Epp said as much at the will reading when he became upset you had gotten the land? He's a geologist. He should know. If he thought he was going to get Duncan's land, do you suppose—"

"He might have risked killing Duncan for it?" Cash finished for her, as he savored every drop of his after-dinner coffee.

"The land is yours now. If you have it checked and it proves valuable, that could be the motive for Duncan's murder."

Cash shook his head. "But whose motive would it be? Gene's? Evan Wahl's? Hal Sawyer's? If the release of mineral rights was at stake, any of those three could have killed Duncan in the anticipation of profit."

Carrie frowned. "I see how Gene and Evan Wahl might have thought there was a profit involved, but how could Sawyer have benefited? He's just a hired hand, isn't he?"

Cash leaned back in his chair. "A chief mining engineer of a big job always gets a bonus. Even with the new methods of getting at previously inaccessible silver deposits, most areas are mined out. Getting a new job on Duncan's virtually virgin and extensive land holdings must have been tempting for Sawyer. Maybe too tempting."

Carrie frowned as her finger made circles around the rim of her coffee cup. "But he didn't even know Duncan had died when he came at me yesterday morning demanding to know where Duncan was. He even claimed to have seen him the night before."

"He could have lied to you, Carrie. By making it appear he didn't know about Duncan's death, he could have been intentionally trying to mislead everyone into thinking he had to be innocent."

Carrie nodded. "I see. So we add Hal Sawyer to the suspect list along with Gene Van Epp and Evan Wahl. Anybody else?"

"Edward Van Epp got over twenty thousand. What do you think?"

Carrie shook her head. "Edward's engaged to a wealthy society woman. Duncan's modest nest egg wouldn't have tempted him."

Cash nodded. "So we're left with Gene Van Epp, Evan Wahl and Hal Sawyer as the top three contenders. Is that how you see it?"

"Yes, although I think Hal Sawyer would be my number-two choice after Gene Van Epp. Evan Wahl is a crusty old tyrant, but somehow he didn't strike me as the poisoning type.''

Cash downed the last of his coffee. "I think I know what you mean. Quietly slipping poison into someone's drink doesn't fit the image he portrays. He'd need the anger of the moment to spur him on to action. Although, if he didn't do it personally—''

Carrie thought over the implication in Cash's words. "Yes, he's a man used to giving orders. I suppose he could have ordered someone else to get rid of Duncan. By the way, did you understand Duncan's words about his inability to pay some kind of debt to Wahl?''

Cash shook his head. "I suppose it means Duncan and Wahl had business dealings in the past. From the few times Duncan mentioned him, I gathered they went back a number of years. Still, the unclean 'slate of debt' struck me as referring to something other than a monetary arrangement.''

She nodded. "Yes, what type of a debt is unpayable? And why didn't Duncan just give Wahl the three thousand some odd dollars he owed him instead of willing it to him?''

Cash watched Carrie's finger still circling the rim of her coffee cup as her mind obviously thought about the facts they had uncovered. And just like them, she continued to be a mystery to him.

As he followed her into the kitchen to do the dishes, he decided to try a gentle probe. "Your town house is very neat. My house's disarray cannot have made a very good impression.''

Carrie was opening the dishwasher. "On the contrary. Seeing your place has made me feel mine lacks character. Yours seems so full of life, reflective of your personality.''

Cash smiled as he closed the dishwasher and started to fill up the sink. "That was a nice compliment whether you realized it or not. Did you realize it?''

She handed him a dish, the corners of her lips turning up ever so slightly. "Yes, as a matter of fact.''

"Well after such an admission I feel I owe you one. Since my divorce, I've felt very empty. I know I've been trying to compensate for that emptiness by making everything around me seem full.''

She was surprised at his candor. "You?"

He heard her disbelief. "Why does that surprise you?"

"It's just that you seem so strong, confident, self-contained. You have your own business, your own home. You don't seem to...need anything."

She felt his deep voice vibrate through her. "I may not need anything, specifically, Carrie. But that doesn't mean I don't need anybody."

A warm flush began to creep up Carrie's spine as she turned her eyes away to find a drying towel. She blurted out her next question before she had time to think about its implications. "What broke up your marriage?"

He didn't answer for a minute and when Carrie looked over at his face again, he was frowning as he seemed to be studying the dish in his hands. "I was a compulsive gambler."

"Was?"

"Yes. Definitely past tense. However, while it was still present tense, my wife yelled and screamed at me to stop what had become my...occupation. I handled the situation by stalking out. Not exactly mature behavior on either of our parts, but mine proved to be the more infuriating."

Carrie received a surprising message in Cash's words. "Your wife divorced *you?*"

He smiled at her, encouraged by the look of disbelief on her lovely face. "Yes. Thank you for being surprised. That's the nicest compliment you've given me yet."

Carrie felt her legs liquefying beneath her at the warmth in Cash's smile. With an effort, she tore her eyes away and they traveled to the unused dishwasher. She decided it was as good a change of subject as any.

"Why don't you use dishwashers?"

He shrugged. "They irritate me. You still have to rinse the dishes. Besides, my hands feel good in hot, soapy water."

Carrie began to imagine herself immersed in that hot, soapy water, which began to agitate as those large capable hands came closer and closer. She blinked out of her momentary fantasy, feeling flushed and transparent as Cash handed her the last dish to dry. He looked at her rising color with a hint of curiosity and she felt extremely thankful at the sudden distracting ring of the telephone from the kitchen wall.

When she answered it, she found it was for Cash and handed him the phone. His side of the conversation was just a series of affirmative grunts. When he hung up and turned back to her, however, a new light of possibility was in his eyes.

"Carrie, that was my friend at First Interstate Bank. Until he called I had completely forgotten about the three-hundred dollar notes he was checking on."

Carrie nodded in understanding. "With everything else that's been happening, so had I. What did your friend find?"

"Nothing. However he said there might be something in a warehouse on the outskirts of town where some records were sent that were considered too old to be computerized. He's given me an okay to check them. It's a long shot but—"

Carrie was already reaching for her shoulder bag. "A long shot is better than no shot at all. What are we waiting for?"

Cash smiled at her eagerness and leaned over to give her forehead a light brush of his lips. His action surprised himself as much as it did her, but he was happy to see she didn't move away. He watched a soft excitement deepening the blue of her eyes and wondered for a moment if she would raise her lips to his. But the next moment she was repositioning the strap of her shoulder bag and stepping away. "Ready?" she asked.

"More than ready," Cash muttered as he ignored the insistent urgings of his body and headed for the door.

CASH'S FRIEND AT THE BANK had notified the night watchman at the warehouse to give them the run of the place. While Cash searched the metal shelves, Carrie shivered beside him as the chilly night air rushed through a million wall cracks. It didn't take him long to figure out why she had suddenly become so quiet.

"Here, take my sweater," Cash said as he yanked the pullover across his shoulders. "I'm too warm with it on anyway."

Before she had a chance to protest, he had deftly slipped his sweater over her head and was holding the sleeves out for her arms to enter. Its instant warmth and tantalizing scent gathered so recently from his body scattered her resistance and she found herself stretching out her arms to accept the rest of the sweater's comforting bulk.

She looked up at him as he rolled the too-long sleeves back on her arms, trying to judge if his offer had been a completely chivalrous one. The knight-in-shining-armor look glinting happily in his eyes settled the question in her mind. "Cash, you shouldn't have. You'll get cold."

He smiled down at her, a smile that cloaked her more snugly than even his sweater. With a featherlike look, his eyes stroked each cheek and then her lips. "Not if you continue to look at me like that, I won't."

Carrie's breath caught at his words. Her heartbeat pounded like a drum inside her chest as she watched his handsome face turn back toward the metal shelves to resume his record search. And all the time she hugged the meaning of his words as she snuggled in the sweater.

He's making love to me, she thought. *With just the touch of his words.*

Cash watched Carrie from the corner of his eye as she began to check the records next to him. It had taken all his control to turn away from her that moment before, to ignore the warmth of her look, to get back to the task at hand when all he really had wanted to do was take her in his arms and—

"Cash, this shelf of records are all from 1951. Maybe we'd best move on to a shelf farther in the back."

He nodded wordlessly, not surprised he hadn't been comprehending what he had been reading. Clamping down on his wandering attention, he concentrated on the labels of the next shelf of old records. They were at the far back of the warehouse before he found anything dated near the time the notes were issued.

They divided the several boxes up between them and Carrie sat on one while she leaned over to search through another. She felt the eyestrain of the dim light as she fought to decipher the faded pen scratches on the age-yellowed paper.

It was over an hour later before Cash's voice broke her concentration. "Carrie, I think I've found something. Come take a look."

Carrie thankfully dropped the nearly unreadable ledger in her hands as she moved to Cash's side.

His voice had a strange quality to it when he repositioned a sheet of paper to an angle that afforded better light. "Read these three numbers here. Do they look familiar?"

Carrie read the numbers and then excitedly grabbed for the envelope with the three hundred-dollar notes in her shoulder bag. She drew them out and compared the numbers on the notes with the numbers on the typed list. They matched exactly.

"Cash, you've found them! This is terrific!"

Carrie's eyes sought his face. His expression told her there was nothing terrific about what he had found.

Carrie's stomach somersaulted. "My God, Cash, what is it?"

For one interminably long moment Carrie stared at Cash's quiet face. When he finally spoke, she had no difficulty deciphering the disillusion which punctuated his words.

"This attached note explains it all, Carrie. That list of serial numbers was for money that was part of a one-hundred-thousand-dollar ransom."

Carrie sucked in her breath in shock. "Ransom money?"

Cash passed his hands over his eyes, as though he might be able to erase what he had seen. "A payoff to kidnappers who snatched a child back in 1931. And this wasn't just any kidnapping, Carrie. Or any child. Read the note. The baby's father was Evan Wahl."

Chapter Nine

Carrie couldn't have spoken then if she tried. With stiff, cold fingers she took the note from Cash's hand. It was addressed to the bank tellers warning them to be on the lookout for currency being passed that bore any of the listed serial numbers. As an inducement, it reminded them that Evan Wahl would pay ten-thousand dollars for any information leading to the arrest of the kidnappers of his baby daughter.

Carrie slumped back against the cold metal of a dusty shelf as the teller's note slipped from her hand to the floor. Cash's next words caused a clammy perspiration to break out on her skin.

"My godfather had ransom money from a baby's kidnapping."

Duncan's gentle, smiling face flashed before Carrie. Her words came out in a sigh. "There's got to be some mistake."

Cash's tone was strained. "Well, there's no mistake in these serial numbers. There's correspondence in this same file that says the serial numbers were recorded by the bank at the request of the local Reno police when the ransom was being gathered for the payoff."

Carrie reached for the file pages in Cash's hand, glancing through the sketchy data as her mind formed new questions.

"What happened to the baby? Were the kidnappers caught?"

Cash exhaled heavily. "There's nothing in this file to say. We'll have to look for other records back in that time."

Carrie put the papers down. "Other records?"

Cash shrugged. "Maybe old newspapers will help. Strange, I've lived my whole life in this town and I've never heard of a story about Wahl's child being kidnapped. Still, since it happened sixty years ago, I suppose time does distance things."

Cash's words hit Carrie like a hard slap, both stunning and sharpening her wits. *Sixty years ago. 1931. The money. The kidnapping. The missing journals.* She licked dry lips, almost afraid to put her thoughts into words.

"Cash, your grandmother yelled out at Duncan's will reading that he was right, 'past sins must be revealed.' In her 1933 journal, she used that phrase 'past sins.' Could Duncan's call to her on the afternoon before his death have been about this past sin of kidnapping? Could that be the reason she sought her missing journals, one of which is from the year 1931? Was she trying to better remember the events? Cash, could all this be connected?"

She saw her words register on his face in unwelcome surprise. "My God, Carrie, I hate to think it but you could be right. It all seems to fit, doesn't it? What were Grandmother's other words at the will reading? Oh yes. 'Dear God, he was right! Our silence has been wrong!'"

Carrie nodded. "Their silence about the kidnapping. Maybe it was the 'awful terror' of Ann's journal description."

Cash put his head in his hands. "God, Carrie, what was Duncan involved in sixty years ago?"

The question sent an icy chill up Carrie's spine, joining with the cold drafts swirling around her legs. She shivered.

"Come on, Carrie. Let's get out of this freezing place. I think we've learned all we're going to from these records."

Cash made quick work of restacking the cardboard storage boxes on the shelves, and he and Carrie were soon in her Jeep with the heater on high, thawing out their chilled limbs.

They remained quiet through most of the ride. But Cash knew he couldn't go much longer without saying what was on his mind.

"Carrie, I think we've found out all we're going to."

Carrie's hands gripped the steering wheel. "You don't believe that any more than I do. You think we're going to find out something about Duncan that will be too hard to face, don't you?"

Cash exhaled heavily. "Haven't we already? We've got to ask ourselves the all-important question—how did Duncan come into possession of ransom money in a sixty-year-old kidnapping?"

Carrie knew the question was coming, and belief in her friend had already formed the answer in her mind. She sat up straighter, stiffened by a new resolve. "It must be that somebody passed that money to Duncan. More than likely, Duncan never even knew where it came from."

Cash's voice was full of hard pain. "If he didn't know it was part of the ransom money, why did he hold on to it all these years?"

Carrie bit her lip. "I don't know. But there must be a dozen honorable explanations for Duncan having that ransom money."

"And are there a dozen honorable explanations to the words he left in his will that described a slate of debt to Wahl that couldn't be washed clean? Carrie, don't you see those words he said to Wahl probably directly relate to Duncan's involvement in the kidnapping of the man's child?"

Carrie shook her head vehemently. "Not Duncan. Not the man I knew. Not ever. There has to be another explanation."

Cash liked her defense of Duncan, but he knew the tone of his response didn't hold much conviction. "I guess anything's possible."

Carrie could feel the dark shadows of Cash's skepticism swirling about them as she pulled up her drive. She glanced over at the strong, beautifully shaped bones of his profile, marred by the sad lines of disillusionment etching around his expressive mouth.

She took a determined breath. "We know only one thing for certain. Duncan was a decent man. Isn't that true?"

Cash nodded, not just understanding her words but feeling the strength of her challenge behind them. He turned in the passenger seat to study her face, finding himself in renewed admiration for her fighting strength. Despite the odds against them, he suddenly knew he had to offer whatever support was his to give.

She was still wearing his sweater and she took a moment to slip it over her head. In the darkness she couldn't read his expression, but she heard a new note in his voice when he took the sweater from her hands. "You're right, Carrie. We can't let unsubstantiated suspicions drag down our spirits. Tomorrow right after your early morning class, we'll visit the Washoe County Library and check the newspaper records. We'll even go see Evan Wahl if we have to. One way or another we'll find out exactly what happened sixty years ago."

Cash bid Carrie good-night, and after leaving her he put his sweater back on—not because he was cold but because on his drive home he wanted to feel her warmth and smell her scent still clinging to its fabric.

"THE SIGN ON the library's front says it's not open until ten, Cash. We've got forty-five minutes to kill," Carrie said as they both turned away in disappointment from the locked doors Thursday morning. "Any ideas?"

Watching the morning sun glowing through her skin and hair, Cash found several ideas coming to mind, but he pushed the more appealing ones aside as he spied the public telephone booth. "Let's call Wahl. Maybe we can get in to see him."

Carrie nodded somewhat doubtfully, remembering her difficulties in even trying to speak to the man by telephone. It made Cash's success at securing an immediate appointment all the more surprising.

"He'll see us *now?*" Carrie said, not believing her ears.

"Curious, huh? Evan Wahl's secretary was more than eager to accommodate. I no sooner identified myself when he said Wahl had just tried to reach me and would be happy to see us both right away if that was convenient. I wonder what gives?''

Carrie shrugged. "Let's go find out before he changes his mind.''

They arrived at the corporate offices of Wahl Mining a few minutes later. It was an old and elegant white stone building, beautifully kept with gleaming marble floors and tall, clean Doric columns. Evan Wahl's office was on the seventh and top floor. As Carrie and Cash got off the elevator, they found both his and his secretary's office were the only ones on the floor.

Carrie looked at the three bigger-than-life portraits that lined the paneled entry hallway as she and Cash made their way to the secretary's desk. Soon she found herself stopping in front of the first portrait, recognizing the picture as one she had seen in the pages of an early Nevada history book.

"Joseph Patrick Wahl," she read aloud from the engraved metal plate on the picture frame. "I read about this man in high school. And there's his wife, Geraldine. Did you know they were immigrants who reached Reno in the latter half of the nineteenth century with less than a dollar between them?''

Cash nodded. "Yes. Joseph was the mining engineer, Geraldine the business manager. Together they bought and organized most of the state's small, waning silver mines into a conglomerate of steady, dependable income. Their savvy and hard work were what caused Wahl Mining to grow into a large, wealthy corporation.''

Carrie studied their stern expressions.

"Funny. They looked just like anyone else, Cash. Good, strong, bone structure, even familiar in a way. Still, no special sparkle of greatness lights their eyes, just determination. Although I guess plain, old down-to-earth determination might be the true mark of greatness in anyone, the one common aspect of humanity that can make any individual's efforts rise above mediocrity into greatness.''

Carrie's eyes turned to the third portrait on the wall, the son of the two pioneers, Evan Wahl. She guessed him to be about thirty-five when the portrait had been painted. He had the same stern countenance as his parents, but in his eyes the determination seemed to have turned to obstinacy. Carrie wondered how much of Wahl's mistreatment of Duncan colored her reaction.

"What do you see in him?" Cash asked at her side.

"I'm not sure," Carrie said. "Maybe I'm seeing what I expect to see. Perhaps that's all any of us see in people."

He nodded in understanding and agreement as they walked the final few steps to the secretary's desk in silence.

Wahl's fiftyish, male secretary was square-shaped and stern looking. He could have been an ex-Marine sergeant from his impeccable grooming and sharp, crisp movements. He said nothing when Cash identified them but showed them right in to an enormous office where Carrie was sure echoes would be heard if a voice was raised.

In its far corner, behind a massive mahogany desk, sat Evan Wahl. She and Cash advanced together across the dark, highly polished wooden floor, the rhythmic slap of their leather soles like an ominous drum beat in the otherwise quiet atmosphere. Before they reached Evan Wahl, he stood up and circled to the front of his desk to greet them. He offered no hand in welcome, continuing to grasp his sturdy, black cane. However, he was wearing an expression that was probably as close to a smile as the man ever got.

"Good of you to come, McKendry, Ms. Chase. Please be seated. Don't let my standing annoy you. Doctor advises me that frequent position changes are most important at my age."

They sat down and Carrie looked up at Evan Wahl's towering, well-dressed figure, ancient and bony yet still powerful looking, and wondered if it were truly his doctor's advice or Wahl's own desire to look down on them that made him stand.

"A regrettable incident that business with Van Epp's forged signature," Wahl said with a rueful shake of his head. "You were quite right, Ms. Chase. When I confronted my chief engineer, he admitted forging Van Epp's name after learning of his death.''

Carrie leaned back in her chair, so surprised at Wahl admitting to the forgery of the mineral rights agreement that her thoughts scattered like leaves buffeted in a powerful wind.

Cash's immediate question proved he was less easily swept away. ''Why did Hal Sawyer forge Duncan's signature?''

Wahl gripped his cane before answering. ''He thought he was acting in my best interests. He knew I wanted Van Epp to sign. He decided to make it his business to force the issue.''

Carrie found her voice, even if it was a bit too high. ''Are you saying that's why he ran his heavy machinery near Duncan's home trying to *coerce* him into signing? To insure *your* best interests?''

Wahl looked uncomfortable at the distinct hints of outrage in Carrie's delivery. Once again he shifted uneasily on his feet. ''Yes, Ms. Chase. The damn fool did admit to annoying Van Epp as you described, precisely because he thought the ends justified the means. I certainly didn't direct his behavior. I'm as appalled as you are, and I have severely reprimanded Hal for it.''

''Reprimanded?'' Carrie's anger for her dead friend brought her to her feet. In some surprise she realized that despite the age-bent bones of Evan Wahl, he still was taller than her. She put the slight surprise behind her and let the anger show through.

''How could you possibly convince yourself a reprimand is adequate punishment for the deliberate harassment of a kind and wonderful man and the calculated, criminal act to falsify—''

Evan Wahl raised a raw-boned hand. ''What would you suggest, Ms. Chase? Shall I draw and quarter him?''

Carrie blinked in surprise at the seriousness in Wahl's tone. She looked into the steady expression in his eyes and understood he was trying to throw her off balance with his outrageous statement. She felt her backbone stiffening to meet the challenge of his words. ''I recognize what century

I'm in, Mr. Wahl. The police should be notified to lay charges against him. A *normal* employer would have fired him. Why haven't you?''

Wahl's eyes never dropped from her face as he once again repositioned himself, leaning up against his desk this time as though he needed to give his legs a rest. The only change Carrie could detect was a small tiredness in his voice.

"Maybe because I'm not a *normal* employer, Ms. Chase. You see, Hal Sawyer isn't just my employee. He's my grandson.''

The surprise of Wahl's words caused Carrie to drop back into her chair with an audible plop. Hal Sawyer—the grandson of Evan Wahl? The two men were so remarkably unalike in personality and physical structure, she just couldn't believe it.

But Wahl's surprising admission explained a lot to Cash, who had been sitting quietly watching the exchange between Carrie and the elderly man. Cash now understood why Wahl had so quickly changed his mind about seeing them. Having had time to check out their allegations of the day before, he wanted to be sure no one pressed charges of forgery against his grandson. Cash listened to the old mining magnate's next words from the benefit of his new perspective.

"So you see, Ms. Chase, McKendry, as much as I abhor my grandson's methods and have made this fact painfully clear to him, it was his loyalty to me that formed their impetus. So in point of fact, I am the one to blame. Consequently, I would take it as a personal favor if you would direct any and all need for retribution to my door.''

Carrie exhaled in frustration at the old man's ability to deflate the angry sails of her indignation. How could she even consider calling this man to task when he laid himself so open to protect his grandson?

Cash, however, seemed to be made of sterner stuff. "Perhaps we can avoid bringing this matter to the sheriff's attention, Mr. Wahl. If you are willing to assist Ms. Chase and myself in some discreet inquiries, the matter need go no further.''

Wahl eyed Cash steadily, a sharp light flashing in his eyes. Cash felt as though he was being newly assessed, and from the small lift to Wahl's mouth, that he had not been found wanting.

"Perhaps I'd best hear your questions first," Wahl said.

"They're not very complicated, Mr. Wahl. Duncan made a small bequest to you in his will, a bequest that was identified as a final payment on a debt. We'd like to know what that debt represented."

Evan Wahl frowned slightly as he used his cane to reposition himself once again. "I have no idea what Van Epp meant by that past debt statement. He and I had no business dealings."

Carrie spoke up. "That sounds odd. Why would Duncan have left you money in final payment of a debt when there had been no debt?"

Evan Wahl exhaled and recircled his desk to sit down again. He lowered himself carefully into his chair and looked over at Carrie. He seemed annoyed, but she couldn't tell whether it was with her or with Duncan.

"He was an... unpredictable man. In all the many years I've known him, I never really figured out what made Duncan Van Epp tick."

Cash thought Wahl sounded as though not understanding Duncan had been a major failure in his life. "What do you mean 'unpredictable'?"

Wahl looked like he was going to decline to answer, but then thought better of it. "No point in keeping it a secret anymore I suppose. For some reason Duncan Van Epp rendered me a large financial favor about forty years ago."

"A financial favor? How did he do that?" Carrie asked.

Wahl leaned forward in his chair so that he could still rest his palms on his cane. He ground his teeth for a moment in what looked like unresolved annoyance before speaking.

"Silver mining had gone bad. Railroad was gone. I should have seen it coming sooner, but I didn't. Had too much capital sunk into the mines to scrap enough together to diversify to get me through the bad times. I needed a loan, but the banks turned me down. Then out of the blue one called and offered me the loan in the exact amount I needed at a quarter of the asking interest rate with a payback over thirty years instead of ten."

"And you took it?" Carrie asked.

Wahl's sharp eyes flashed over at her. "I would have been crazy not to. Only I found out later that Duncan Van Epp had put up the money himself, using the bank employee just as a front. That was the first time I even heard of him."

"Weren't you curious as to why he did it?" Cash asked.

Wahl looked at Cash in irritation. "Of course I was curious. I had him checked out. He was a local lawyer, born and raised in Contention. Finished up his formal training in an Eastern law school. Done quite well for himself in representing corporations around the Reno area. But there was nothing in his background that gave any reason for his loan to me."

"What about Duncan's comment in his will about there being a slate of debt he owed you that couldn't be washed clean?" Carrie asked.

Wahl's forehead sank into deep furrows as he once again ground his teeth in apparent agitation. "It made no sense to me when Burney read it then and it makes no more sense now. If one of us owed the other, it was I who owed him for that loan those many years ago. Perhaps he had me mixed up with someone else. Perhaps he was beginning to lose his grip toward the end. Pity. In his day he was a smart one. Still for all his legal logic, he was a strange sort of bird. Refused to live anywhere but that old house on the outskirts of Contention. Bought up the land around it years before, even though it was obvious the town was closing."

"When was that?" Cash asked.

"Late thirties. His brother had gone to California in '31 to find his fortune and never returned. Only family Duncan had was a nephew he had been left to raise."

Carrie was immediately intrigued. "You say Duncan's brother went to California? How do you know?"

"I told you. I had Duncan checked out. When my investigator found an Edward Van Epp worked for me once as a laborer in my silver mines, he identified the man as Duncan's younger brother and discovered Edward had deserted his wife and gone to California.''

Carrie's tongue circled about her lips as her thoughts speculated. "Could Duncan have considered your hiring his brother as the debt he owed you? The slate that couldn't be washed clean?''

Wahl took turns smoothing back the long ends of his mustache with the back of his hand. "Hardly. I fired Edward Van Epp less than eight months after I hired him.''

"Over a disagreement?'' Cash asked.

"No. Never met the man. Silver prices lagged so I laid off. Simple economics.''

Cash leaned forward in his chair. "Laid off? I thought you said a moment ago you fired him?''

"Fired. Laid off. It all meant the same in those days. Didn't have all these unions yowling about payoffs and compensations then. When there was work, I paid men to do it. When the work disappeared, the last men hired were the first to be let go. Sometimes a few stayed around waiting to be rehired when the work returned. Sometimes they left for greener pastures like Edward Van Epp.''

Cash was shaking his head. "I'm finding it hard to believe there was nothing more to your relationship with Duncan, Mr. Wahl. My godfather had his full mental faculties right to the end. Something had to have been behind that three-thousand dollars he left to you and those strange words about an unclean slate.''

Wahl seemed to bristle as he sat up straighter. "I've told you, McKendry. There was no debt. Duncan did me a favor once, helped me get back on my feet and didn't ask for anything in return. He never even knew I knew. Finding a man like that is a rare thing in this life, I can tell you. I... kept tabs on what happened to him. That's all.''

"But that wasn't the extent of your contact,'' Cash said. "I distinctly remember Duncan becoming very upset about your attempt to mine minerals in Contention several years ago. Are you going to tell me you two didn't clash over that matter?''

Wahl shrugged as he repositioned himself in his chair, seeming to ignore the slightly accusing tone in Cash's voice. "It was a minor thing. I bought the mineral rights to Contention decades ago. When I decided to exercise those rights a few years back, Van Epp found out and started talking sentimental slop. Said he didn't want his beloved town being dug up. Shouldn't have interfered."

"What did you do about his interference?" Carrie asked.

Wahl watched her cleverly, as though he knew she was trying to bait him. "I didn't have to 'do' anything. The law was on my side. Both Burneys, father and daughter, told Duncan to back off. Kept trying to get him to see he didn't have a chance. But Duncan wouldn't listen to them. As it was, Duncan's legal maneuvers just kept me tied up in the courts for three years before I could move my machinery in. No big deal."

"And is your desire to gain the mineral rights on Duncan's land no big deal, either, Mr. Wahl?" Cash asked.

The corners of Wahl's mouth turned up. "Surely after yesterday's outburst you're not going to try to tell me you're interested in striking some deal with me on those rights?"

Cash watched the old man's shrewd eyes. "No, I'm not."

Sensing Cash had satisfied his curiosity and no further comment from Wahl was forthcoming, Carrie leaned forward in her chair, her mind alight with another subject.

"I'd like to know about the events surrounding the kidnapping of your daughter, Mr. Wahl. I—"

Carrie got no further. Wahl shot to his feet, the quickness of his movement and the immediate fire in his eyes telling Carrie she had just wandered into some very nasty conversational quicksand. His words spat out at her, their volume seeming to vibrate the very chair in which she sat.

"You presume too much, Ms. Chase! You have my apology for Hal's behavior. The rest of my family affairs are not subject to discussion. You've asked all the questions I will answer. Now you and McKendry may leave!"

Wahl was neither giving his permission nor making a request. He was demanding their withdrawal. Thoroughly stunned, Carrie scrambled to her feet, more than happy at the moment to oblige.

It wasn't until she and Cash were outside in the hallway with the door closed behind them that she leaned against the wall to catch her emotional as well as physical breath.

Her first words were said with a dry tone. "Do you think I might have asked the wrong question?"

Cash gave the irony in her words a big smile, but Carrie soon noticed his look changed to one of disturbed concern as he glanced over her shoulder. Carrie followed his eyes back to the corner of Evan Wahl's secretary's desk where attorney-at-law Nora Burney temporarily rested her behind. She was in animated conversation with the secretary as though they were old friends, seemingly unaware of Carrie and Cash's presence.

"What's she doing here?" Cash wondered aloud.

"Let's ask," Carrie said as she headed in the woman's direction.

Nora Burney's face took on a wary look as she suddenly lifted her head and saw Carrie and Cash closing the distance. She immediately scooted off the edge of the desk and stood uncertainly. Reading the woman's uneasiness, Carrie pasted a smile across her lips and decided to try as non-threatening an approach as possible. "How's the fingernail, Ms. Burney?"

Burney's wariness turned to undisguised appreciation as her eyes traveled from Carrie's face to Cash's. Carrie was pleased to note that Cash's expression did not return the woman's obvious regard.

Burney didn't look so pleased as she redirected her attention back to Carrie. "The fingernail's fine. I just need to wear a Band-Aid until it heals. What brings you here?"

Carrie kept the smile on her face. "Mr. Wahl wanted to explain to us how Hal Sawyer forged the mineral rights agreement between himself and Mr. Van Epp."

Burney's face wrinkled into a half-guilty look as she shifted uneasily. "Yes, I heard about that. I guess I should have checked the signature more closely. Still, who would have thought the fool would attempt something so stupid as an outright forgery? He is a bit of a birdbrain.''

Carrie's smile was feeling strained. ''For my part, I wouldn't insult our feathered friends that way, Ms. Burney. What brings you here?''

At Carrie's question, Burney rose to her full height, adopting her most supercilious air. ''I thought everyone knew. My family's law firm has represented the Wahl family's legal interests for two generations.''

The news both surprised and disturbed Carrie, but it was Cash who spoke both their thoughts. ''Is that right, Ms. Burney? But I also thought your firm was the one representing Duncan Van Epp?''

''So we represented them both. There's nothing wrong with that.''

Both Cash's eyebrows and tone raised in mock surprise. ''Really? What happened when Duncan went up against Wahl's attempt to mine minerals in Contention several years ago? How were you able to represent both their interests then?''

Whereas Nora Burney's look had seemed wary before, now she looked positively stalked. Carrie watched her visibly gulp as she grasped the edge of the secretary's desk.

Even the formidable-looking secretary seemed to take his cue that this was a good time to be elsewhere and quickly got up and disappeared.

''You don't understand the situation,'' Burney finally said.

Carrie stood before the lawyer crossing her arms about her chest. Her voice was steady, but she knew it held an edge. ''Why don't you explain it to us then?''

Burney licked dry lips. ''It's not what you think. I... My father and I tried to reason with Van Epp. Clearly Wahl had the law on his side. There was no use in fighting the inevitable. It was all just a waste of money. We knew Van Epp couldn't win.''

''Did you even try to win for him?'' Carrie asked.

Burney had obvious trouble getting her answer out. ''No.''

"Why not?" Cash asked before Carrie had a chance.

Carrie was surprised at the pointed vehemence of the attorney's next answer. She suddenly reminded Carrie of a child who was being forced to tell the truth and didn't like it. "Because Van Epp fired me! He handled the case himself. All the filings. All the appearances. We were totally free to represent Wahl in the matter. There were no longer any legal ties to Van Epp. Are you satisfied?"

"Not quite," Carrie said. "If Duncan fired you several years ago, why did he draw up his will with you this July and why is your firm handling the disposition of his estate?"

Burney's dark eyes shone brightly as she just stared at Carrie, her lips clamped shut so tightly that they began to turn white. Something was on the tip of her tongue, Carrie could tell. She could also tell that Nora Burney wanted desperately to say it, but for some reason couldn't.

"Well, Ms. Burney?"

Nora Burney did not answer. In ill-humored frustration, the attorney abruptly turned away from Carrie and Cash and headed for the door leading into Evan Wahl's office. After two introductory knocks and a sullen backward glance at them both, she yanked the back door open and slammed it behind her.

Chapter Ten

"Could it be Nora Burney is hiding something?" Carrie asked.

Cash looked over at her and smiled. "You have a decided gift for understatement this morning, Ms. Chase. Are you getting the same impression I am that the law firm of Burney and Burney might have been indulging in a bit of conflict of interest?"

"At the very least, Mr. McKendry," Carrie said with equal mock formality. "I'm very concerned when I think about the fact that the law firm was handling Duncan's financial matters as well as his legal ones. Why didn't Duncan just get rid of them once and for all when they refused to represent him against Wahl?"

Cash shrugged. "I don't know how we'll be able to find the answer to that question. What do you say we tackle the library now and see what we can find out about the kidnapping business?"

Carrie nodded. "You bet. After Wahl's reaction to my probe, I can't wait to see what we dig up."

CARRIE AND CASH HUDDLED in the back corner of the second floor of the Washoe County Library, going through the listings of microfilm until they found 1931.

They had learned from the librarian that the present-day *Gazette Journal* was a combination of the older *Reno Gazette* and the *Nevada State Journal*. Each took a different newspaper, placing their individual rolls of film within the microfilm reader and beginning to replay the daily headlines through the viewer. Carrie was up to November before the story broke.

"Here it is!" she said. "Sunday, November 1, 1931. Front page, banner headline." She read the story aloud as Cash quickly abandoned his machine to look over her shoulder.

"INFANT DAUGHTER OF MINING MAGNATE GRABBED

"Mining industrialist Evan Durnell Wahl's nine-week-old daughter, Milicent Emory Wahl, was snatched from her carriage, and her nurse, Edith Toomey, was brutally struck down while nurse and child were taking a walk in the park near the home of the child's father last Tuesday.

"A ransom note demanding $100,000 was left in the carriage with delivery instructions and warning the child would be killed if the money was not paid. The money was paid as instructed, however Wahl contacted the authorities when the child was not returned.

"Police..."

They read the rest of the article to themselves. When she was finished, Carrie was frowning.

"I don't understand. It talks about the Reno Police Department handling the case. I thought all kidnappings were federal offenses and that the FBI had jurisdiction."

Cash nodded. "Not until after the Lindbergh baby was kidnapped and killed, receiving national attention. That occurred in 1932. This earlier kidnapping would have been handled locally. I wonder if the little girl was ever recovered."

They read the follow-up stories, which continued until the spring of 1932. With each new report, the situation got worse.

The nurse died several days later from the injuries she sustained. Then the badly decomposed body of a baby girl was found in a shallow grave near the very park where she had been taken three months before. And with the news of her child's death, the baby's mother became ill and died soon after.

Carrie sat back in her chair and sighed. "Horrible. I can't imagine anything so vicious. What kind of fiend could cause such suffering? I tell you, Cash, I'm appalled at such cold-blooded cruelty. Whoever took that child's life and that money—"

She stopped as she heard her own words. "Whoever took that money," she repeated, remembering full well how she had come into possession of it.

His hand sought her shoulder and gave it a squeeze. "There must have been some police reports pointing to a suspect. Perhaps there are still some around. Do you think your brother would look at the Reno police records for us?"

She chewed the inside of her cheek in contemplation. "Look for us, no. But I'm sure Tom would probably be more than willing for us to look, particularly if he thinks it will distract me from investigating Duncan's murder. I'll go call him."

Carrie found a public telephone booth and got her brother on the line. When she told him she wanted to look at the Reno Police Department's old unsolved case files from the 1930s, he didn't seem surprised. "Looking for a new lead on Ernie?" Tom asked.

Carrie tried to answer as truthfully as she could. "Anything's possible. We just thought we'd take a look."

"We?" Tom repeated.

"Cash is with me."

Carrie heard silence on the line for a moment. "I had him checked out, Carrie. You know he's a gambler? Got his nickname 'Cash' because he always has a fistful of money for the tables?"

She smiled, knowing her brother's efforts on her behalf were because he cared. "He *was* a gambler, Tom. All past tense. Don't worry. He's not an emotionally weak man. Quite the contrary. So there goes your theory about me."

Tom grunted. "Maybe. Anyway, I'll give a buddy over at the Reno police a call and clear you through. But you won't be able to get in until after-hours—say eight tonight. I don't want your presence interfering with officers trying to do their job. And, I'm sure I don't have to remind you not to remove anything."

"Now that you've reminded me, you can be sure you don't have to remind me," Carrie said with light sarcasm.

Tom took it in stride and she thanked him before hanging up. When she returned to Cash to tell him about the delay, he looked as disappointed as she felt. She decided it was her turn to try to prop up his spirits.

"I don't know about you, but I didn't have time for breakfast. What do you say we go to my place and I'll fix us some brunch before I have to leave for my afternoon class?"

Cash's face immediately lit up at the invitation as he casually draped an arm over her shoulder. "Best offer I've had since last night."

CASH WATCHED CARRIE take out a coffee grinder and put in some fresh beans of French roast and chocolate almond.

"You grind your own coffee beans?" he asked.

"On occasion."

He made an audible sniff. "What else smells so good?"

"Eggs Benedict," Carrie said, trying not to sound too proud. She knew she was showing off her cooking skills shamelessly, but she couldn't seem to help it. She wanted to impress Cash. Good cooking was so much more satisfying when she could do it for someone special.

Cash was certainly that. She counted every second of careful preparation well spent when she saw the look of pleasure on his face as he took his first bite. A few minutes later not even a drop of hollandaise sauce remained on his plate. Carrie filled his coffee cup for the third time and brought in the fresh, chilled, honey-glazed blueberries with a dash of freshly whipped cream for dessert just as though she had them every day.

"You should weigh three hundred pounds," he said a few minutes later after the blueberries had disappeared and his coffee cup was again empty. "I've been trying to take these meals you've prepared casually, but I can't any longer. Where did a physical anthropologist learn to cook like this?"

Carrie tired to mask the very real pleasure she got from Cash's compliment. "Oh . . . just here and there."

"Your mother must have been a good cook," Cash said.

She shook her head as she got up to begin clearing the dishes away. Cash noted the cloud that had descended on her countenance at the mention of her mother. It began to concern him when the cloud didn't immediately dissipate.

His tone was serious, not just polite when he asked his next question. "What was she like?"

He didn't think Carrie was going to answer for a moment. When she did, the words were said sadly. "She wasn't a very successful person. Her education was minimal, her desire to work outside the home nil. She burned our dinners, except the pizzas that were delivered. The house looked a mess and so did she."

Cash heard no bitterness in Carrie's sad delivery. "What did you like about her?" he asked.

It had been a lot of years since Carrie had thought about what it was she had liked about her mother, yet the image came to her in crystal clarity in response to Cash's question.

"She was gentle with people and animals. Never raised her voice to me or my brother. Every stray dog or cat always found its way to her door. Unfortunately, they'd make a mess of the house and then my father would be angry again. He was always yelling at her to clean up her act. She was always doing something that made him mad."

"Didn't his yelling make *her* mad?" Cash asked.

Carrie put the dishes on the table as she sank into her chair. "I don't think it ever occurred to her she could be mad. When my father would yell, she'd just sit with her head bent and take it. I hated to listen to it, see it. I always retreated to my room."

"You sound like you're still angry about it, Carrie."

His words took her by surprise. "Why would I be angry? It all happened over twenty years ago."

"Where are your parents now?" he asked.

She shrugged. "My mother died when I was eight. My dad retired to Florida a few years back."

"Which one do you miss the most?" Cash asked.

Carrie was surprised at his question, appalled at her answer. "Neither. My father was always a perfectionist, never satisfied with anybody's effort. And my mother..."

"Your mother?" Cash prompted.

Unbidden tears flew into Carrie's eyes. "She was so weak! I wanted her to be strong. I wanted her to stand up to my father, for her sake, for my sake. I wanted her to show me how to be strong."

Cash came over to her and put his arm around her shoulders. His voice was gentle. "My mom died when I was young, too. I relied very heavily on my father afterward. Tried my very best to do what would make him happy so he wouldn't end up leaving me, too. Was it like that for you?"

"Yes," Carrie said, remembering now other thoughts she had long ago suppressed. "I worked very hard to keep the house in order and prepare meals that would satisfy him."

"But he wasn't easily satisfied, was he?"

"No."

Her look of defeat said it all. Cash understood now why her house had been so neat, why she fought so hard to keep in control. She was still trying to avoid her mother's mistakes and please her father. "Thank you for telling me, Carrie."

She managed a small smile in return. "I didn't think I wanted to talk about this, but I'm beginning to realize I should have long ago. And you know what's really funny? I now realize I loved my mother, despite my father's disapproval of everything she did. Only, I've been afraid to admit it to myself. I've been afraid it would make me weak like her."

Cash massaged the back of her hand very lightly with his index finger. "I think we all come from dysfunctional family experiences of one kind or another. Perhaps what really counts is how we deal with them. You've emerged a strong, caring woman, Carrie. You obviously made the best of what you were given. I think that's all any of us can do.''

She gave him a real smile then, her look warm and loving. She leaned over to gently kiss his cheek and her fragrance filled his senses. His breath caught at the warm, moist touch of her lips.

He was just about to claim her mouth with his when she pulled away and stood up. "I'd best get these dishes cleaned up and head for the university.''

Exhaling a deep breath, Cash realized she was oblivious to what her nearness had just done to his physical expectations. He got up and started to assist in the dishwashing, reminding himself there was plenty of time and realizing more than ever that it was Carrie who had to make the first move. But for his sanity he hoped she would make it soon.

"Why don't you come by here tonight and we can go to the police morgue together?'' she asked.

Cash nodded as he started to fill the sink with hot water, doing his best to quiet the insistent urgings of his body while he felt her continued nearness playing havoc with his resolve.

FROM THE MOMENT Cash arrived at Carrie's place that night, she could tell something was wrong. Even after he assured her his grandmother's condition was unchanged, the worried look still cloaked his countenance.

Finally as they got in the car and started toward the Reno Police Department's archives, she could keep quiet no longer. "Cash, what is it?''

"I contacted my friend at the bank this afternoon. I wanted to find out if any of the ransom money had turned up there.''

"And?'' Carrie prompted.

"As far as their records show, the bank never saw it again. Some banking employees were still checking notes up until ten years later according to the records.''

"Ten years?''

"Yes. Evan Wahl's ten-thousand-dollar reward for information leading to the identification and apprehension of the kidnappers apparently kept people interested in checking their money for some time. Things didn't really die down until ten years after the tragedy when Wahl remarried."

"Wahl has a second wife? Do you know who she is?"

"Was," Cash amended. "She died several years ago. I found the announcement of death as well as of the wedding in the newspaper society column when I went back to the library this afternoon after talking with my friend at the bank. Wahl's second wife was Cara Maximova, a widow of a business associate."

"They must have had children for Hal Sawyer to be his grandson," Carrie said.

"Just one. A daughter from Cara's previous marriage. Wahl formally adopted her."

Carrie ran her hands over the smooth leather of the steering wheel. "So Hal Sawyer is his adopted daughter's son. Well, that explains the lack of physical similarity between Sawyer and his grandfather. Do you know anything more about Wahl's family?"

"No. The newspapers carried very little. The only reason the marriage and adoption information found its way into print was because they occurred around the time Wahl was running for governor. As soon as he retired from political life, however, his personal life went back underground. The newspaper reports said that a desire to keep his personal life private was one of the reasons he declined to run for a second term."

Carrie nodded, thinking she understood. "Didn't want to give any more kidnappers a chance."

"Yes, I thought that, too."

Memories of the kidnapping made Carrie feel sad once again. Cash accurately read the look on her face and felt bad that he was going to have to add to it. He shifted in the passenger seat.

"Let's get it all said, Carrie. The kidnapper was never caught. The money was never found. Yet we know who had at least three hundred dollars of it."

Carrie had begun to shake her head.

"Hear me out," Cash said. "There's something I haven't told you yet. I asked my friend at the bank about the loan Duncan arranged for Wahl. He found records of it in the files. Wahl saved nearly ninety-seven thousand dollars on that loan because of the reduced interest rate and extended payback period."

Carrie gripped the wheel in sudden dread. She knew what Cash was about to say. She stared ahead and waited for the words that could dim even the sun-bright banner in the night sky across Reno's main street, proclaiming it the Biggest Little City In The World.

"Duncan's bequest to Wahl was just over three thousand dollars, Carrie. Ninety-seven thousand plus three thousand adds up to one hundred thousand dollars."

She had begun to shake her head in denial, but Cash went on knowing it all had to be aired.

"In his will's bequest, Duncan said the three thousand dollars was the final payment on a debt, yet Wahl claims no such debt existed. But there may have been a debt that Wahl never associated with Duncan's payment—a debt that as Duncan said prevented the slate between them being washed clean. Carrie, there's no getting around it. One hundred thousand dollars was the exact ransom amount Wahl paid to the kidnapper of his baby daughter. All the evidence points to Duncan being involved in the kidnapping of that child."

Carrie shook her head vehemently. "He didn't do it, Cash. You'll never convince me Duncan could have been so cruel or caused such pain."

He exhaled, feeling as unhappy as she. "I loved him. He was my godfather, my friend. I guess in my heart I still don't believe it. But the facts are rather hard to ignore."

Carrie straightened with new resolve. "All right, let's not ignore them. But let's also add a few more. If Duncan had really been responsible for the ransoming of Wahl's child, why did he go to such pains to pay back the hundred thousand dollars? That doesn't fit in with the harsh, cruel nature of a child murderer, does it? And his giving those three one-hundred dollar bills to me—wasn't that also opening him up for possible exposure?"

Cash scratched his chin. "I've been trying to reconcile those facts myself. I think although Duncan was involved in this business, he was ready to let it all come out. Remember my grandmother said he wanted to expose 'past sins'?"

" 'Past sins must be revealed,' " Carrie quoted.

Cash read the changing tone of her voice. "What is it?"

Carrie licked her lips. "Cash, if you had done a terrible thing like being responsible for a child's death and guilt and remorse had overcome you, would you speak about it as past sins being revealed?"

He frowned as he considered her words for a minute. "No. I think admitting to personal blame would cause me to be more specific. I'd be inclined to say, 'I must confess my past sin.' "

"If it was *your* sin," Carrie said.

Cash heard the new speculation in her voice and turned to watch her face as she drove. "Carrie, are you saying you think Duncan was covering up for someone else?"

Carrie nodded. "Duncan was a lawyer, Cash, subject to the constraints of attorney-client confidentiality. What if the kidnapper hired Duncan just in case he was accused? What if the kidnapper gave Duncan some of the ransom money as a retainer? Wouldn't that explain why Duncan had some in his possession?"

"You could be right," Cash said, as he thought of her words. "It fits in with the facts and with the type of man we knew Duncan to be. He might have even gotten hold of the rest of the ransom money and tried to return it to Wahl in a way that kept its origin confidential."

Carrie nodded. "And that explains Duncan's loan to Wahl when he was in financial trouble. Duncan was the type of man to try to right as much wrong as he could. I can picture him insuring Wahl got the loan when he needed it, can't you?"

"Yes, Carrie, I can. But if Duncan didn't commit this kidnapping, then you know what that means?"

Carrie nodded gravely. "Yes. He knew who did. And it was the sins of the real kidnapper he was about to expose."

ONCE INSIDE the Reno Police Department's archives, Carrie and Cash were escorted by a records clerk who was in charge of overseeing the very old case material in the basement. He was round, bald and close to retirement, with obviously something less than zest for his current assignment. As Carrie and Cash headed for the big rolls of microfilm in the back, he quickly returned to his desk to prop up his feet and resume eating baloney sandwiches while watching football reruns on a portable TV.

Their search soon proved to be painstaking work. The older years were often separated by neither year or crime. Hours passed and each had put a lot of rolls in and out of their respective microfilm viewers before Carrie finally found the right one.

"This is it," she said. Cash quickly scooted his chair to her side.

"See here, Cash? It's very close to the newspaper account of the kidnapping, except that it mentions two additional things. One, the police department thought that the kidnapping was pulled off by two men and, two, that they made an investigation into the background of a twenty-two-year-old man named Fred Koske, a Reno resident."

"Koske? Why him?" Cash asked.

"According to this detective's report, Koske was a Reno resident and one of several miners fired by Evan Wahl just the week before."

"Like Wahl's firing of Edward Van Epp?" Cash asked.

She nodded. "Right. It was just a drop in silver prices that brought cost-cutting measures by Wahl. Koske was relatively new on the job and therefore one of the first workers to be fired. Apparently, however, he got extremely angry when he was let go and other miners overheard him saying he'd get even."

"Is that the reason the police suspected him?" Cash asked.

"That and one thing else. A second nurse walking her baby in the park on the day of the kidnapping said she saw two men—one short, one tall—talking to the Wahl nurse just a few minutes before the attack and abduction. She knew Koske and thought the shorter man looked like him."

"She couldn't be sure?" Cash asked.

"Not completely. She was strolling on the other end of the park when she looked over and saw the two men with the Wahl nurse. The tall man was dark and seemed to be limping. The short man was stocky, bowlegged and had red hair and buck teeth. As she explained it, the extended upper lip of his profile, the hair color, the short, stocky shape, and the fact that he was swinging a tree branch with his left hand, made her think he was Koske."

"What did the investigation uncover?" Cash asked.

Carrie shrugged, pointing to the entries. "Not much. As it says here, Koske had left his Reno lodgings the week before, telling his landlady he was heading for California to join some family there. The police talked with a local relative of the man and contacted the authorities in Sacramento, California, but it proved impossible to track Koske down. The police considered it a dead end."

"Did he ever come back to Nevada?" Cash asked.

"No one heard from him for the duration of the investigation at least. A lot of other people were questioned, but there were no other leads. The police closed the file after five years."

Cash was reading over her shoulder now. "What's that comment there?"

Carrie paused before answering, finally saying the words as though they gave her pain. "That after months of a dignified demeanor and reserved manner, when they found his child dead, Evan Wahl broke down and cried in front of the officers. Like a baby, they said."

Cash was quiet for a while, contemplating Carrie's words. "It's hard to imagine the man we met doing that," he said.

She sighed as she rewound the roll of film back onto its spool. "Yes, but he's had sixty years to harden. Perhaps that hardening is what has allowed him to survive the tragedy.''

Cash saw the sad look on her face. ''What is it?''

She slowly got to her feet. ''I never should have asked him about his daughter's kidnapping. Now that I understand the real story, I also understand how insensitive such a question was. He's suffered so much and I brought it all back.''

Cash shook his head. ''Maybe not, Carrie. I think Wahl would be equally unwilling to discuss other aspects of his family. Most wealthy men keep their personal lives as private as possible. These tragic memories are probably quite faint for him now.''

''Well they're fresh and new for me. I feel I owe him an apology.''

''Even though his desire for the mineral rights on Duncan's land ended up hurting Duncan?''

Carrie shook her head in indecision. ''I'm still feeling confused about all that. The way Wahl talked about Duncan made me think he really liked him. Maybe I'm gullible, but I believe he really didn't know about what Hal Sawyer was doing, and when he found out he was truly sorry for it.''

She brushed against Cash as they turned to go, and before he could stop himself he found his arm around her shoulders. With an effort he tried to make his words sound casual. ''I like your special brand of gullibility.''

Carrie felt the warmth of his words and strength of his nearness as the comfort he offered invaded her on many levels. Her senses sharpened in awareness and she had the sudden impulse to lean against his broad chest and let those strong arms surround her.

She saw the unmistakable invitation in his gold-brown eyes as her body drew toward his. She couldn't resist it. She didn't want to resist it. She wanted to touch the muscles tightening across his back, to inhale the clean, male scent of his skin, to feel his warm breath on her cheek, to taste his full mouth. Her hands circled his body. In eagerness, she lifted her lips to his.

But she was unprepared for the strong arms crushing her to him, for the hunger of his mouth that branded hers with its urgency. The force of his desire raged through her like a powerful current, singeing her blood and setting her flesh on fire.

Shock gripped her like a vise. Then suddenly she felt a rush of cool air on her burning cheeks and opened her eyes to see Cash had stepped back. She blinked, trying to gather her stunned thoughts and bring his face into focus.

His voice was a husky whisper. "That's not exactly what you were expecting, was it?"

Carrie dumbly shook her head, finding no words on the erased blackboard of her mind.

Cash took a deep, audible breath, letting it out slowly as his hands dropped from her arms. "Time for us to go."

She nodded then turned toward the exit. When she sat behind the driver's wheel, her movements became automatic as she headed for home. As the blocks passed by, she felt a growing trembling inside and a tardy awareness of what this man sitting so powerfully still beside her represented.

He was a major disturbance in her neatly ordered life.

His raw desire and need had flowed through her unrestrained. She had put up no fight to the immediate and complete takeover of her body and such total surrender had brought immediate shock to her normally controlled, disciplined mind. Now in the aftermath of his scorching kiss and embrace, all her stunned senses were reawakening with new intensity and desire.

Yes, he was disturbing. In an incredibly exciting and totally disorganizing way. And she never felt more alive or more willing to be so disorganized.

Cash stared straight ahead, but he wasn't seeing their route. He was cursing himself for letting his passion completely wipe out his caution. When she had come so willingly into his arms, he had lost all thought but to make her his. Her shocked response told him just how unsuspecting she had been of the full brunt of his desires.

They didn't speak until they reached her place. Cash reached across to the driver's side and took the keys from her hand.

"Come on. I'll walk you to your door."

He stood on its threshold as she hesitated in the doorway. He was just about to just say good-night and walk away when she stood on tiptoe and quickly brushed his lips with hers before turning to go in. As he watched the door close, he smiled.

However off balance his earlier embrace had caught her, she was not retreating. He found a happy little tune to whistle as he walked back to the Seville.

CARRIE FOUND SLEEP very elusive that night. She kept reliving the feel of Cash's hard body pressed into hers. And even once she had put the memory of Cash's embrace to rest, many more memories concerning the discoveries they had made that day rose up to disturb her.

Duncan's face drifted in and out, first young then old. He kept telling her it was all right that he had been hoarding money tainted by innocent blood. She tossed and turned as a sad little smile lifted his lined lips while he assured her he was still the same man she knew in her heart.

Then in the dim twilight of consciousness, she saw a young Evan Wahl crying in front of police officers who stood around not knowing what do. That's when she knew she had to do something.

Her chance came. She was in the park. A little baby girl was being snatched from her carriage by a man's hands, rough and blackened from the mines.

In desperation Carrie found herself running after him, shouting for him to stop and reaching out to grab at him from behind. She strained and strained, feeling her heart about to burst inside her chest until finally, in both surprise and terror, her hand touched the running man's shoulder.

Only he wasn't running anymore. He was turning toward her, an evil grin twisting his blackened face.

Chapter Eleven

Carrie shot up in bed at the sound of the sudden crash beside her nightstand. Perspiration soaked her nightgown, her breaths were coming in short little bursts and her heart was racing hard against her rib cage. Disoriented, she tried to reconcile her reality to her shadowy nightmares. Had there really been a noise that awakened her?

Shaken, she fumbled for the switch on the table lamp. When her slippery, unsteady fingers succeeded in turning the lamp on, her eyes blinked in the sudden brightness, then did a quick search of the hardwood floor. She immediately spied the obsidian figurine of the dappled-gray mustang. Then she realized that in her fitful sleep, her flailing arms had knocked the shiny figurine off the nightstand.

She swung her feet onto the floor and padded over to pick it up. As she reached for it, however, she noticed, much to her dismay, that a sliver of silver from the flying tail had broken off.

When she had originally seen the silver strips of the stallion, she had thought them to be paint. But now as she felt this sliver in her hands, she could tell it wasn't like any paint strip she had ever felt before. She brought it over to the light and felt its cold, metallic surface.

Cold? Metallic? Could it be what it seemed? Were these silver strips, adorning the mane and tail of this beautiful stallion? And if they were, where had Duncan gotten silver?

She went back to bed, but the new possibilities that invaded her thoughts kept her agitated for a very long hour before the healing draft of a dreamless sleep finally overtook her.

CASH WAS WAITING for Carrie in her office after class the next morning. He was eager to find out what it was she had found and sounded so excited about when she'd called that morning. But the moment she stepped inside and closed the door behind her, all thoughts save one fled his mind.

She looked so damn beautiful. Her long, rich brown hair danced around her shoulders as she approached and her blue-gray eyes sparkled with a warm welcome.

Let her make the first move, he told himself again, but when she stood before him and he smelled the light, sweet fragrance that was all her own he could feel his resolve once again slipping.

Before he knew it, his hands had circled around her waist, luxuriating in the warmth they found.

Carrie forgot her news. She was indeed finding it hard to think of anything clearly but Cash's closeness and the feel of his hands. The quickened beat of her heart had begun to pulse through her ears as she remembered the strength of his embrace the night before. She raised her hands to circle about his neck as she smiled into the gold-brown of his eyes.

His look was enough to liquefy the ligaments in her knees, but she saw, too, the constraint that held his desire in check. He was letting her know his feelings, but this would not be like last night's embrace. He was waiting for her to guide his response.

She found the control he placed in her hands incredibly exciting. A burgeoning omnipotence grew in her, the knowledge that it was totally in her command to unleash both their passions.

The power pulsed through her veins, heady and hot. She slowly bent his head toward her, feeling the heat of his skin as he came closer, the exciting feel of his breath as it caressed her forehead, then her nose. His lips lightly rubbed against her cheek, and she closed her eyes, moaning as she lifted her mouth to his.

His lips melted against hers, ever so deliciously gentle as his hands leisurely pulsated down her back. She felt his light touch ripple through her body in warm and exciting waves. This exquisite slowness, which heightened the tension in her every cell, was so different from that first embrace and even more exciting. She moved in for more.

As his hands worked their way to the outside of her hips, however, they suddenly stopped their massage and he leaned away.

Carrie opened her eyes to see him looking down at her right hip with undisguised curiosity. She became aware that something bulky was digging into her right hip bone and memory flooded back in a flash.

Amazed she had forgotten everything she had been about to share with him just because he had touched her, she gave herself a mental scold. But no admonition could diminish the excited pulsing through her body. Nor did she want it to.

She reached into the right-hand pocket of her overblouse and brought out Duncan's shiny gray obsidian mustang stallion.

"Well, that explains that eccentric bump," Cash said, his voice amused but a little husky. "I was beginning to wonder just how different you anthropologists could be."

Carrie smiled. "This is what I wanted to show you. Look at this sliver that fell off the stallion's tail. I thought it was some kind of paint at first, but now I think it's... Well, you give me your expert opinion."

Cash's eyes had traveled toward the obsidian figurine as she spoke. What he saw caused his forehead to pucker in a frown. He took the sliver from her hand and studied it and the other strips like it still on the figurine. "That's not paint. All of these thin strips along the mane and tail are silver. I wonder where Duncan got silver."

"I've been wondering that, too. Cash, do you suppose Duncan found silver on his land? Could that be the reason Evan Wahl is so eager to gain the mineral rights?"

Cash shrugged. "I don't know. I'm pretty unsophisticated when it comes to silver mining, but one thing I do know. It doesn't come out of the ground like this. These streaks through the horse's mane and tail are pure silver. They've been extracted from the rock where they were originally embedded. Such mining takes the proper equipment and expertise. I wasn't aware Duncan had either."

Carrie hooked her hair behind her ears. "Still, he was brought up in Contention, a town that grew up on a silver strike. Surely he could have picked up some knowledge just from being around miners?"

Cash nodded. "Yes, he could have. But he'd need something to crush the rock, and then a centrifugal device of some type to separate it, and a smelter. Where is the equipment?"

"Good question. I don't have a good answer. Still, the land he bought around Contention was the site of lots of mines. Perhaps he found a new vein in a previously closed or lost mine."

"Duncan wouldn't have wasted his time hacking away inside some old silver mine. Those things never interested him."

She shrugged. "Maybe not. But if Duncan didn't mine this silver, where did it come from?"

Cash was shaking his head. "I've never seen Duncan use silver on any of his figurines before. And come to think of it, I've never seen him use this mottled-gray color of obsidian stone before, either. I didn't think there was any on his property. He always showed me obsidian the color of black or green or brown when he returned from his rock-hunting trips."

Carrie's eyes took on a new sparkle. "Maybe that's it, Cash! Maybe the spot where Duncan found the gray obsidian is also the spot where he found the silver. Maybe we could find it, too."

His voice sounded doubtful. "Maybe. But Duncan's land is nearly five thousand acres. Finding that mottled-gray obsidian rock, if there is more of it, would be like trying to find the proverbial needle in the proverbial haystack."

"Still, if we could find it and prove a valuable vein of silver exists on that land, that coupled with the forged mineral agreement would be a strong motive for Duncan's murder. We could go to Tom and have him reopen the case."

Cash looked over at her, hearing the exuberance in her voice but knowing she had forgotten something.

"Neither of us is a geologist, Carrie. How could we possibly find a lost silver mine?"

She looked undaunted. "We could hire a geologist. I'll get the Yellow Pages."

He shook his head. "It's Friday. We don't have a prayer of getting anyone today and the weekend is coming up. I'd say the soonest we could arrange for any kind of technical advice would be Monday, if then."

Carrie nodded as the truth of Cash's statement sank in. Cash watched her as she replaced a thick strand of hair behind her ear in what he now knew was a typically characteristic mannerism. He was just resisting an impulse to step over and nuzzle that exposed ear when he saw the changing expression on her face.

"Why didn't I think of it before!" she said.

"Think of what?" he asked.

"Bonanza."

"Bonanza?" Cash repeated.

"Yes, he can show us. Don't you see? The dog's been out with Duncan on all his rock hunts. He'll know where Duncan was last. He'll lead us to the place where the gray obsidian came from and the silver, if there really is any."

Cash was shaking his head. "He might if we knew how to let him know what we needed."

"But he will know. Don't you remember Duncan bragging that Bonanza always took him to where they had been before? That was how he helped Duncan remember where they had looked last time so Duncan wouldn't repeat it. All we have to do is give Bonanza his head and let him lead us to the spot."

"But how do you know Duncan went to the spot of the gray obsidian last?" Cash asked.

Carrie fingered the stallion. "This was the last piece of obsidian he carved. Chances are good he and Bonanza found the stone on their last walk. Besides, what have we got to lose?"

Cash looked at the hope in her eyes and smiled. "You're right. What have we got to lose? Do you have a class this afternoon?"

"No, and I've got a good pair of walking shoes in the Jeep and an old sweater I can bring along in case we're out late. All we need to do is pick up Bonanza."

When Cash brought Bonanza out of his house a few minutes later, however, he was also carrying a thermos and a backpack with a shovel sticking out the end. He put all three in the back seat of the Jeep and answered her questioning look. "It could be a long day and you never know what we might find."

Despite a mild weather report, Carrie began to feel quite warm from the hot desert air blowing into the Jeep. Bonanza panted behind her and Carrie soon found her clothes sticking to her as she squirmed in the driving seat.

She watched in jealousy as Cash unbuttoned his shirt to let the breeze cool his chest. As the air whipped back his shirt, exposing his smooth muscle and golden brown hair, Carrie's initial envy rapidly began to change into admiration for the view. Unfortunately, it did nothing to keep her cool.

She was relieved to pull up in front of Duncan's house about fifty minutes later. No sooner did she park than Bonanza jumped out and headed for the door, barking excitedly.

Carrie was instantly dismayed. "I should have anticipated this. He thinks he's going to see Duncan, doesn't he?"

Cash nodded as he watched the animated little terrier scratching at the door with his front paws. "Not much we can do about it now. We'd better let him in before his excitement has a chance to do any more damage to his ribs."

"You go ahead," Carrie said. "I want to bring in the mail."

Carrie joined Cash inside just a moment later. He was watching helplessly as Bonanza ran into each room, tail wagging, looking for Duncan. The little dog kept it up for a couple more minutes as though he couldn't believe his master couldn't be found. Then he came whimpering over to Carrie and Cash.

"It's going to take some time, for him and for us," Cash said as he leaned down to pat the terrier's head. "Anything in the mail?"

Carrie placed the mail on the kitchen counter. "Just Duncan's new bank checks and the advertising circulars that were there Tuesday."

Cash looked up at the preoccupied tone of her voice. "What is it, Carrie?"

"There seems to be something missing from the mail you showed me on Tuesday, but for the life of me I can't think what."

Cash shrugged. "I don't remember, either. Doesn't seem logical Tom would have removed just one piece."

Cash had begun to collect several of the obsidian figurines that lay on the floor next to him. Carrie knelt down beside him to assist.

"They're as I remembered them," Cash said to her as they both began picking up the scattered figurines and replacing them back on the display shelf. "Most are black. Some have a tinge of green or brown. But the horse is the only figurine that is the mottled-gray obsidian. And it's the only one with the silver. Did you bring it along?"

Carrie pulled it from her pocket. Cash took it from her hand and put it next to some of the others. "It's a darker gray around the horse's legs, but the neck and back are definitely a mottled gray when compared with these others. Well, this is our clue. Let's go track it down."

The enthusiasm in Cash's voice seemed to infect the little white terrier. As soon as they opened the front door, Bonanza immediately took off down the front stairs of the house and started toward the mountains far in the distance. Carrie and Cash made a quick detour back to the Jeep to collect the backpack, which Cash adjusted over his shoulders. Both he and Carrie shaded their eyes with dark sunglasses.

Bonanza had obviously become used to Duncan's slower pace because he immediately adopted a circular path around Carrie and Cash. He'd run ahead a few steps then circle around to their right or left, sniffing out a rock or plant until they caught up. Then he'd run ahead again.

"He does appear to have a direction in mind," Cash said. "I'm beginning to think this just might work."

As Carrie walked along in the still air after the terrier, she watched the desert earth turning a white-gold in the full rays of the afternoon sun. The muffled sounds of their footsteps were the only noise in the miles of expanse all around them. Carrie felt a dreaminess come over her, a feeling of peace.

"It's relaxing out here, isn't it?" Cash said, his words mirroring her feelings, as his large fingers gently entwined with hers and their palms brushed lightly as they walked side by side. She could feel his flesh warm and firm against hers, exerting a gentle but persistent pressure, like he didn't want her to forget for a second that he was beside her.

"Yes, lovely," she said, experiencing an expanded sensuality just from holding hands with him. The energy and strength of his body seemed to flow through her skin. She tried to remember when she last held a man's hand but found it difficult to recall.

Hand holding must have seemed too tame to the often too-aggressive men she had dated. Perhaps that's why she hadn't found a lot of pleasure in dating them. But strolling along the desert and holding hands with Cash felt exciting, like a continuance of their earlier embraces. His touch brought back all the pleasure of those moments and made her look eagerly forward to the next.

"Have you been out here before?" he asked.

"Farther north for an anthropological outing in graduate school some years ago," she said. "There are caves around Pyramid Lake where early man lived at the same time giant sloths and reptiles still roamed the earth. Your grandmother wrote two books about them."

"What were the people like?"

Carrie laughed. "Your grandmother is probably the world's leading authority and you're asking me about them?"

Cash smiled at the good-natured ribbing. "I know it's crazy, but I haven't read her books. Grandmother didn't like to talk about her work to me. She was a very ordinary grandmother while I was growing up, bringing hugs and presents at Christmas and birthdays. I'm afraid I wasn't that curious about her profession."

Carrie shook her head. "Tsk. Tsk. And you call yourself a history buff. Still I think I can understand your grandmother's reluctance to discuss her work. Maybe she enjoyed just being a grandmother around you. You were her only grandchild?"

"Yes, and my mother was her only child. And now that I've been properly chastised for my previous lack of curiosity in my grandmother's profession, help to educate me by telling me about these ancient Indians of Pyramid Lake."

Carrie smiled at the lightness in his tone, needing no more encouragement to discuss a subject she loved.

"They were hunters. Made their clothes out of pelican skins, their hats from plant fibers and their moccasins out of deerskin. Their weapons were obsidian-tipped spears. Duncan gathered a lot of their discarded spears on his earliest walks. It was noticing how they fashioned those spear tips that first gave him the idea of how to make his obsidian figurines."

Cash nodded. "Now that you mention it, I seem to remember Duncan telling me something about that. What else?"

"Well, they used to eat a special prehistoric fish called the cui-ui. As a matter of fact, the cui-ui fish still lives in Pyramid Lake, and the pelicans still populate one of the islands."

Cash nodded. "Indians know how to subsist on the land and still leave it for future generations to enjoy. Pyramid Lake is quite a bit north of Duncan's property though, isn't it?"

"Yes. But the Indians migrated into what was Duncan's desert property during the winter to escape the heavy snowfall. Have you decided what you're going to do with the land?"

He nodded. "I'll preserve it for the wildlife, just as those Indians have done for centuries and just as Duncan was trying to do."

Carrie stole a look at his face. "You knew Duncan all your life, didn't you?"

"Not on an everyday basis like one gets to know one's close family. Duncan was the godparent who visited me two, maybe three times a year while I was growing up."

"And you said earlier that your mother died when you were young. Did your father ever remarry?"

"Yes, after I had grown up and was on my own. He moved to Idaho with his new wife about twelve years ago."

"Do you feel cut off from his new life?"

Cash nodded. "In a way. I was glad he had found someone to love, but I'm selfish enough to wish she had been someone who wanted to stay in the Reno area. Still, he's happy and that's what's really important. His moving away is probably one of the reasons why I found myself getting closer to Duncan. That and the fact that his great-nephews didn't seem to care he had trouble getting around and needed help."

Carrie's brow puckered. "They do seem quite callous considering all he did for them. I'll never understand it."

"No, I suppose a caring person like yourself wouldn't."

She pondered his words. "Caring? I wonder. My brother accuses me of being drawn to weakness."

Cash thought about her words for a moment and gave her hand a squeeze. "Maybe your background has caused you to be the champion of the weak against the excesses of the strong. If that's the case, then everyone should be so sensitized. It would make for a much nicer world."

She exhaled, feeling relieved by his words. The picture her brother had painted of her had not sat comfortably on the easel of her mind. She liked the image Cash had just described so much better. He certainly knew how to make her feel special.

Cash pointed. "Bonanza is scurrying around in a haphazard manner. Let's hope he settles down to a straighter line soon."

But after an hour and a half of walking, Carrie began to have her doubts about Bonanza settling down or Duncan's claims of the dog's ability to return to their previous site. The little white terrier had done a lot of backtracking and he was obviously tired and thirsty.

"Shall we stop and have something to drink?" she asked.

Cash nodded and removed the pack from his back. Bonanza came bounding over to drink from the cup of water Cash poured for him.

"Were we expecting too much?" Cash asked Carrie as he sat down next to her.

She felt the exciting draw of his body and she sighed. "Maybe. He seems to be angling off in various directions. Still he keeps coming back to a general heading toward the foothills there."

Bonanza's tongue licked Carrie's hand, as he seemed to understand he was the topic of discussion. The whiskers on his chin were dripping water from his recent drinking. Cash watched her gently smooth the excess water over the dog's head in an effort to keep him cool, her hair glistening like molten bronze in the sunlight.

With an effort he reordered his thoughts. "Maybe we've been interpreting Duncan's comments a little too literally. Perhaps what he meant was that Bonanza would keep Duncan in the right direction. What would you say to our heading for the foothills in a straight line to see if he follows?"

Carrie nodded as she finished her cup of water and got up to leave. "I'm for it. I don't imagine Duncan could get too far when he walked. You remember, the doctor said his limp gave him pain. Wherever he went can't be much farther."

After they reloaded the backpack, they took off in the direction they had decided upon and set the pace a little faster. Bonanza bounded ahead of them eagerly.

They made it to the far section of the foothills in just under an hour. Carrie was hoping Bonanza would take it from there, but he seemed to stop at every brush and rock for the next five minutes. Carrie was just about to suggest they give up when the little dog jumped up onto a small rise and began wagging his tail and barking excitedly.

Carrie and Cash looked at each other and then followed the dog up to the raised area. It was a flat ledge about thirty feet long, just slightly higher than the surrounding desert but at just the right position to see the ghost town of Contention in the valley directly due east.

"What is it that's got him so excited?" she asked.

Cash frowned as he continued to survey the area. "No doubt Duncan's scent is strong here. Maybe it was a favorite place for the two of them to stop."

Carrie bent down on one knee and called Bonanza over to her. He came obediently enough, but seemed dissatisfied when all she offered him was a pat. He scurried away from her and began to dig at the base of some ordinary sagebrush, kicking up the desert dust in a whirl.

She shook her head in disappointment. "Well, it certainly doesn't look like the site of an old silver mine to me."

Cash was surveying the earth carefully. "Maybe not, Carrie, but look here. This ground has been disturbed, and recently, too. See its darker shade and how loose the soil is compared to the earth several feet to your right? I think Bonanza may be digging here because he's repeating what he and Duncan did when they were here last. They dug something up."

She looked at the difference in the texture of the earth and nodded. "I think you're right. I've never known Bonanza to be much of a digger. Perhaps he did learn it by watching Duncan. Maybe the entrance to the silver mine is buried here. I did see a small shovel in the backpack, didn't I?"

Cash removed the small shovel. He got down on his knees and began to dig into the desert dust. "The ground is really pretty soft. There's no doubt it's been turned over recently. I wonder how far down it goes?"

Carrie sat down on a large gray rock and watched him dig. He'd removed his shirt and soon she found the sight of his hard golden muscles lubricated by his exertion a delicious sensual delight. Bonanza kept up his own digging for only a few minutes and then seemed to become tired. He joined her next to the rock.

Cash dug for nearly twenty-five minutes. The hole he managed to make was about five feet deep. He leaned back on his heels in the middle of it and passed the back of his hand over his sweat-filled brow. His flesh gleamed in the hot sunlight.

As much as she'd been enjoying the view, Carrie felt guilty. She stood up. "Take a break and have some water. I'll take over for a while. I'm used to digging out in the hot sun."

He smiled and nodded as they changed places. She made good progress. But in about ten minutes, her cotton blouse was sticking to her, soaked in perspiration. Then she felt the shovel hit something. In some surprise, she stopped, her voice reflecting her excitement.

"There *is* something here," she said.

She threw the shovel aside and began to carefully smooth away the dirt with her bare hands as her anthropological training automatically took over. By working carefully with her hands, she could be sure not to damage whatever it was she had found. Cash dropped down on his knees next to her and started to mimic her movements.

As soon as her hand brushed away the dirt from the bone, exposing it to the sunlight, she knew. She sat back against her heels just staring at the part of exposed skull, a sick feeling creeping into her stomach.

"An animal?" Cash asked.

Her voice was low and subdued. "A human."

"Are you sure, Carrie? We've only uncovered a small part."

"I'm sure. What you're looking at is a side piece of a human cranium parietal bone. This isn't the entrance to a lost mine we've been digging in, Cash. This is a grave."

Chapter Twelve

Cash sat back on his heels to watch Carrie's worried frown as she leaned over the skull. She had become very quiet as she studied their find. He tried a probe to assess her thoughts. "It must be a recent burial judging from the disturbed earth."

Carrie shook her head. "The body wasn't recently buried. It's been underground a long time. It's the earth that has been recently turned. We'll have to be very careful in uncovering the whole thing to be sure, but people don't generally rebury skeletons. Would you mind giving me a hand?"

He reached over to brush a speck of dirt from her chin, smiling. "I'm not squeamish, if that's what you mean. Tell me what to do."

She gave him a returning smile and then described the gentle feathering away of the dirt around the bones using fingertips and they started to work. The entire skull and upper chest were exposed in just a few minutes.

Carrie sat back. "It looks like that's the cause of death."

Cash's eyes followed her pointing finger. "That large dent over the eye socket?"

She nodded. "A powerful blow to the left frontal area probably by a right-handed person using a very hard substance. Look at the deep radiation of cracked bone from the impact point. And no healing took place, which means this individual died soon after the blow."

"Could this be one of your ancient Indians?"

Carrie shook her head. "No. The bones haven't had time to completely fossilize."

"How can you tell?" he asked.

Carrie flipped a recalcitrant strand of hair back behind her ear. "Fossilization takes place when the protein material in the bone is replaced by the percolated mineral material from the ground waters in the enclosing soil. With this relatively dry alkaline soil, it takes a while. If you look at this piece of the upper vertebrate column you can see the molecular substitution in the crystalline lattice of apatite—"

"Oh, yeah. I can see that real clearly," Cash said as he leaned back on his heels grinning.

Carrie caught the light, mocking tone of his words and laughed. "Sorry. Didn't mean to get off into the technical jargon. What I meant to say is that the fossilization indicates the bones have probably not been buried longer than, oh, sixty years. Consequently, this cannot be an ancient Indian."

"Do we dig farther?" he asked.

She nodded. "You know, this is sort of coincidental. Ernie, the skeleton from class, had been buried for about sixty years, too, when they unearthed him just over to the east there in Contention."

"The man with the bullet in his head."

"Yes. And now we find this one with his head bashed in buried around the same time. Doesn't that strike you as a little odd?"

Cash's hands found his hips. "It strikes me as a little bloodthirsty, but those were wilder times, I suppose."

Carrie bit her lip, her thoughts distracted. "Hmm. I suppose. Well, let's get the rest of his skeleton exposed before the sun sets and we lose the light. You start digging a few feet in that direction. I'll begin here."

They worked steadily away for the next half hour to unearth the skeleton before Carrie leaned back on her heels to observe their work. "The thick heavy bones on this skeleton appear to—"

Cash's voice interrupted her observation. "Look at this."

She diverted her attention away from the leg area of the skeleton where she had been working to look at the rifle he held up. He was fingering the long barrel.

"You found that in the grave?"

Cash nodded. "Just now. Last time I saw one of these it was hanging in a museum. It's one of those old-time, single-shot, trapdoor loaders. See the insignia? Made by Springfield. Set any memory banks in motion?"

The setting sun seemed to blind Carrie's eyes for a moment as his words revolved around in her mind like a squeaky Ferris wheel. "A Springfield trapdoor loader?"

He heard the disbelief in her voice and turned to her. "Yes, Carrie. Just like the one that caused the bullet hole in Ernie's head. A bit coincidental, don't you think?"

Carrie's voice rose in excitement. "Cash, do you think that could be *the* Springfield rifle that was used to murder Ernie?"

Cash looked back at the weapon in his hands, continuing to finger its long barrel. "There may be no connection. These rifles were still common right up into the early 1930s."

She nodded at his words and exhaled heavily. Suddenly what she thought was clear became foggy. "Yes, Tom said so, too. It's just that for a moment . . . knowing both bodies were buried around the same time—I guess I jumped to the conclusion too quickly."

He looked back at the skeleton and the weapon in his hand. "Maybe not. You say Ernie's skeleton was buried around the same time as this one?"

She nodded. "Dating the bones isn't precise, but the ossification is almost identical. And despite the fact that this soil has been recently turned, the imprint on the packed sediments beneath the skeleton show it has remained untouched since the time of its burial, around sixty years ago. My educated guess is that both bodies were interred very close to the same time."

Cash was obviously considering her words as he munched on his bottom lip. "Two people are murdered around the same time just miles from each other. Both are buried, but not in the town graveyard. Obviously, their deaths were never recorded."

Carrie nodded. "Yet my brother's investigation into Ernie's death revealed no sheriff's record of a missing person from the town of Contention sixty years ago. Who were these people?"

"Drifters?" Cash suggested.

She shrugged. "Maybe. But who killed them?"

"Could be another drifter," Cash speculated.

"No, I find that hard to believe. Remember, Ernie was found in the concealed cellar of an old boardinghouse in the ghost town of Contention, and he had a cross above his grave. How would a drifter get in?"

"So you're thinking whoever killed these two was a citizen of Contention and knew the other victim, hence the cross over the grave. Did your brother find out who owned the boardinghouse?"

Carrie nodded. "First thing he checked. They were an elderly couple, killed in a fire that burned most of the structure in the days just prior to the town's closing. Of course, Tom couldn't be sure they even knew about the concealed cellar or the body buried there. They may not have even owned the boardinghouse at the time of Ernie's death. But Tom wasn't able to find out who did so it became a dead end."

"So what we've got is a man killed with a Springfield rifle about sixty years ago and another person killed by a bash in the skull around the same time buried about eight miles away with the possible murder weapon of the first man."

Carrie was shaking her head. "Doesn't make much sense, does it? If their deaths are connected, why were the bodies buried separately? And why bury that rifle in this grave?"

"Maybe the rifle belonged to this dead person."

She shrugged. "If you've killed somebody, would you balk at stealing his rifle?"

Cash was looking at the rifle more closely. "No, but maybe the rifle had a distinguishing mark that would enable it to be traced. In that case the murderer wouldn't dare keep it. Look at this carving along the handle. What does that look like to you?''

Carrie leaned over to take a closer look. She scraped some of the soil off the roughly carved surface with her fingernail. ''Seems like R—O—S—K—E.''

Cash shook his head. ''I think the first letter is a *K*. See, what you thought was the top of the *R* is just a scratch.'' A light seemed to pop on in his eyes. ''*K?* Koske? Carrie, could this be Fred Koske's rifle?''

The meaning in his words caught her all at once, like a mental jolt kicking her off balance. ''Fred Koske! The suspected kidnapper of Evan Wahl's baby daughter! The man who supposedly went to California and was never seen again. My God, Cash. Is it possible he never went to California? *Was* he one of the kidnappers? Is this his grave?''

All the same questions were occurring in Cash's mind at the same moment Carrie was voicing them. His hands turned the rifle. ''If this is Koske's grave, I'd like to know who put him in it. You're sure this individual was murdered?''

''Yes. That severe blow to the skull couldn't have occurred accidentally. And his was not the only body buried here.''

Her matter-of-fact comment took him by surprise. Cash looked up at her, shielding his eyes from the slanting rays of the setting sun. ''Another body was buried here?''

In answer, she squatted next to the spot where Cash had unearthed the rifle, and pointed to a pattern in the packed dirt below.

''See those indentations? They were left when the other body was removed. There's the spine and the back of the head.''

Cash's eyes followed her pointing finger. What he saw made his stomach queasy. The imprint of the tiny bones was unmistakable. ''Was it the skeleton of a child?''

He felt relief when Carrie shook her head. ''No, it looks like a small dog. I can't be sure, but from where it lay on the packed earth beneath, you can just barely see the spinal column and front and back legs if you look closely.''

Despite how closely Cash looked, he decided it would take a trained eye to see what Carrie was able to see. Finally he gave up the attempt and straightened to his full height. Carrie was shaking her head.

"Let's try to piece this together, Cash. Assuming that Bonanza has led us back to the last site where he and Duncan were, we have to conclude that Duncan knew of this grave. Add to that the fact that he removed the skeleton of a dog and there's a new dog's grave in his own pet cemetery—"

"There is?"

Carrie nodded. "Yes. I noticed a sixth cross on Monday. I thought it was strange at the time, but Duncan's death claimed all my attention. Now, however, it seems pretty evident to me that Duncan reburied the dog's skeleton. The importance Duncan attached to it seems to imply—"

Carrie was interrupted by the sound of loose rock coming from a steep ledge about fifteen feet above them. Startled, both Carrie and Cash looked up in surprise. What she saw sent a sudden chill along her skin.

Gene Van Epp scowled down at them. "You've found it, haven't you? I knew if I followed you, you'd lead me to it."

She felt her throat go dry as she heard the sneer in the man's voice and looked into the double barrels of his shotgun.

Bonanza must have sensed the fear and tension in the air. He bounded forward and began to bark up at Gene.

"Shut that damn dog up!" Gene yelled.

Carrie, fearing Gene might try to hurt the dog, climbed out of the newly dug grave and called for Bonanza to come to her, leaning down to pet and quiet him. Cash also climbed out of the grave and stood next to her as he answered the man up on the ledge.

"And what exactly is it you think we've found, Gene?"

From the gentle pressure on her arm, Carrie understood Cash was trying to get her to step behind him out of the line of fire. She rose to her feet and slowly responded to his urging.

More loose rock tumbled down in front of them as Gene stepped forward on the ledge.

"Don't play dumb with me, McKendry. Where's the money?"

"Money? What are you talking about?" Cash asked as he continued to gently urge Carrie behind him.

She was halfway there when Gene's next words caused her to halt in her tracks.

"I want the ransom money, McKendry. The hundred grand. He didn't hide it in the house otherwise I would have found it when I tore the crummy place apart. It was just like the old desert rat to hide it somewhere out here. I just didn't know where until now."

Carrie had stepped forward in front of Cash without realizing it, circling the rim of the grave to get a better look at the face of the man on the ledge. The only thing that was real to her at that moment was the implication in Gene Van Epp's words.

"The Wahl baby ransom money, Gene?" she asked. "Is that what you're talking about?"

Gene sneered. "Yeah, I figured you must have found out about it, too. Something had to be keeping you around. So you know. Big deal. You've waited around for nothing. The money's mine. Now hand it over or you'll be dead, too. Both of you."

Carrie was still confused. More than anything she wanted to understand. "Duncan told you about the kidnapping? He told you who did it?"

Gene's voice turned sarcastic. "The fool said it all had to come out. All of the wrongs had to be righted. Can you imagine? He sits on the truth for sixty years and suddenly decides to open his mouth and give everything away. Crazy old coot! Didn't die too soon for me."

She knew she was in danger, but Carrie didn't feel afraid anymore. Or maybe she was still afraid, but the anger welling up inside her had overridden it. It was the same anger that always had overtaken her when faced with a bully. A furious voice that dwelt deep inside her yelled up at the man on the ledge.

"You're a fool, Gene. A stupid, blind fool! All your life Duncan gave you his love, a treasure far more valuable than any money and you threw it away."

Carrie stepped back from the grave and pointed at the fully exposed skeleton lying there.

"There's what you've followed us to find, Gene. That's all your greed has led you to. There's no money here, only death. It's all yours."

No sooner had she gotten the angry words from her mouth than she saw a terrified look flash onto Gene Van Epp's face. For an instant his arms extended and he seemed to poise in midair above her like some giant bird of prey ready to swoop. Then the next thing Carrie knew, his body began falling toward her, his loud, terrified screech freezing the blood in her veins.

In absolute horror she scrambled backward, out of the way. Her foot caught on the edge of the rock and she lost her balance and fell just as Gene Van Epp's body hurtled past her into the ready grave. Then, for Carrie, everything went blessedly black and silent.

IN IMMOBILIZING SHOCK, Cash heard Gene's unearthly screech and then watched the man fall from the ledge above them headfirst. Gene's scream died on impact, a heavy hushed thud that left waves of a suffocating silence in its wake.

Cash stared in disbelief at the man's body slumped over the skeleton he and Carrie had just unearthed. Gene Van Epp was not moving. From the open, staring eyes and twisted position of his neck, Cash knew he never would again.

As Cash raised his head, he suddenly saw Carrie lying motionless on the other side of the grave. He rushed immediately to her side, an awful suffocating feeling clenching at his chest. Her face looked so white, so deathly still. He dropped to his knees beside her, frantically probing for the pulse in her neck as he said a silent prayer.

He put his ear close to her mouth, but heard nothing. With encroaching dread, he felt his own heartbeat slowing to a stop until suddenly he detected the faint, but rhythmic pulsing through his probing fingertips and the whisper-soft warmth of her breath on his cheek. She was alive! He released his trapped breath as an immense relief swept through him.

He was just about to start rubbing her hands to try to bring her back to consciousness when suddenly his head rose again as he heard an engine starting up. In the instant before Gene Van Epp had fallen, Cash had thought he heard another noise, like footsteps on the ledge behind Gene. Now the significance of those footsteps took a very sinister turn.

He released Carrie's hand and shot to his feet, running to the edge of the incline, toward the sounds of the retreating engine noise. He got there just in time to see the old, beat-up Ford Bronco he recognized as belonging to Hal Sawyer tearing off toward the ghost town of Contention.

CARRIE GRADUALLY BECAME conscious of a pounding in her ears and a sharp pain radiating from the back of her skull. She wanted very much to ignore both and allow herself to drift back to oblivion but she kept hearing a voice. She couldn't make out what the voice was saying because it came from so far away, but it seemed insistent so she tried to concentrate. Then she opened her eyes and although everything was a blur, the voice seemed closer and more intelligible.

After a moment her eyes focused on Cash's worried face and she heard him distinctly say, "Carrie, can you hear me? Answer me, please."

She opened her mouth to find her voice was a dry croak. "Yes, Cash. I hear you and the entire percussion section of a rehearsing orchestra."

He exhaled heavily and gave her a small smile. "I'm not surprised. You whacked your head quite hard."

His words confused Carrie as did the fact that she suddenly realized her face was wet. She raised her hand to wipe away a drop dripping off her brow. "What happened?"

He used his shirtsleeve to gently wipe the excess moisture from her face. "You tripped. I'm sorry for the bath, but

Bonanza and I began to worry when I couldn't get you to come around. I contributed the cold water. The wet tongue was his idea."

Bonanza was whining beside her so she gave his head a pat. He must have felt reassured because his whining stopped and he snuggled up against her side. She realized that she was propped up against Cash's knee.

"I don't understand. You said I fell? I don't seem to remember..."

She felt his strong arm circling her shoulders as she glanced around. Suddenly, she sat up straight and stiff as she recognized the desert terrain, and her memory came striking back like an uncoiled rattlesnake. Her head jerked up toward the ledge where Gene Van Epp had stood. And then her head slowly turned toward the grave she lay beside to see the hunched body of Gene Van Epp over the skeleton of the man with the crushed skull.

She shivered, only partly from the rapidly cooling air, and the pain shooting through her head at its every movement. She felt Cash's arm tighten around her. "He's dead?"

Cash nodded. "Do you feel well enough to stand?"

In response Carrie moved her feet and found them steady. Cash helped her up. He wrestled her sweater out of the backpack and helped her put it on. Then he put on one himself and adjusted the backpack over his shoulders. He leaned down to retrieve the old Springfield rifle and Gene's shotgun, which had fallen with him. He turned back to Carrie.

"Sun's going down. It will be cold and dark soon. We've got to start back to the house. I'll call your brother from there."

"We're going to leave... Gene here?"

Cash exhaled heavily. "There's nothing we can do for him now, Carrie. Nothing anybody can do."

She took one last look into the grave before turning to go. It was just then that the sun's setting rays caught the large rock she had both sat on and tripped over that afternoon, reflecting its light like an uncut diamond. She did a double take and then walked over to reach out a hand across its glassy surface. A moment later she sensed Cash at her side.

"It's the gray obsidian, isn't it?" he asked.

She nodded. "Look, there's a place where a piece has obviously been carefully chiseled off the end. It must have been the piece Duncan used for the mustang stallion. See the mottling in that part of the stone? I can't believe I sat on this rock, even tripped over it and still didn't recognize it until now."

He took her hand as they turned to go. "I can believe it. Often it's the things that are right in front of our faces that are the hardest to see."

"ALL RIGHT, CASH," Tom said as he put down the old candlestick phone in Duncan's desert home and reopened his notebook. "I've just sent out an A.P.B. for Hal Sawyer. Are you sure it was his vehicle you recognized?"

Cash nodded.

Tom turned to Carrie. "And did you see Sawyer or his vehicle up there in the foothills at the time of Gene's death?"

Carrie looked up at her brother through a cloud of constricting pain. "No. I guess the noise of our digging masked the sounds of the truck engine. And when it drove away, well, I was out cold by then. I didn't even realize Sawyer had been there until Cash told me on our walk back here."

Tom nodded. "Are you sure you don't want to see a doctor?"

Carrie exhaled. "For the tenth time, Tom, I'm sure."

Tom didn't look pleased but he let further argument go. "Did you hear anything just before Gene Van Epp fell?"

Carrie realized now that she had been in shock when she had regained consciousness out in the desert. But on their walk back, the shock had unfortunately worn off. It was unfortunate because now all the horror of Gene's death was closing in on her. She tried to keep her voice calm.

"I was too busy yelling to hear anything, Tom. And after I had finished, suddenly he was falling...."

A chill shook her shoulders. She felt Cash's arm circle around her back and was immediately grateful for the warmth.

"So you heard nothing?" Tom asked.

"No," Carrie said. "Like I told you before, he seemed to think we were after the ransom money from that sixty-year-old kidnapping of the Wahl baby."

Tom was shaking his head, the tenor of his voice rising with every "and" coming out of his mouth.

"You should have told me about the Wahl kidnapping before this, Carrie. *And* about the forged mineral rights contract. *And* about the silver on the gray obsidian figurine. *And* about the money Duncan gave you."

Carrie watched Tom impatiently turning over the white envelope containing the hundred-dollar notes, his every movement conveying his irritation. But no matter how hard he was trying to put Carrie in the wrong, this time she felt confident of her innocence.

She reached down to stroke Bonanza who was curled around her feet. It had been a full day for the little dog and he was sound asleep. Carrie envied him. Despite two aspirin, her head was still pounding and her entire spine felt like someone had been beating it with a sledgehammer. But she was determined that she was not going to lose her temper, no matter how lousy she felt.

"Tom, the last time we spoke of Duncan's death, I told you he had been murdered. You didn't believe me. Since you refused to look for his killer, you left me with no choice but to do it myself."

"When you uncovered evidence, it was your duty to—"

"To tell you?" Carrie interrupted. "No, Tom. If I had come to you when Cash and I discovered that the money Duncan gave me was from that sixty-year-old kidnapping, you would have told us it had nothing to do with Duncan's death. Wouldn't you?"

"You still can't be sure it did."

"Oh, but I can be sure, Tom. Gene Van Epp made me sure this afternoon. What he said to us has made me realize that it must have been Duncan himself who told Gene about the Wahl kidnapping. Gene believed Duncan still had the ransom money and—''

''You figure Gene killed Duncan to get it?'' Tom asked.

''I think he might have. At the will reading, Cash's grandmother implied Duncan was going to reveal past sins. In light of what Cash and I have discovered and Gene's admission, I believe Duncan was talking about the Wahl kidnapping.''

''You believe Duncan was in on it?''

Carrie sat forward. ''Oh, no, Tom. But I believe he knew who was. I think just before he was killed, he was about to reveal who the real kidnappers were.''

Tom eased his large frame into one of Duncan's hardwood chairs and faced his sister.

''I don't like bursting your bubble, Carrie, but it's much more likely that Duncan was one of the kidnappers than some innocent party who just happened to find out what went on. From your statement and Cash's, Gene even said Duncan had confessed to him—''

Carrie sat up straight, despite the renewed pounding it brought. ''Duncan only told Gene that the truth about the kidnapping had to come out. Even Gene said nothing about Duncan being one of the instigators of that dreadful affair.''

Tom slapped his thigh and rose to his feet impatiently. ''Come on, Carrie. Duncan gave you three hundred dollars of the ransom money. Then the old man's dog leads you to an unmarked grave with the remains of a man killed just about sixty years ago on Duncan's land. If the rifle and your subsequent examination identify him as Fred Koske, we've got a pretty open-and-shut case.''

Tom paced as he continued. ''And even discounting everything Gene said, which implicates his great-uncle, the money and the grave are sufficient evidence to tell me Duncan Van Epp was one of the men who took the Wahl baby sixty years ago and subsequently murdered his partner—that skeleton you dug up.''

Carrie rose to her feet in indignation. ''No, Tom. Not Duncan!'' Her head felt like it was about to split open. That pain plus her brother's words were becoming unbearable. Tears born from both circled in her eyes. It was then she felt Cash rise beside her to face her brother.

"Tom, if you had known Duncan as we did, you would understand. There's an explanation for Duncan's unwillingness to come forward and reveal the circumstances that led to his involvement in the kidnapping. We've told you how he returned the hundred thousand to Evan Wahl. Does that sound like a heartless kidnapper and cold-blooded killer?"

Tom scratched his chin. "Old age can sometimes bring remorse."

Cash shook his head. "Duncan began returning the money to Wahl over forty years ago. He was hardly into his old age then."

Tom shrugged. "Perhaps Duncan Van Epp never intended to hurt the child. Perhaps Koske murdered her. Duncan could have turned on his partner, killed him, and in a way of partial restitution to Wahl, surreptitiously returned the amount of the ransom money."

Tom's words had a ring of probability that circled about Carrie uncomfortably. She could see they had given Cash pause. For a moment, her mind had an image of Duncan as a young man standing next to a shorter red-haired man talking to a child's nurse as they planned to steal the baby from the carriage she pushed. Then, like broken glass, the image shattered before her mind's eye. Duncan would not have been able to plan such a thing. She was sure of it. There had to be another explanation.

But what?

Chapter Thirteen

Cash took a step forward. "Tom, we can stand here all night and speculate about the past. The truth is we'll probably never know what really happened sixty years ago. But I know what's happening right now. Carrie is in a lot of pain and—"

"I'm okay," she said, wanting to forestall what she anticipated would be Cash's suggestion they leave. There were still things that had to be said. But she let him ease her back onto the couch.

"Okay," Tom said. "We'll forget about sixty-year-old crimes for the time being. Let's get back to current history. Do I take it you now believe Gene Van Epp poisoned his great-uncle?"

Carrie's head throbbed. She raised a hand to her forehead as though she could direct the drumbeat into a slower percussion. "I don't know, Tom. He admitted he tore Duncan's place apart looking for the ransom money."

"So you don't think a lost silver mine was the motive? You're ready to discount the forged mineral-rights agreement?"

Carrie brought her other hand to her head. Even her jaw and tongue were beginning to ache. "I'm not discounting anything, Tom. It's just he seemed to be so interested in the ransom money that—"

"Gene had reason to be interested in a quick hundred thousand," Tom said. "And it doesn't necessarily preclude his interest in a lost silver mine."

Carrie tried to focus through the pain. "What do you mean?"

Tom shrugged. "I mean one hundred thousand is what Gene Van Epp currently owed to a very unforgiving lender around town."

Cash leaned forward on the couch. "Kurt Mofatt?"

Tom nodded. "Yes. I heard you had dealings with him, Cash. You might be able to help us later when we bring him in."

Carrie's head was pounding so hard she could barely hear what the men were saying. "Tom, what's going on?"

He turned to her. "Just routine checking. Ever since we traced the hypertensive medicine to Gene—"

Carrie shot forward in her seat. "What?"

Her brother shrugged. "My people have been trying to contact the doctor who prescribed the metoprolol found in Duncan's body and in his medicine cabinet. Dr. Haskell has been on vacation. When he returned this morning we learned the Van Epp on the prescription bottle was Gene, not Duncan."

Carrie's voice rose excitedly. "So it must have been Gene who put both drugs in the whiskey! He was the one who murdered Duncan!"

Tom shrugged. "Looks like it. I've just been trying to piece together how Gene figured he'd benefit from killing his great-uncle. Now that the ransom money has come into the picture, it's a little more complete. Still this afternoon's fiasco hasn't contributed a satisfactory ending."

Cash looked at him quizzically. "What do you mean?"

Tom paced around the small living room with his hands in his pockets. "Why would Hal Sawyer push Gene Van Epp off that ledge?"

Cash shrugged. "I guess that's something you'll have to ask Sawyer. Now if you don't need us for anything else, I'd like to take Carrie home."

She summoned all her strength to resist the suggestion. "Edward Van Epp must be told about Gene. No matter what Gene did, he was Edward's only family. You can't just expect to send a deputy—"

Tom frowned. "Are you sure you're feeling well enough?"

Carrie stood up gently this time and found Cash right beside her. "I think I should be the one to tell Edward, Tom."

Her brother eyed her, still frowning.

Cash anticipated an argument and realized that would probably be the worst thing for Carrie now. He spoke up. "I'll make sure she gets home okay. Now, I think the sooner we leave the sooner Carrie will be getting the rest she needs."

Cash smiled at Carrie's look of unspoken gratitude and tightened his arm around her. Tom shrugged as they made their way to the door. Bonanza was up like a shot following in Carrie and Cash's wake.

Once outside Cash noticed that Carrie automatically headed for the Jeep's passenger seat. It told him just how bad she must be feeling. He settled Bonanza in the back and climbed behind the wheel. He noticed Carrie leaned her head back and closed her eyes.

When they pulled in front of Edward's town house about an hour later, Carrie opened her eyes to a feeling of déjà vu. It had only been a few days before when she had told Edward of Duncan's death. Now here she was back again to tell him about his brother.

Edward opened the door almost immediately after Cash rang the bell. He looked at them in obvious surprise. "What the hell are you doing here?"

"May we come in, Edward?"

When Edward just stood there, Carrie re-asked her question and he finally waved them inside with some irritation. "You can't stay. I'm getting ready to pick up Margaret."

In stockinged feet he led them into the living room where he sat on the couch and proceeded to put his shoes on, something Carrie and Cash had apparently interrupted.

Carrie could see that Edward's hair was still slightly damp from a recent shower.

"Well, out with it," he said. "What's going on?"

Carrie sat next to him and turned sideways on the couch so that she could face his profile. "Gene died this afternoon, Edward. He fell from a ledge on Duncan's northern property and broke his neck."

As he looked over at her, Carrie watched Edward's eyes flickering like fluorescent light bulbs unable to make up their mind whether to come on or off. His voice was toneless. "What?"

Carrie repeated the message and went on to explain how Gene had pointed a shotgun at her and Cash and demanded the ransom money from the Wahl baby kidnapping. She gave Edward the background on the sixty-year-old crime. Her voice faded only when she began to describe Gene's fall. Cash finished the story.

Edward stared at the shoe in his hand, his face expressionless. "I don't believe it."

Carrie was taken aback both by his words and the vehemence behind them. "Edward, I saw him fall. Gene is dead."

Edward waved the shoe in irritation. "Oh, I believe that part all right. But this garbage about Gene being responsible for Duncan's death is dribble. Just like all that old kidnapping crap."

Carrie was surprised at Edward's denial, but not disappointed. She was glad to detect he had some family loyalty after all. "Duncan told you nothing about the Wahl kidnapping?"

Edward was still staring at the shoe in his hand, his voice laced in irritation. "There was nothing to tell." He turned to look at her. "The story's a farce. You knew the old man. Can you see him kidnapping some kid then murdering it?"

Carrie shook her head, more than relieved at Edward's support for Duncan's innocence. "I agree that Duncan would not be a part of such a terrible thing. But I think he knew who was involved. He did have some of the ransom money in his possession."

"What are you talking about?"

"He gave me three hundred dollars that was part of the ransom money. Cash traced it."

Edward looked back down at the shoe in his hand. His face was still expressionless, but Carrie could see the vibrant throbbing of a vessel in his temple. He didn't say anything for a few minutes, just stared at the shoe. Then finally he slipped it on and stood up, looking down at her as she remained seated on the couch.

"Duncan could have gotten that money anywhere and at any time. It proves nothing. You'd best tell that to your brother, the cop, before he starts slinging accusations around about my family."

"But Gene said—" Carrie began.

"I don't care what Gene said. He wasn't himself. His hostile actions toward you and Cash should be sufficient proof how far he had descended into his own personal hell of gambling and drink."

"Do you think he could have killed Duncan?" Cash asked.

Edward swung toward Cash, looking angry at the suggestion. "Gene could have shot you if he had gotten drunk enough, but Duncan was family. Gene wouldn't have killed a member of his own family."

"Did he know Hal Sawyer?" Carrie asked.

Edward swung back to her. "He never mentioned him to me."

"So you don't know why Hal Sawyer would kill him?" Cash asked.

Edward turned to face Cash again. "No, I don't. And there's no reason to think that Sawyer did try to kill my brother."

"What do you mean?" Cash asked.

"All you saw was Sawyer's truck driving away. You don't know if Sawyer was driving it. You don't know if he was on the ledge behind my brother. It seems a lot more likely to me that Gene had been drinking and slipped off that ledge all by himself."

Carrie sat forward. "But Duncan knew about an old grave in the foothills, Edward. The remains might be—"

Edward put his hands up to halt Carrie's words. "I don't care to hear any more. They're dead. That's it. Nothing you can say or do is going to bring back Duncan or Gene. Let them rest in peace."

As Carrie left with Cash, she wondered whether Edward was right. Should she leave well enough alone?

Her head pounded as she approached the passenger side of the Jeep. Once again she was happy to relinquish the driving to Cash. She took a quick look at Bonanza on the back seat. He was curled up and fast asleep. She leaned back, her throbbing headache giving her no peace. Neither would the words of Edward Van Epp III. He said Duncan was innocent of kidnapping and Gene was innocent of murder. She agreed about Duncan. But what of Gene?

By the time Cash pulled the Jeep in front of her place, Carrie could neither see nor think through the pounding pain.

"Feeling pretty rotten, aren't you?" he asked as he opened the passenger door and held out a hand. Carrie took his hand, feeling its steadying warmth and strength. "Is it that obvious?"

"Matter of fact, yes. It's the first time you've waited until I've walked around and opened the door for you."

Carrie slipped her legs over the seat to get out. "It's the first time I've questioned my ability to do it."

She managed to get into her house and get her shoes off before she collapsed onto the couch, but her thoughts remained active. "Did Gene really do it, Cash? Did he poison Duncan in an effort to steal the ransom money?"

Cash sat across from her, watching the pain etching its way on her face. "Tom's evidence certainly seems to support that conclusion. But why don't we forget it for tonight and get some rest?"

Carrie wanted to nod but her head wouldn't cooperate. "I'd like to keep Bonanza with me tonight if you don't mind. Do you suppose you could open a can of dog food for him before you go?"

Cash got up and gave her a reassuring smile. "I'll do better than that. I'll open a can of something for all of us. Lie down and I'll bring you yours on a tray."

Carrie sighed. "I should resist, but I have no strength to."

It was the worst headache she'd ever had. She closed her eyes against the pain, but even her eyelids throbbed. Just when she thought it was hopeless, she felt cool, gentle fingers stroking her temples. Slowly they worked their way to the back of her head and then around the top, seeming to draw out the pain as they passed. She sighed, just content to enjoy the magic they were working. And at some point when the pain eased, she fell into a dreamless sleep.

The next thing she knew, tantalizing smells of hot soup were invading her consciousness. She opened her eyes to see Cash standing next to the couch, placing a steaming bowl in front of her. Cautiously she sat up, finding the pain was now just a dull ache.

"Feeling better?" he asked.

"Much, thank you. The soup smells terrific. But where's your bowl and Bonanza's?"

He smiled. "Bonanza and I ate a few hours ago while you were still snoozing."

Her hand paused as it was bringing the soup spoon to her lips. "Hours ago?" she repeated.

He nodded. "It's two in the morning."

A quick glance at her watch confirmed his words. She was amazed she'd slept so long. "Where's Bonanza?"

Cash pointed over to an easy chair where a white, circular bulge rested. "He gave out a little while ago."

She swallowed her spoonful of hot lentil soup. "I'm sorry I fell asleep. You should have just left and gone home to get some sleep yourself. You must be very tired."

"I couldn't leave until I was sure you were okay. Head injuries can be very serious, Carrie. I'm glad to see you've weathered the worst of yours. How's the soup?"

She didn't miss the warm look in his eyes as she scooped up another spoonful. His gentleness and concern for her sent an agreeable warmth through her body. "Best soup I've ever tasted."

He gave her that special grin of his and her heart began to beat deeper and faster. She finished the rest of the soup without tasting it. When he returned from taking the dishes back into the kitchen, she stood up to face him.

He watched her eyes silently for a moment and then raised his hands to gently release the strands of hair she had imprisoned behind each ear to keep them from flopping in the soup bowl while she ate. His fingers traveled to her cheekbones, tracing their line as his thumbs lightly feathered the outline of her lips. She felt his light touch travel along her nerves in an exciting wave.

"Feel in need of a good night's rest?" his words asked, but Carrie read a different question in his eyes and in the slight tremble of his hands.

He wanted her, but she realized he was waiting for her to tell him it was time. That delicious, addictive feeling of having the power to control his passion rose inside her making her feel incredibly alive and aroused.

Her hands circled his. "I think we could both use a good night's rest," she said, the warmth in her voice and look answering the question in his eyes and touch.

Effortlessly, he picked her up and held her to him possessively, as though she might slip away, and carried her into the bedroom.

He gently deposited her on the bed and knelt down before her. He leaned over to kiss her cheek, circling behind her until his lips reached the bump at the back of her skull. She felt his mouth, moist and warm, tenderly drawing out all the remaining pain. Then she moaned softly as his warm tongue traveled down the back of her neck sending thrilling waves of sensation down her spine.

She reached for him, her hands becoming frantic in her need to hold him close. He was instantly in her arms, his ragged breaths whispering her name, and everything faded away but the feel of him and their shared, all-consuming need.

As she finally lay back spent in his arms, slowly she began to become aware of herself as a separate entity again. Only a part of her seemed unwilling to reform back into Carrie Chase. It stubbornly clung to the warmth and strength of his body, safe and complacent in its newfound home.

Emotionally, she gave it a tug, trying to bring it back, but it stuck fast. She gave up and sighed. Then she heard his deep whisper next to her ear.

"You feel perfect in my arms, Carrie, like a part of me I've been searching for and have finally found."

She raised a fingertip to trace the line of his jaw. "Cash?"

"Yes?"

"Do you know you have a wonderfully strong mandible?"

His eyes blinked open in surprise. "What?"

"Lower jawbone," she explained.

He laughed. Carrie felt his arms tighten about her. "Damn, now I know I'm in trouble. No one warned me you anthropologists had such sexy pillow talk."

Carrie cuddled up to his broad chest. "Hmm. Wait until I tell you about your clavicles."

His hand stroked her hair as he chuckled. "I'm looking forward to it. Carrie, it feels so good to be with you. I know those people fond of quoting odds say there are at least a dozen individuals any one of us could be happy with in the billions on this earth. But at this moment no one would ever be able to convince me there could be anyone for me but you."

Carrie's smile slowly rippled into a spreading arc that circled about her happily beating heart.

"I'VE GOT SOME unpleasant news, Carrie," Tom's voice said into her sleepy ear much too early that morning.

Carrie rolled over in bed, only then becoming aware she had answered the phone while still half-asleep. She immediately saw a tousled, golden brown head leaning in her direction and took a moment to enjoy Cash's light, good-morning kiss and the deliciously sensuous feel of his fuzzy, unshaven chin as it brushed hers.

"Carrie, are you awake?" Tom's voice asked in her ear.

"Becoming more so by the second," Carrie said as she felt Cash's mouth beginning a slow exploration of her exposed neck as his hand caressed spots farther down on her anatomy.

Understandably, Carrie missed her brother's next few words. But something finally registered and she found herself suddenly sitting straight up in bed, away from the enticing distraction of Cash's touch.

"Tom, did you just say you found Hal Sawyer's *body?*"

"Yes. Early this morning. He died in a car crash."

"Dear God," she said.

"Carrie, what is it?" Cash's worried voice asked.

Carrie cupped the phone and repeated Tom's words.

"What was that again, Tom?"

"I said Sawyer's body was burned along with his truck."

"Where did it happen?"

"On a side road off of Highway 445. Could have occurred right after Cash saw him drive off yesterday. Coroner's report isn't in. They only took in the body about an hour ago."

Carrie brushed some warm brown hair out of her eyes. "I guess now we'll never know if he pushed Gene."

"Not from him, anyway. I've called Evan Wahl and asked him to come down for questioning. Since Sawyer was his grandson, maybe he can shed some light on the man's motivations."

Carrie was troubled. Now that her headache was gone, some things were beginning to occur to her that hadn't the night before. "Can I come down and be there for the questioning, Tom?"

"Carrie, you have no official role—"

"Tom, please. What Evan Wahl says could help me in identifying the bones Cash and I found in that desert grave."

Carrie heard Tom's exhaled breath. "All right. He'll be here in thirty minutes. If you can get here in time, I'll put you in a soundproof box next to the interview room so you can listen."

Carrie thanked Tom and quickly hung up the phone. In as few words as possible, she told Cash what had happened.

"Will we both have time to shower and dress?" she asked.

"We will if we shower together," Cash said smiling.

Carrie's eyes gleamed. "Sounds good to me. We Reno citizens should always be looking for opportunities to conserve water."

THEY ARRIVED at the third-floor entrance to the detective unit about forty minutes later. Carrie saw Tom immediately. He was standing near the entrance intently studying a report of some kind. She walked up to him.

"Not too late, I hope?"

Tom's head came up as he looked from her to Cash. He didn't seemed surprised she hadn't come alone. "Cash and Carrie. Never see one of you without the other these days. Have you two noticed that together your names sound like some major warehouse clearance sale?"

Carrie heard the note of good-natured teasing in her brother's voice and knew it meant he was feeling good about something. Her interest was instantly peaked. "What's up?"

Tom smiled. "I've found out something interesting about Hal Sawyer. Watch me question the old mining magnate. He's holding up well considering his grandson's death. Said he'd tell me whatever he could. Still, I suspect his lawyer's probably on the way."

"Where do you want us?" she asked.

Tom looked over at Cash and shrugged in defeat as though he knew any attempt to try to exclude Cash would turn into a fight with Carrie. He gestured.

"Wahl's waiting in here. Go through that door and you'll be able to see and hear everything."

Without further explanation, Tom disappeared into the first room. Carrie and Cash opened the door Tom had pointed out.

It was a small room, about eight feet long and six feet wide. A long counter with chairs positioned beneath it extended the eight feet. Carrie and Cash each pulled out a chair and sat at the counter that looked into a two-way mirror. On the other side sat Evan Wahl. Next to him was Tom. Prominently displayed on the ceiling was the video camera that would be recording the interview.

"Mr. Wahl, I appreciate your willingness to speak to me about your grandson, Hal Sawyer. I understand he's also been in your employ ten years. Trying to teach the boy the business that would one day be his, I imagine?"

Evan Wahl's handlebar mustache twitched. Carrie watched the stony expression on his face and the dark blue veins on the bony hands gripping his sturdy cane. If Tom wanted a response from the man, she was thinking he'd better ask a more direct question.

Tom got up from his chair and began to pace about the small interview room. "Sawyer's recent behavior has proved confusing to us. As his grandfather and employer, we thought perhaps you could help us understand his peculiar actions."

Tom paused to look at the old man but Wahl still said nothing.

"Over the past week and a half Mr. Sawyer has been running the heavy mining machinery of your company at irregular hours and in close proximity to the desert home of the late Duncan Van Epp. Were you aware of Sawyer's activities, Mr. Wahl?"

Wahl gave a small nod. "I became aware something was going on at Van Epp's will reading."

"And what did you discover?" Tom asked.

Evan Wahl looked at Tom with a curious dignity, almost as though he pitied the detective sergeant. "That Hal had harassed Duncan Van Epp in an attempt to coerce him into signing a mineral-rights agreement with me. And when he found Van Epp had died, he forged Van Epp's signature to the document."

"Why, Mr. Wahl? Why did Hal Sawyer do these things?"

Wahl passed a bony hand over his eyes. "A mistaken sense of duty. He heard me offering Burney a bonus if she could convince Duncan Van Epp to sign those mineral rights over to me. No doubt he thought he was doing me a favor."

Tom paused at Wahl's words then began pacing again. "Sawyer had the reputation of a troublemaker. Couldn't you have anticipated his taking matters into his own hands?"

Wahl spoke irritably. "Did you expect me to read his mind?"

Tom's voice remained even and conversational as he continued to pace. "Reading his mind shouldn't have been so difficult. On six occasions in the past year your secretary bailed Sawyer out of jail on various charges of drunkenness and assault. Your personal intervention with a certain local judge and substantial financial reparations are all that's kept Sawyer from standing trial for a number of property damage and personal injury suits."

Wahl exhaled heavily. "Sawyer had his good points, too. He knew the mining business. He was loyal."

Tom's voice continued conversationally. "Hmm. That's a rather high price to pay for loyalty, isn't it?"

"He was family, Sergeant. And loyalty can't be bought."

"But apparently Sawyer could be bought. As a matter of fact, Kurt Mofatt, a local loan shark, bought Sawyer's services as one of his 'enforcers.' You know what an enforcer is, don't you, Mr. Wahl?"

Wahl gripped his cane with a new vehemence.

"Yes, I see you do," Tom continued. "So your grandson was moonlighting as a loan shark enforcer. And Gene Van Epp was in debt to Kurt Mofatt. Did you know these things?"

Wahl's shoulders remained rigid. "Gene Van Epp was always trying to squirm his way out of some gambling debt. And Hal did beat a man several months ago at Kurt Mofatt's direction. But it wasn't Van Epp. And when I heard about the incident, I confronted Hal and made it clear such behavior was not to continue. It didn't."

Tom stopped pacing. "Just like that?"

Wahl's stare was as uncompromising as forged steel. "When I gave him a direct order, Hal didn't disobey me."

Hearing the tone and delivery of Wahl's words, Carrie could believe it. Tom began to pace again. "But you admit your grandson was a violent man."

"Sergeant, as I've told his mother many times, Hal is . . . was wild and undisciplined, just like his father. But he was no killer."

"Where is his mother?"

"She is with a patient at the hospital. I've left word for her to join me here."

"And Sawyer's father?"

Wahl waved a hand. "Who knows? My daughter eloped at the age of eighteen. I had overprotected her, driven her away, she told me. So she took up with the first motorcycle-riding sleaze bag she found. She returned when Hal was eight and her husband had run out on them. She had learned, even grown from her mistakes. She went to medical school and made something of her life. But her son's wild, sometimes mean streak was too much a part of him."

"Are you telling me Sawyer went out of his way to harass an old man because he was mean?"

Wahl's mustache twitched. "His motive grew out of his loyalty to me. I'm not condoning it. I'm explaining it."

Tom paced for a minute before he asked his next question. "Mr. Wahl, even if you had been aware Sawyer was harassing Duncan Van Epp, it wouldn't have made any difference, would it?"

Carrie saw a new twitch in Wahl's cheek. "If you've got something to say, Sergeant, say it straight."

Tom continued his rhythmic pacing. "You hated Duncan Van Epp, didn't you?"

Wahl did not answer immediately. When he finally did his words were spoken evenly. "On the contrary. I liked him very much."

"Liked him?" Tom said, his voice ascending into the tonal realms of incredulity.

Wahl watched Tom with narrowing eyes.

Tom stopped his pacing and leaned over the table toward the elderly man. "Surely you're aware that Duncan Van Epp not only had knowledge of your daughter's kidnapping and murder, but also that he was probably one of the men who carried it out?"

Tom's words sucked Carrie's mouth dry. But from the way Evan Wahl flew to his feet, she could see they had shocked him severely. His deep voice boomed.

"I'm aware of nothing of the sort!"

Carrie could see Tom perceptibly backing away from the strong old man. He paused briefly before he asked his next question.

"But it would explain why you directed Sawyer to harass Duncan. You might have even directed Sawyer to poison him. And when Sawyer found out Gene Van Epp was trying to get the ransom money, it might explain why Sawyer pushed him to his death. Mightn't it, Mr. Wahl?"

Wahl's scowl mirrored the agitation of his hands, which were grasping the handle of his cane like he wanted to use it against Tom. Carrie saw her brother's small involuntary flinch.

"What stupidity is this? Do you really think I sent out my grandson to murder people? Do you really think a harmless old fool whose heart was too soft even to discipline his jerk of a great-nephew could kidnap and murder a child?"

Tom leaned across the table. "If Duncan Van Epp had nothing to do with your baby daughter's kidnapping, why did he go to such pains to return nearly a hundred thousand dollars to you, Mr. Wahl? You didn't know him from Adam. Supposedly, he didn't know you, either. Only guilt could have motivated such behavior. And only revenge could have answered such guilt. You killed him, didn't you?"

Evan Wahl directed his sledgehammer eyes at Tom, beating him down with every one of his snarling words. "If Duncan had been responsible for my baby's murder, for my young wife's broken heart, do you think I would have waited all these years to seek my revenge?"

"You might have if you'd only just found out he—"

"You're a fool, Sergeant! Don't make the mistake of thinking me one. I had Duncan Van Epp thoroughly investigated before his first check to me cleared the bank."

"You suspected him?" Tom asked.

"Of course I suspected him! When a man comes out of nowhere and offers you low-interest money, you'd better suspect him! But you're dead wrong about his involvement. He was in a courtroom back East arguing a case for an old college friend at the precise moment of my daughter's kidnapping. He returned to Contention only after the ransom had been paid and my child murdered."

"But the money—" Tom began.

"I don't know why he arranged for me to get the money, but he had no part in the kidnapping. You're beating a dead horse, Sergeant. If Duncan Van Epp had done that to me, I would have found out. And he wouldn't have gotten off easily with an overdose of pills. I would have sent him to hell long ago with just the strength in these two hands."

As Evan Wahl extended his long, bony fingers toward Tom, a look like Carrie had never seen descended on the elderly man's face. It was fierce, sad, tortured, and it wrenched at her insides. She found she had to look away. In understanding and comfort Cash's arm extended about her shoulders.

There was a moment of quiet before even Tom appeared sufficiently recovered to go on. His voice held a visible strain. "Then supply me with the reasons, Mr. Wahl, as to why your grandson murdered Gene Van Epp?"

"Hal killed no one!" Evan Wahl snapped as he clutched and unclutched his cane in continued agitation. "Damn it, man, he's dead! And just like your stupid predecessors of sixty years ago, all you can do is stand around and badger the bereaved family."

Carrie heard the pain in Wahl's words. The anger was in him, but the sorrow overrode it. And suddenly the room faded and she could see him clearly as a young man sixty years before, tears falling down his unlined cheeks as he faced the death of his child.

Tom did not meet the old man's eyes as he began to mutter something that sounded like an apology. But in any case he never got a chance to complete it because suddenly the door flew open and Nora Burney barged into the room. She stood in the doorway and looked from Tom to Wahl. Seeming satisfied she had gained their attention, she spouted her lines as though she had often rehearsed them and had just been waiting for a center-stage opportunity to deliver them.

"As your attorney, I advise you to answer no more questions, Mr. Wahl."

Any reply Evan Wahl was about to make was interrupted by a shuffling behind the attorney. She turned around only to be literally pushed aside as Dr. Eileen Packer charged into the room. Eileen ignored the lawyer's squawk of protest, and headed directly for Wahl. She dropped to her knees in front of him, her face contorted and drenched with tears.

"Evan, he's dead! My baby's dead!"

Evan Wahl's voice was infinitely gentle as he reached down to stroke Eileen's wet cheek. "I know, my child. I know."

Chapter Fourteen

"Dr. Eileen Packer is Evan Wahl's adopted daughter and Hal Sawyer's mother. Cash, do you know what this means?" Carrie asked as they stood around trying to drink the bitter-tasting coffee from the dispensing machine outside Tom's office.

"Yes," Cash said. "It means Duncan selected her because of her relationship to Sawyer or Wahl. But which one? And why?"

Carrie stared at her cup. "'Past sins must be revealed.' Those are the words Ann spoke at the will reading. And remember how nervous Eileen Packer seemed when I asked her why Duncan had selected her? Cash, I think Duncan must have gone to see Evan Wahl's adopted daughter to tell her about the kidnapping sixty years ago!"

Cash frowned. "But why Eileen Packer? If Duncan wanted to tell someone, why didn't he tell Wahl? After all, Wahl was the kidnapped child's father? Surely he was the one most concerned. Why did Duncan visit Wahl's adopted daughter instead?"

Carrie exhaled a frustrated breath. "You're right. We know he told Ann and Gene, but Edward says he didn't tell him and Wahl sure acts like he didn't tell him. So why did Duncan just select certain people to tell about the kidnapping? Could it be what he had to say had significance just for them?"

"Maybe," Cash said as he frowned over the taste of the machine-vended coffee. After having a cup of Carrie's freshly ground coffee, everything else was falling far short in comparison. And after having a taste of Carrie he knew, just like her coffee, the richness of the woman she was had spoiled him for any other. With an effort he tried to refocus his thoughts on her supposition.

"Except for my grandmother, no one else was alive sixty years ago. How could the circumstances around the kidnapping have significance for anyone, except Ann?"

Carrie sipped coffee without tasting it. "I don't know, but it now seems very unlikely to me that Duncan went to see Eileen Packer just to get some pain pills. There's got to be something—"

Carrie snapped her fingers as another thought occurred to her. "Wait a minute. Remember when we first looked at Duncan's mail on Tuesday? And then again yesterday before we began the hike into the foothills?"

"Yes. You said you thought there was something missing."

Carrie's eyes were sparkling. "And now I know what it was! Remember the letter without a return address? The one in the plain, white envelope?"

As soon as Carrie described the missing piece of mail, Cash could see it clearly. "Carrie, you're right! I remember now. There was an envelope like that on Tuesday and it was gone when you brought in the mail on Friday. I wonder who took it?"

Carrie's face wore a satisfied look. "If it was the person who wrote it, it was Dr. Eileen Packer who took the letter back."

Cash frowned. "Are you sure? There wasn't a return address."

"I knew the scribble looked familiar. And now I remember where I saw it before. It was the same scribble on Duncan's medical file. I only caught a glimpse of it when we were in her office, but now I realize that writing and the writing on the letter were the same. And that means the letter was from Dr. Eileen Packer."

Cash studied her face. "You don't think she wrote to him about his medication?"

Carrie felt herself on firm footing. "No. If Eileen Packer wrote Duncan about his treatment, her secretary would have prepared it. That would mean his name and address would have been typed and the envelope would have had her embossed return address like those envelopes we saw on her desk. No, I think that letter I saw in Duncan's mailbox contained a personal message. And to my mind that means it related to the real reason Duncan went to see Eileen Packer."

Cash nodded. "Now the only questions are, what was in the letter, and who took it?"

"I bet Eileen Packer could answer those questions."

Cash's jaw locked. "We should try to speak with her now. She may be still in the station. I heard Wahl telling Burney to arrange for a chauffeured car. He didn't want Eileen driving herself."

Carrie looked doubtful. "It's tempting to corner her, but I doubt she'll talk to us. She's just lost her son. This is not the best time to be asking her what was in a letter she wrote to Duncan and if she stole it back."

Cash looked at her, appreciating her natural compassion, but seeing the situation a little differently. "It may not be the best time for her, but it could be the only time we get. If she doesn't have a clear conscience, then the sooner we find out the better. For Duncan's sake, Carrie, I think we need to give it a try."

Carrie nodded, the conviction behind his words convincing her. They both threw their cups of partially drunk coffee in the trash can and took the elevator to the ground floor. They walked the hall until they found Evan Wahl standing near the back by the detention area conferring with Nora Burney in lowered tones. Eileen Packer was nowhere to be seen. Carrie took a deep breath as they approached the man and his lawyer.

"I'm sorry to hear of your loss, Mr. Wahl," Carrie said.

Evan Wahl nodded curtly in her direction, not ungraciously but not exactly friendly, either. Just as Carrie was trying to think of how to ask about his adopted daughter, Cash spoke up.

"We'd like to express our condolences to your daughter also and speak to her for a moment. Has she left?"

Burney quickly answered. "She's in the ladies' room washing her hands and face. Your sentiment is fine, but rest and family will be far more soothing than a stranger's well wishes."

Wahl turned to his lawyer and frowned. He looked decidedly put out at her presuming to answer for him. Carrie took a deep breath, determined to complete what she and Cash had begun.

"We need to talk with Eileen, Mr. Wahl," she said. "Your daughter may be the only one who knows why it happened."

Wahl frowned at Carrie. "What are you talking about?"

"Your grandson's death," she said. "Gene Van Epp's death. Maybe even Duncan's death. Eileen may hold the key to them all."

Wahl shook his head. "You're talking rubbish. The deaths are not related and Eileen knows nothing."

Burney stepped between Carrie and Wahl, obviously trying to use her position to intimidate. Her bluff meant nothing to Carrie. She stepped around the shorter woman to lay a hand on the elderly man's bony arm in an attempt to reach him. She willed her voice to carry the conviction she felt.

"Mr. Wahl, I don't want to hurt Eileen or you, but I believe Duncan came to see your daughter last week to tell her something that may relate to the kidnapping of your natural child. Won't you help us find out what it was? It could have some bearing on why Duncan, Gene and now your own grandson, Hal, have died."

He looked at her suspiciously, as though he was trying to understand what she really wanted but wasn't saying. When Burney started to protest beside Wahl, he waved her silent.

"Go home, Nora. You're not needed here."

The lawyer's head rose and centered between her shoulders, as though it was righting itself after a blow. She stalked away.

"You must ask my daughter nothing," Wahl said. "If you try to question her, you could do irreparable emotional harm. Whatever Eileen wants to say, I will listen to. If she has any information concerning these tragic deaths, I will inform the sheriff. Now if you'll excuse me—"

Wahl began to turn from Carrie and she knew she did not have the right words to stop him. She watched him in silent defeat when suddenly her head jerked up at the sound of a woman's scream. She whipped around in the direction of the ladies' room. For an instant there was quiet and then another terrible scream pierced the air.

Cash didn't hesitate but ran toward the entry, colliding with a woman who was running out and letting out yet another scream. Cash blocked her way and grabbed the woman's shoulders. He looked into her face and saw horror and disbelief written there.

"What is it? What's happened?" he asked. Evan Wahl's voice coming up from behind him demanded the same information almost simultaneously.

The woman's white face just stared at them both for a moment. Then she extended an arm behind her and pointed. Her voice came out in a strained croak. "She had a knife." Then the woman brought her hand up to her mouth, balling it into a fist as though she had to fight against screaming pain.

Cash looked to Carrie. "Can you take her?"

Carrie nodded as Cash relinquished his hold and bounded through the ladies' room door. He found Evan Wahl at his side.

It was a small facility with just two stalls, but the two men didn't need to check either to locate Eileen Packer. She was draped over the single sink, the bright red blood pouring from the deep slashes on her wrists.

"WILL SHE MAKE IT?" Carrie asked as Cash returned from consulting with the emergency-room duty nurse scarcely fifty-five nerve-racking minutes later.

He nodded. "The doctor says the chances are good for her recovery if they can keep her from trying it again.

Wahl's going in to see her briefly. Want to sneak in behind him?''

Carrie was a bit taken aback by Cash's suggestion. She still felt shaken by the image of Eileen Packer's slashed wrists. "We weren't invited, were we?"

"We weren't told to stay out, either," he said. She heard the urgency in his voice. "This suicide attempt means something important, Carrie. If we don't take the opportunity unfolding before us, we may never get another. Come on. Let's be bold."

His reasoning fortified her courage and they followed Evan Wahl in, standing behind him as he leaned over the bed. Eileen Packer's pale face immediately turned to Wahl, her bandaged wrists raised above the IV feeding her arm. Carrie thought the change in the woman's normally strong demeanor was striking.

"I know he wasn't your blood, Evan. I know he's been a trial at times. But he loved you. I swear to God he loved you!"

Wahl's big bony hands returned Eileen's outstretched hands to her sides. "Never a doubt about it in my mind, Eileen."

Eileen's head drew an arc back and forth across the pillow like an agitated windshield wiper. "It's all my fault. I sent him back when I remembered the letter. He must have read it, Evan. That's why he went out there. That's why he—"

"The letter?" Wahl said, interrupting. "What letter?"

Eileen Packer's head stopped dead still against the pillow as her eyes magnetized on Wahl's face. Carrie saw them enlarge in fear as her mouth began to quiver. "I couldn't tell you, Evan. When Duncan Van Epp told me about it, my first thought had to be for Hal. You understand that, don't you? My child's future was at stake. Everything that he had ever worked for, hoped for—"

Evan Wahl stood up very tall and very straight next to Eileen's bed. Carrie heard his tone turn into that of a scolding father. "What did Duncan Van Epp tell you? What is it you haven't told me?"

New tears filled and overflowed Eileen's eyes, washing her face in an uncleansing salty guilt. Her voice came out in a wail. "It doesn't matter anymore! Hal's dead, don't you see! He's dead!"

Evan Wahl began to say something just at the same moment the door was opened by the emergency-room nurse and she ordered the three of them out. She immediately went to Eileen Packer's side and tried to quiet her. The doctor followed the nurse in calling immediately for the administration of a sedating shot.

Carrie turned to Cash as soon as they were out in the hall. "Duncan did tell her something, Cash. Something important. And it was tied into that letter I saw, the one she mailed to Duncan and later had Hal retrieve."

Carrie could see Cash's eyes were not focused on her face. He was looking over her head at someone behind her. Carrie turned and looked at him, too.

Evan Wahl's dark eyes glistened above hers in the hall light, the pain leaking slowly from their centers. "What was in the letter, Ms. Chase? I must know."

Carrie felt the hurt in his look. She took a steadying breath before responding. "I don't know. It was in Duncan's mailbox on Tuesday. It was gone on Friday when next I looked."

Wahl squinted at her a moment before he spoke. He sounded tired, defeated. "If my grandson had it on him when he died, it was probably burned along with everything else in his truck. Unless Eileen—"

His comment was interrupted by the approach of the doctor. "I've just sedated your daughter. In her agitated state, it's best if we can keep her this way for the next couple of days. I'll be having her moved out of emergency into the psychiatric wing in a few hours. If you wish to arrange for a private room, see me within the next ten minutes."

Wahl's responding "thank you" sounded flat. The doctor nodded and returned to Eileen Packer's room. Carrie could see the recent tragic events had etched the lines deeper in the mining magnate's face. His head bent for a moment in a sign of uncharacteristic vulnerability. It gave Carrie the impetus to ask something she might not have otherwise.

"Mr. Wahl, does Duncan's land really contain precious minerals?"

Wahl looked from her face to Cash's and then back to hers with sad and tired eyes. He leaned heavily on his cane as he spoke.

"It might, but I honestly don't know. The mineral-rights agreement was a way I could insure Duncan had sufficient money when he needed it, without letting him know where it was coming from. Mike Burney and his daughter, Nora, were both instructed to perform their legal services for Duncan for free. They told him it was a firm's tradition for anyone they represented over twenty years. In reality, I paid their salaries, instructing them to leave Duncan with the impression his investments were doing well and he could spend whatever he wanted."

"You mean you were supporting Duncan?" Cash asked.

Wahl shrugged. "Not supporting exactly. I was just there in the background in case he needed me these last ten years or so. Only happened a few times."

"When was the last time?" Cash asked.

"When Duncan decided to pay off a gambling debt for Gene several months ago. Amount was close to forty-five thousand. Nora paid the gambling debt from my sources, leaving Duncan's money intact."

Carrie thought she was beginning to finally understand. "So Nora Burney acted as the attorney for both of you so she could arrange for that type of transfer to take place unnoticed by Duncan?"

Wahl exhaled as he nodded. "It seemed the simplest way for me to help him."

"To pay him back for when he helped you?" Carrie asked. Wahl didn't answer her, but the look in his eyes was soft and a little sad. She knew then that Evan Wahl had been and still was mourning the death of Duncan Van Epp, and she bowed her head in shame for the injustice of her earlier thoughts. Without additional comment, Wahl turned back to reenter his daughter's hospital room.

Carrie sighed as she watched him go and immediately felt Cash's warm arm circle her waist as his words circled about her own thoughts.

"For all his money, he hasn't found a lot of happiness in his life. I feel sad for him. I wish there was something I could do."

Carrie and Cash walked slowly to the hospital parking lot. They were both lost in thought over the events of the past few minutes. Carrie began to express hers first. "Duncan had something important to say before he died. Something about that sixty-year-old kidnapping. Something that involved the people he told. What could it have been, Cash? And why is it the more we find out, the less we seem to know?"

"Hmm. Yes, it does sort of increase the frustration level. I'm still wrestling with the question of why Sawyer felt compelled to follow us? And if he did push Gene, could it have had anything to do with his working for Kurt Mofatt?"

Carrie thought she understood what Cash was implying. "You mean because Tom discovered Hal Sawyer was moonlighting as an enforcer for Mofatt and Gene owed the loan shark money?"

Cash nodded. "I suppose that's a distinct possibility. Still, I think the part that's bothering me the most at the moment is his accident. It seems just a little too coincidental, doesn't it?"

Carrie considered his words. "Maybe you're right. What caused him to turn over his truck? Did he read the letter his mother wrote? Was there some terrible secret in it about his family or his birth that made him destroy both the letter and himself?"

Cash shook his head. "Hal Sawyer never struck me as the type to commit suicide. Murder maybe, but not suicide."

They were at the Seville and Carrie automatically headed for the driver's side, just as she had been doing all day. Cash had been very happy to see it. To him it meant she had completely recovered from the very hard knock she had gotten the day before.

But once behind the wheel, she just sat there. He was content to watch the sunlight skip along the line of her cheek and play hide-and-seek within her long strands of warm brown hair. Despite the developments in Duncan's murder, Cash found his thoughts kept returning to their recent night of lovemaking and the pleasure of having her in his arms. When this business got straightened out, he would need to talk with her. They had a future to discuss, a future made clear to him last night.

Carrie finally started the car, a look of decision on her face. "I need to take a look at that skeleton we found yesterday. Tom must have had it brought to the forensics group at the county morgue by now. Do you want to come along?"

He smiled. "With you, anywhere. But what can a skeleton tell us?"

"You might be surprised," she said.

BY THE TIME Carrie had finished examining the bones, Cash found he was very surprised indeed by her ability to discern some very interesting facts.

She began with the major one. "The bash on his forehead did kill him all right."

"He?" Cash said.

"Yes, he. An adult male. The epiphyses are all closed."

"Epiphyses?" Cash repeated.

Carrie frowned. "Perhaps I'd best not use the technical terms."

Cash moved over to put his arm around her shoulders and plant a kiss on her hair. "I've the distinct impression that there are lots of old bones rattling around in my future, as well as some luscious, young ones I'm holding right now. Might as well get acquainted with them all. What are epiphyses?"

Carrie relaxed into his warm arms, happy at the promise in his words and excited about sharing her work with him. "Epiphyses are the ends of the long bones in the body. As a human being grows, these epiphyses ossify separately. At maturity, they become ankylosed to the main part of the bone.''

"Wait a minute. Ankylosed?"

"It means unified. In this skeleton the separate hard parts have unified into the single bones."

"Okay, got it. His bones have hardened so that makes him an adult. How old?"

"Over twenty. Under thirty. My guess, early twenties."

"And you know this because . . . ?"

"The sutures are still quite visible on his skull. See these wiggly lines at the top and sides of his head?"

"Those are the sutures?"

"Yes. When we're born the cranium is made up of thirty separate pieces of bone. During growth, these gradually grow together to form a solid case that protects the brain. The joints or sutures where they knit together are visible until sometime in the thirties when they slowly fade and disappear."

"So since they're quite visible, you think close to twenty?"

Carrie nodded. "There's another check, too. I'm not finding any osteophytosis on the lumbar vertebrae. Here, look for yourself."

"And what am I supposed to be seeing?" Cash asked.

Carrie took hold of his right index finger and gently scraped it across the vertebrae in question. "Not seeing. You're supposed to be feeling a buildup of the bone if osteophytosis had begun, but since it hasn't you won't. The bony buildup comes with age in all of us, somewhere between thirty and forty. Since this skeleton doesn't have it, again that helps to place his age at death."

Cash removed his finger and nodded. "And taken with the visible sutures, we're confident he was probably in his early twenties. Okay. I'm getting the hang of this. What next?"

Carrie smiled. "Well, he was malnourished during his formative years. The bowing of the leg bones was caused from rickets, a deficiency in calcium and/or vitamin D. He didn't have sufficient protein, either, otherwise the bones of his arms and legs would have been longer and he would have been a taller man. This nutritional deficiency tells us he was from a poor family."

Cash was amazed and a little amused. "What, you can't tell me how many brothers and sisters he had?"

She pursed her lips in thought, undaunted by the teasing challenge in his remark. "I'd say he had one or more older brothers. While his bones were forming, he experienced several injuries in his fingers, his right wrist, his left elbow and both of his knees and shins. He also had a nasty break in his right radius."

"Radius?"

Carrie pointed. "Main bone in his forearm."

"But you're kidding about the older brothers, right?"

"No, logically they probably existed. Look at the radius bone. You can see the scar tissue that built up when the break healed. Scar tissue has also collected around these other breaks and cracks. Numerous bone injuries in a malnourished body is generally a sign of older male siblings."

"I don't understand," he said.

"Well, in a poor family during the time in which this individual was growing to manhood, large families were the norm and frivolous play very unlikely. He would have been needed for chores and consequently the companionship he would have shared would have been with members of his own family. Sisters would have had duties in the house. Roughhousing with brothers outside would have been a natural outgrowth of working with them and a likely cause for these bone injuries. Their severity indicates he roughhoused with larger, hence older brothers."

Cash's look of amusement was gradually turning to amazement. "Your deductions sound convincing. I suppose next you're going to say you can tell me what line of work he went into?"

She nodded. "He did manual labor and he was left-handed."

"Seriously?" Cash asked.

"Oh, yes. The manual labor is easily discerned from the extra thickness of the bones in the shoulders, arms and hands. And you see these grainy ridges? They appear where muscle attached to the bone. The most prominent attachments show up on the left arm bone, indicating more massive muscles and consequently left-handedness. I've also run some shoulder-girdle measurements with these vernier calipers that also point to left-handedness.''

Cash was watching as she measured the bones with an instrument that had a shape similar to a wrench but had calibrations to indicate the size of its jaws. He noted the size difference and was nodding until her next comment.

"He also didn't smile much.''

"Now, wait a minute,'' Cash said, shaking his head. "I admit I can buy the other stuff, but how can you possibly know whether the guy smiled or not?''

She laughed, enjoying her inside information. "Easy. He had a very pronounced overbite and buck teeth. His right lateral incisor was missing, apparently due to trauma, and he had several bad cavities in his upper and lower molars. Since he did manual labor, we know he worked outside. If he smiled, he would have let cold air into his mouth which would have aggravated the pain in his teeth.''

Cash nodded. "So naturally he wouldn't smile.''

"Right,'' she said. "And if the pain didn't get to him, comments regarding his buck teeth probably would have and could have embroiled him in a fight. Such an earlier fight was probably the reason for his missing incisor.''

"Amazing,'' Cash said. "When you explain it, it sounds so obvious. So this was a left-handed, short, muscular, bowlegged man in his early twenties with buck teeth. You know who this description fits just like a glove?''

Carrie put down the calipers as she nodded. "Yes. This man's physical description matches everything we know about Fred Koske. Considering the name on the rifle found in the grave beside him, I think we can be ninety percent sure this is him.''

Cash leaned back against the table. "So Koske never made it to California, if that was indeed where he had intended to go when he left his lodgings sixty years ago. You realize Duncan had to have known it was Koske buried in that grave?''

Carrie bit her lip. ''Yes.''

Cash continued to watch her face. ''Your brother, Tom, brought up an interesting theory last night. He said that Koske and Duncan pulled off the kidnapping together and then when Koske killed the child, Duncan killed him.''

''Cash—''

''Let me finish, Carrie. The nurse described the second kidnapper as a taller man with dark hair, a man who limped. We both know Duncan limped, and I've seen pictures of him as a young man. He had a full head of dark hair and compared to other men of those times, he did look taller—''

''No,'' Carrie spoke up quickly. ''Don't you remember Wahl saying he'd had Duncan checked out? Duncan was back East at the time of the kidnapping and the child's murder. It had to be someone else. After all, Duncan wasn't the only tall man who limped—''

A light seemed to come on in Carrie's eyes. She stepped over to Cash and grabbed his arm. ''He wasn't the only tall man who limped! Why didn't I see it before? I've been so blind!''

Cash's hands grasped her shoulders. ''What is it, Carrie?''

''Cash, it's Ernie, the skeleton unearthed in the ghost town of Contention last year. Do you remember my lecture about his congenital hip dislocation? The man limped, Cash! And he was tall. And he was shot with the same type of rifle Koske had. And he was buried in Contention sixty years ago. Don't you see? It was Ernie who was Koske's partner in the kidnapping!''

Cash wore a contemplative look. ''I guess it's possible. But why would Koske have murdered your Ernie?''

She shrugged. ''Maybe they quarreled over the money. The entry and exit angle of the bullet tell us a left-handed man shot Ernie and we know Koske was left-handed.''

Cash wasn't convinced. ''I admit the bone examination lends some support to the two skeletons being those of the two kidnappers, but if Koske made Ernie kneel down and then coldly shot him that way, it doesn't follow he'd be the kind of man to bury the body in the cellar with a cross over the grave. That's how Ernie was found, remember? And how did Koske die? And where does Duncan come in?"

She smoothed her long strands of hair behind her ears as she attempted to think it through. "We know Duncan knew about the kidnapping because Gene told us he had admitted keeping his knowledge a secret for sixty years. We also know that Duncan knew about Koske's desert grave. If Duncan wasn't involved in the kidnapping, only something very important would have made him remain silent for sixty years."

Cash watched her face. "You know what that was?"

"I think so," she said.

She moved away from the warmth of his touch as though something else, something unpleasant had taken hold of her. A pink tongue darted out to wet her lips. "Remember Dr. Packer telling us that Duncan had a congenital hip dislocation?"

Cash nodded. "She said something about that being the reason he limped."

"Right. Well until she told me, I hadn't known that about Duncan. I assumed his limp was due to an injury."

Cash shook his head. "I still don't understand. What does Duncan having a congenital hip dislocation mean?"

"Remember my lecture Monday? Remember my showing you Ernie's femur and talking about his hip dislocation?"

Cash shrugged. "So Ernie had it, too. Why is that significant?"

Carrie sighed. "That hip displacement is a genetic rarity and much more common in females than in males. The chances are greater than one in a hundred thousand that two males, Duncan and Ernie, contemporaries in the small town of Contention, would just by chance both have the same rare bone disease. All my training as an anthropologist tells me another explanation must exist."

Cash thought he was beginning to see the light. "You're thinking Ernie and Duncan had to be related?"

Carrie looked up at him then, her eyes large and sad. "Yes. And if Ernie and Duncan were related, that means Ernie can only be one man—Edward Van Epp I, Duncan's brother, and the other kidnapper of Evan Wahl's baby daughter sixty years ago."

Chapter Fifteen

Cash digested Carrie's words. "Fred Koske and Edward Van Epp I were both laid off from the silver mines about the same time."

Carrie was nodding. "And remember Wahl told us his investigator said Duncan's brother, Edward Van Epp I, left his pregnant wife and went to California never to be seen again?"

Cash chewed his lip. "Except there's no real evidence he did, is there? So perhaps if Koske didn't leave, neither did Duncan's brother. Two men whose families both said they left in order to cover up their participation in the kidnapping of the Wahl baby?"

"Yes. And when they had a falling-out and Koske killed Edward, Duncan found out about his brother's murder and maybe..."

Cash said the words for her. "Killed Koske?"

She sighed, obviously uncomfortable with the fact but facing it nonetheless. "It makes sense from the skeletal evidence, Cash."

Cash's finger tapped his teeth. "But we know Duncan went to Koske's grave recently and removed the skeleton of a dog. What significance would that have?"

Carrie scratched her head. "I assume he planned to lead the authorities to the spot where he buried Koske. I think he first wanted his earlier Bonanza to be given a proper burial. Somehow the dog must have been involved in the—"

She was interrupted by Tom's entry through the swinging door. "You through yet, Carrie? I'd like to drive Cash over to the office and have him sit in while I interview Mofatt."

"Yes, I'm through," Carrie said. "We'll both come."

Cash glanced at Tom, saw his look of disapproval and concurred. He turned to Carrie. "That's not a good idea. I know this loan shark. He's coarse, crude and lewd. He's not fit company for..."

Cash paused, temporarily at a loss for words. Carrie spoke up to fill in the blank. "For an anthropologist?"

He grinned. "Yes. My very thought."

Carrie wasn't fooled. She assumed an unconcerned air. "No need to be concerned about us. We're used to dirt."

A look of slight irritation crossed Cash's face. "C'mon, Carrie. You know what I meant. Make this easy on Tom and me and stay here. I'll be back soon."

He reached over to give her cheek a quick goodbye kiss, but she leaned out of reach. Without thinking, he grabbed hold of her arm and pulled her to him forcibly.

Carrie yanked her arm free, a deep resentment welling up inside her. To her own surprise, she was blazingly angry. "Let go of me! If you don't want me along, you've got your wish."

Cash stood before Carrie's flushed face and fighting words, so taken aback that he was unable to think. Too late, he realized his mistake in trying to physically coerce her. Then, in a flash of insight, he thought he understood the true meaning behind her need to always be in control. She feared domination. Of any kind.

It was a lesson she had learned from her parents' uneven relationship. Perhaps it was even the reason she had not married. Perhaps she thought marriage would mean such domination.

Tom interrupted his thoughts. "We've got to be going."

"Do you really need me?" Cash asked. He didn't want to leave Carrie, not until they could sort this thing out together.

"I thought you could help us judge how far the slime might have gone if Gene Van Epp had been unable to pay him off."

Cash nodded, convinced, but first he looked back again at Carrie, standing so quiet and still. As his eyes sought her face, she turned away and sank down into one of the straight-back chairs, all earlier traces of warmth gone from her expression.

He reached for her with what he now knew was his only safe approach, his voice. "Wait for me, darling. Please."

But he could see his words were not penetrating her newly erected shield. Then he felt Tom's hand on his shoulder. They were in the adjacent hallway when Tom spoke. "I'm sorry, Cash. Perhaps I should have just let her come along."

"It's not that. It was when I tried to—"

"Yes, I saw," Tom interrupted. "Ever since she was small she's hated being forced to do anything. Dad and I could convince her with logic, but never a strong arm or ultimatum."

Cash didn't respond as he followed Tom. He was remembering her look of resentment and pain, and feeling a growing emptiness.

CARRIE SAT for a long time on the hard, wooden chair in the autopsy room as the anger gradually receded, leaving her feeling sad and limp. She hadn't wanted to feel the anger, but it had come on her unbidden. She began to see that it always did when someone tried to force her.

In her heart she knew Cash hadn't meant to hurt her. But when he grabbed her arm, she couldn't think straight. All she could see was her mother sitting at the kitchen table, being beaten into submission by her father's rough, grabbing words.

Only, what was clear to her now was that her real target was the need to fight weakness. Her mother's. Her own. And anybody else's that had come along. Tom had said she was drawn to it. But now she understood that what she was really drawn to was the need to be strong.

Only, in her latest attempt to be strong, she had sent away the man she loved. Loved? Yes, as soon as she thought it, she knew it was true. It was the part of her he had claimed last night as their passion had fused them into one. He filled her heart with love. What a way she had chosen to show it!

She began to laugh at her own absurdity. It was a sick, tragic little chorus that soon turned into sobs as her heart pinched tightly inside her chest.

"Hey, you okay?"

She looked up to see the morgue attendant standing over her solicitously. Carrie nodded in embarrassment and groped for some Kleenex in her shoulder bag. "I'll be all right," she said as she got to her feet, but her words carried no conviction.

The morgue attendant's profession must have inured him to tears. He nodded as he started whistling and tidying up. Carrie escaped his happy whistle by going into the hallway outside the autopsy room where she began to pace, trying to regain her control and composure.

As she turned toward the morgue's outer doors, she heard a familiar mocking voice behind her.

"Didn't know this was one of your hangouts," Edward said. "Although I must say it seems to fit."

Carrie turned and walked the few paces separating them, ignoring his baiting tone. "I was just attempting to determine who the old skeleton in the desert might be," she said. "You here to make arrangements concerning Gene's body?"

Edward nodded. "So did you have any luck?"

"Luck?"

"Identifying the old skeleton," Edward said.

"I've thought of some possibilities."

Edward's dark eyes narrowed. "You still think my great-uncle was involved in the Wahl kidnapping, don't you?"

Carrie shifted uneasily on her feet. This was one time when she would have preferred the authorities playing messenger. "Yes, I think Duncan was involved, but not as one of the kidnappers."

Edward's look did not waver. "What, then?"

Carrie didn't see any point in hiding the truth. She shared her thoughts about what she had found in the two skeletons and what she had deduced from them. "So I think it was Koske and your grandfather who kidnapped the child. And it looks like Gene killed Duncan to get hold of the ransom money when he learned of it."

Edward watched her with glassy eyes for a moment, almost as though he hadn't taken in her words. Carrie was getting uncomfortable under the stare.

"I'm sorry, Edward, but it's what I'll tell Tom when he's through questioning Gene's loan shark."

Edward's voice was flat, unemotional. "You're that sure?"

Carrie nodded. "I just wish I could find the rest of that ransom money. Since Gene admitted to Cash and me that he didn't come across it when he searched Duncan's place, I wonder where it's hidden."

"You mean the hundred thousand minus the bills you told me Duncan gave you?" Edward asked.

Carrie nodded. "Duncan paid Evan Wahl back ninety-seven thousand in reduced interest on a bank loan, but he wouldn't have used the actual ransom money to do it. The sheriff's office and the bank had a listing of the notes. Were he to have passed—"

Carrie stopped in the middle of her explanation as a frown dug into her forehead. "No, wait a minute. Maybe I'm wrong."

Edward was watching her face. "Wrong?"

"Yes. Duncan made his bank loan to Wahl twenty years after the kidnapping. By then the sheriff's office and the banks had both stopped looking for the notes. That means Duncan could have used the original ransom money to arrange for Wahl's loan. What would it matter? By then, no one was checking money!"

Edward shrugged. "What you've just said proves Gene had no motive to kill Duncan. If Duncan gave the original ransom money to Wahl in that loan, there can't be very much of it left."

Carrie shrugged. "Except maybe Duncan didn't tell Gene he had returned most of the money to Wahl. Let's see, how much money would have been left?"

Edward supplied the answer. "Duncan gave three thousand, one hundred and eight dollars in his bequest to Wahl. Assuming he used the original ransom money in the loan to Evan Wahl, that would mean the three thousand, one hundred and eight dollars was all that was left from the one hundred thousand. If I subtract the three thousand dollars he gave to you, that would leave two thousand, eight hundred and eight dollars of the original notes."

Carrie was amazed. "That was quick figuring, Edward. Your business training is showing. I wonder where it could be."

"If it's anywhere, it's in Duncan's house."

Carrie looked at him. "You think so? Gene didn't find it."

Edward shrugged. "Still where else could it be? Duncan had no safe-deposit box. His home was everything to him. It must be hidden there. And if it is, I think I might just know where."

Carrie was surprised. "You've thought of a hiding place?"

Edward had started to crack his knuckles. "Possibly. I watched Duncan go down there once when I was a kid. I followed him and fell down the stairs, banging myself up pretty good. He scolded me and told me I was never to go down there again. As a matter of fact, I can't remember the trap door ever being opened again."

Carrie blinked at Edward's words. "The trapdoor? What trapdoor, Edward?"

"To the cellar beneath Duncan's house."

An excited little pulse beat in Carrie's neck. "There's a cellar beneath the house? I never knew. But wouldn't Gene have checked there?"

Edward shook his head. "I was seven and Gene was only four when Duncan nailed it shut. Gene probably never knew it was there."

Carrie thought over Edward's words. He made sense. If there was a cellar to Duncan's desert place, it would be a logical hiding place. "I'm going to look," she said, heading for the door.

"I'm coming with you."

Carrie looked over her shoulder at him. "What for?"

His voice turned harsh. "Look, you've made some pretty strong accusations against my great-uncle and my brother. If there really is evidence supporting any of your wild claims, I have the right to examine it, too."

Carrie nodded, understanding that was probably how she'd feel too. "I have to make a call first."

Edward pointed to the phone on the wall. "So call."

But when Carrie dialed her brother's office, she found both he and Cash were already conducting the interview with Kurt Mofatt. Not wanting to interrupt or leave a long, involved message, she just told the clerk to let Cash know she had called and would call back.

She didn't like leaving without speaking with Cash first, but there was no telling how long he and her brother would be involved in the interview. Taking Cash's car now was out of the question in case she missed him and he came back for it.

"Edward, can you take me by my place first to pick up my Jeep?"

Edward nodded. "Suits me. Come on, we're wasting time."

TOM TURNED TO CASH after their quick session interrogating the loan shark. "Well, I'm satisfied he told Sawyer to take care of Gene as an example to other late payers."

Cash shook his head. "I don't know, Tom. Men like Mofatt generally beat up the people who are late on their payments. They don't kill them. You can't collect from a dead borrower."

Tom nodded. "Still, Sawyer may have only been trying to break Gene's arm or leg when he pushed him off that ledge. When he found out he killed him, that could have been what panicked him into running. He wouldn't have wanted

Mofatt to know he made such a mistake. I'm surprised you ever got mixed up with him, Cash."

Cash exhaled heavily in remembrance. "It was a holiday. The banks were closed. I needed some betting money. I considered it a sure thing. It turned out to be, and I returned what I borrowed plus an exorbitant interest to him the next day."

"You were a very successful gambler, weren't you?"

Cash looked at Tom as though he was crazy. "Successful? I lost everything that was important to me."

"I thought you won a lot of money?" Tom asked.

"I did. But money couldn't buy my loss of self-control and respect. I couldn't stop gambling. That's why I borrowed from a man like Mofatt when I found myself short. I couldn't let even one day go by without placing a bet."

"It never occurred to me gambling was bad for a winner."

Cash looked at him painfully. "There are no winners with a gambling addiction, Tom. I think that's why I understand the internal battle Carrie wages. She and I both fight to maintain control over our lives."

Tom nodded in delayed understanding. "Are you going to find her and try to patch things up?"

Cash exhaled. "As soon as possible."

Tom met his look, smiled and held out his hand. "May you be a winner this time."

Cash released Tom's hand when he heard his name called. "Yes?"

"A call for you, McKendry," the sheriff's office clerk said.

Cash picked up the nearby extension. "Your grandmother's regained consciousness," the doctor's voice said. "She's quite lucid and very eager to talk to you. Can you come right away?"

ANN TINTORI LOOKED painfully frail and weak as she lay back against the pillows of the hospital bed. But the moment Cash's warm hand cupped her small, cool one, her eyes blinked open, clear and sharp.

"Granny, you look wonderful."

Ann smiled sweetly, but soon frowned as she tried to sit up straighter in the bed. An urgency coated her croak of a voice. "Dear, I must tell you I—"

Cash's hand sought to hush her. "The doctor says you must rest. You've had a very close call."

Ann's snow-white curls shook in agitation. "This cannot wait. It concerns Duncan, child, and the secret that we buried together sixty long years ago. In all that time I've not spoken of it. I remember now I even destroyed the personal journals that recorded those sad events, thinking I could destroy their very existence. But those memories are ones that will never fade."

Cash found his caution being overrun by curiosity. He watched his grandmother's head rest against the pillow, her faded eyes misty and knew he would not stop her words. "Paul took the secret to his grave. I thought Duncan would too. But Duncan was never Paul. To Paul, family was everything. But to Duncan—"

"You're talking about Grandfather Paul?" Cash asked.

Ann looked at Cash patiently. "Of course, child. Only the three of us knew. All these years. Until Duncan—"

"Until Duncan what?" Cash asked, his excitement growing.

She sighed. "Duncan called me the Sunday afternoon before his death to say he was making a clean breast of it all. Said he was telling the people who might be hurt so that they could prepare themselves before he went to the authorities."

"You're talking about the Wahl baby kidnapping?" Cash asked.

Ann blinked, a little surprised. "You know?"

"Only that Duncan was involved somehow."

Ann sighed into her pillow. "When the Reno police came out to question Paul and me, everyone was drawn to the excitement, soaked it up like a thirsty cactus swelling with ground water. Talked behind our backs. Some even had the nerve to say it right to our face."

"Say what?" Cash asked.

"That Freddie did it, of course. That the sheriff wanted him and when they found him they were going to string him up."

Cash frowned. "Freddie?"

"My brother Fred, child."

Cash felt a hollowness expanding in his gut. "Fred Koske was your brother?"

Ann Tintori nodded. "Koske was my maiden name. My two older brothers had gone to California when the depression hit, to try to find work, but my younger brother, Fred, stayed in Nevada because there was an opening in the silver mines. Except one day he couldn't get work any longer. That's when he came to Contention to hide out in a back room of the boardinghouse Paul and I were running and to plan his revenge on Evan Wahl."

Cash licked dry lips. "He told you this?"

Ann shook her head. "Not at first. Duncan's brother, Edward, had lost his job a few weeks before. He and his pregnant wife were living at Duncan's house on the outskirts of town. Duncan was back east involved in a lengthy court case. He had taken Bonanza and gone there purposely trying to forget Elisabeth and Edward's betrayal. Maybe if I hadn't convinced him to go he might have—"

"He might have?" Cash prompted when Ann hesitated.

She sighed as though the weight of the words was very heavy. "Stopped them from taking the child."

Cash passed a hand over his eyes. "Then it was Fred Koske and Edward Van Epp who kidnapped the Wahl child?"

Ann nodded, her voice very sad. "Fred showed her to me as though she were some prize he had won. When Paul and I asked him who she was, he just kept grinning at us and saying he had found her and that there was a reward for her return. Then he told me he'd be at Duncan's place with the child and I was to say he had gone to California a week before to join his older brothers if anyone asked."

"You didn't know the baby was kidnapped?"

"No, dear. Not until a few days later when the story broke in the papers. The moment I saw the headlines I knew. Paul and I rode out to Duncan's ranch together and begged them to turn themselves in and return the child, but Fred kept insisting that now that they had the ransom, they had to hold on to the child until they knew they were in the clear. Elisabeth was scared to death, holding the Wahl baby and shaking like a leaf. Paul and I knew that whatever happened now, we were all involved and would suffer. I telegraphed Duncan to come home immediately."

"What were you expecting Duncan to do?" Cash asked.

"He was a lawyer. I thought he might be able to plead with the Wahl family not to press charges if the baby and the money were returned. I thought he could talk some sense into Edward and Fred."

Cash watched the sad lines etch new years into his grandmother's already well-lined face. "It didn't happen that way, did it?"

Ann shuddered. "No, it was too late. The next day we read in the newspaper that the nurse had died. That's when the police came to ask about Freddie and we were so frightened, we just lied like he told us to. I was so ashamed."

Cash stroked Ann's trembling hands as she continued.

"The next days and nights are only a blur. A couple and their baby traveling from the east to California stopped to rent a room. All three of them were sick. The doctor panicked the whole town when he diagnosed them as having smallpox. He quarantined them, closing down our boardinghouse. We became isolated.

"It was almost a blessing because we finally stopped hearing about the kidnapping. Since I had already been exposed, my days became an endless succession of nursing those poor sick people. As their fevers got worse, even the doctor stopped visiting, his fear of contagion convincing him there was no good he could do.

"I suppose I should have been scared, too, particularly after the woman and her husband died and I had only the crying baby to care for. But I remember thinking it mattered little whether I caught the pox. We were doomed. Paul, Freddie, Edward, Elisabeth and I were all accomplices to murder."

Ann stopped and Cash poured her a glass of water, holding the straw to her parched, colorless lips and she sipped.

"Granny? What happened?"

She sighed heavily. "It all came to a head that night the couple's baby finally succumbed to the pox and lay quiet in my arms. I was so weary, I just held her quiet little form as though I expected her to begin crying again any minute. Then I heard Elisabeth's frantic pounding on the back door of the house.

"She had run the six miles from Duncan's place. Seven months pregnant and with a crying baby in her arms, she had braved the cold desert night and smallpox to try to save the child. 'Fred wants to kill the baby,' she told me."

Cash's nerves felt like ants fleeing from a roaring fire. Knowing the newspaper reports of Wahl's dead baby girl, he dreaded what was to come. But as afraid as he was to listen further, he was more afraid not to. Ann continued.

"Elisabeth sat next to the kitchen stove where she and the baby would be warm. Paul brought some blankets and sat beside her as she told us of my brother's insistence that the child had to die because she was the only evidence tying them to the kidnapping. While Edward and Freddie argued, Elisabeth had slipped out and come to us in the hope that we could help.

"She had no sooner told us the story when Freddie was at the back door screaming to be let in. We were all shocked into immobility for a moment until I looked down at the dead child I still carried and over at the live child in Elisabeth's arms. I remember thinking only that Freddie wanted a dead child and if I could give him one, maybe he'd go away. Quickly I snatched the Wahl baby blanket and wrapped it around the child that had died of smallpox.

"Paul understood at once. He took the Wahl baby and went upstairs with her while Elisabeth and I answered Freddie's pounding. I told him the child had died from exposure to the cold while Elisabeth tried to carry it to safety. I thrust it at him and pushed him out the door, yelling that I never wanted to see him again.

"It was a long, frightening night as we lay awake, fearing Fred might come back. At dawn, an injured Edward arrived. Fred had broken his leg when they had argued over killing the child. Edward had spent all night crawling along the ground trying to make it into town to our house to stop my brother."

Cash leaned forward. "Edward wanted to save the child?"

Ann nodded. "We told him about the switch of babies, and he was glad. Paul and I agreed to keep the Wahl baby, planning to pass it off as the smallpox infant until Fred was safely on his way to California. Then we were going to return the Wahl baby to her parents anonymously and bury an empty coffin for the smallpox child.

"We didn't know it then, but Fred took the dead child we had given him and buried it in the same park where the Wahl baby had been snatched. He meant for her to be found so that everyone would stop looking for the child. Only while he was burying her, he noticed the smallpox marks on her body and began to get suspicious.

"He returned that night to threaten to kill us all for the deception. Edward jumped him while Paul grabbed Elisabeth and the baby and hurried them into the buckboard trying to get away. I stayed behind, believing that Fred would not kill Edward or me despite what he said. I was only half-right."

Cash watched the tears wet Ann's white cheeks as her sad, little voice droned on. "It was a terrible fight. Their hands and faces were covered in blood. Normally, Edward could have taken my brother, but his bad leg handicapped him. Finally, they fell down the stairs into the wine cellar. Fred overpowered him there, forcing Edward to kneel down in front of him with his hands clasped behind his neck. Then he shot him through the head.

"Even while I watched it, I couldn't believe my brother was committing cold-blooded murder. Then he looked up at me with remorseless, soulless eyes, and told me to get out of my way."

Ann sat with the horror shining through her eyes and Cash felt a cold chill up his spine. She continued in an empty voice. "Paul had driven Elisabeth and the baby back to Duncan's place. I knew Fred would follow and kill them all, and I ran out and saddled up a horse to follow. He probably would have killed me, too, if Duncan and Bonanza hadn't arrived home just then."

"Duncan was there?" Cash said in surprise.

Ann nodded. "He had come home in response to my telegram. He found Fred pointing a gun at Paul and Elisabeth. He didn't know what was going on, but he could see Elisabeth being threatened and that was enough. He yelled at Fred and my brother turned and fired.

"Bonanza jumped at Fred. He was the one who caught the bullet. It gave Duncan time to pick up a rock from a shelf and strike Fred with it. The blow from the hard, glassy stone felled Fred. It must have killed him instantly because he never moved again. Neither did Bonanza."

His grandmother's words drew the scene clearly before Cash's eyes. And clear, too, was the meaning of the new grave in Duncan's pet cemetery. He had finally given an honored burial to his valiant companion who sixty years before had saved his life.

Ann's voice was now ghostlike. "Despite the death of his brother and his beloved pet, it was Duncan who recovered his wits to rally the tragic remnants of our family.

"He directed Paul and me to take the Wahl child back to town and continue to treat her as the smallpox baby. He asked Paul to bury Edward where he had fallen in the cellar. He told us he would take care of burying Fred and getting rid of his gun."

Cash leaned forward toward his grandmother. "Is that why you became so upset when Ms. Chase told you her skeleton had been dug up from the cellar of an old boardinghouse in Contention? Is that when you realized it was Edward Van Epp I, the man Paul had buried there sixty years before?"

Ann nodded. "In that one moment, I saw again Freddie putting that bullet through Edward's head and the awful look in his soulless eyes as he did it."

Cash nodded. "What happened to the Wahl baby?"

Ann's thin chest heaved. "Duncan's plan was to keep her only long enough to figure out a way to get her to her father, but we misjudged the returning courage of Contention's doctor. After burying the mother, he began to have hope for the baby's survival and came in person to see how she was doing. Before I could stop him, he examined her and proclaimed she had miraculously survived the smallpox and would live.

"Now that the doctor had proclaimed her healthy, we could no longer just return her to Wahl and bury an empty coffin. If we had claimed she had gotten ill again and died, he would have insisted on examining the child. To at least keep her in my custody, I immediately applied to adopt her. We were all fast becoming caught in a net that closed in ever tighter and tighter.

"Two months later, Elisabeth died giving birth to Edward II. Then the little girl's body Fred had buried at the edge of the park was found. Every newspaper's front page was plastered with a grisly picture of the pink bundle pulled out of the ground.

"Duncan, Paul and I were shocked. It was the first indication we had of what Freddie had done with the body of the little smallpox baby. Then, when everyone assumed the badly decomposed body was that of the Wahl baby, we didn't know what to do. Feeling was running so high, one man was even beaten in a local bar because he had spoken against Evan Wahl. It was then that we knew that if we tried to return the Wahl baby girl, we would all go to prison or worse. Our previous silence had made us guilty."

"So you never spoke up?" Cash asked.

Ann nodded. "We couldn't, dear. And soon Paul and I found a fulfilling happiness in raising my lovely baby girl. Duncan poured all his time and heart into Elisabeth's son and as the years passed, I sometimes told myself that the kidnapping was all a dream and that little Grace was my natural child."

"Grace?" Cash said. "But Grace was my mother's name."

Ann's eyes started to fill as she stared at Cash. "Yes, dear. Your mother was Evan Wahl's daughter."

Cash was dumbfounded. "I'm Evan Wahl's grandson?"

Ann's watery eyes blinked. "When I saw you two arguing at Duncan's will reading, I knew Duncan was right. Wahl had been robbed of his daughter. To continue to deny you both the knowledge of your true relationship was cruel and unjust. Forgive me, child."

It took several minutes for Cash to collect himself after hearing the extraordinary news of his ancestry. He just sat next to Ann's hospital bed, white and stiff from shock.

"Dear, please, you must forgive me!"

Cash looked up to see the pain in Ann Tintori's eyes and quickly clasped her cool little hands in his large warm ones, angry at himself for allowing the news to blind him to how Ann must be feeling. He smiled into her worried eyes. "You saved my mother's life and treated me with love. There's nothing to forgive. There is much to thank you for, and as far as I'm concerned, you'll always be my grandmother."

He saw then the relief in her eyes and felt the returning pressure in her hands. "I couldn't have loved my own flesh more than I did your mother and you. You know that, don't you?"

"Yes, I know. When you fell down those stairs and I thought you were dead, Granny, I—"

Cash stopped as Ann's fingers clawed at his hands. "Fell? Child, I didn't fall. I thought you knew. I was standing there waiting for you when that awful man deliberately pushed me down those stairs."

The shock of Ann's words shot up Cash's spine like a knife. His hands grasped her thin arms. "Pushed? Granny, what awful man?"

Ann Tintori blinked at Cash. "Why, Edward Van Epp of course."

Chapter Sixteen

Carrie watched Edward push aside the rug and remove the nails from the trapdoor in the floorboard of Duncan's desert home. As he started down the wooden stairs leading below he paused to look back at her.

"You're not going to see much from up there."

Carrie hesitated. "It looks pretty dark."

"Don't worry. There's a cord to pull for the light just to the right down here a step or two."

"There is? How do you know that, Edward?"

"I remember it from when I was a kid. Here, see?"

Edward switched on the light, proving the excellence of his memory. His pulling of the cord resulted in the dangling, naked light bulb swaying back and forth above the cellar's dirt floor.

As she descended into the deep cellar, Carrie immediately noticed the wood beams shoring up a large rectangular hole on one wall leading into a narrow, underground passage. Excitement laced her voice as she hurried to its entrance. "It's a mine!"

"Brilliant deduction," Edward's disdainful voice said from behind her. "But don't get too excited. The equipment is falling apart and you'll find no silver in its black walls."

Carrie ignored him as she fingered the wheel barrel and other rusted silver mining remnants sitting outside of the abandoned structure. A glint from the dark earth floor had her bending down to pick up a thin strip of light metal. She recognized the feel between her fingers.

"What have you got there?" Edward asked.

Carrie turned and raised her palm toward him. "It's a small sliver of extracted silver like the ones I found on Duncan's figurines. Now I know where he got them. I never realized the house had been built over the entrance to this old mine. These slivers must be all that's left from the mining your grandparents or great-grandparents did so many years ago."

Edward let the shiny strip fall through his fingers to the dirt floor. Carrie was surprised at the sudden contempt in his voice. "They were fools. My great-great-grandfather was the older son. If he had stayed in Europe one-hundred-and-thirty years ago, he would have inherited lands and a baron's title. Instead he dragged his family across an ocean and a continent just to end up in this dark, stinking hole."

Carrie looked over at Edward's face, full of sharp, angry shadows beneath the swinging naked bulb. "I didn't know that about your ancestors, Edward."

His laugh was mirthless. He was looking at her strangely and his tone was openly sarcastic. "But you know about my grandfather, don't you? Duncan didn't even have to tell you. Just from a few old bones, you figured it all out on your own."

It was then that Edward pulled out the gun and a chilling wind of danger swirled out of the darkness to surround Carrie. Too late the truth became plain. "My God, Duncan did tell you!"

Edward's half smile slithered on his lips like a snake. "Oh, yes. Poor Gene begged and pleaded with him to just shut up about the whole thing. But no. The old man was adamant about admitting his cover-up for a kidnapping our grandfather helped commit. Told us about burying Koske and hiding the ransom money. That was when Gene passed out drunk. I put him in the back of my car to sleep it off and filched the high blood pressure pills out of his jacket pocket."

Carrie found her lips were very dry. She knew what was coming, yet she still had to ask. "*You* killed Duncan?"

No trace of Edward's earlier sarcasm remained. His voice was even and controlled.

"Oh, yes. I just walked into the bathroom and dumped Gene's pills and the other pills I had noticed earlier in the medicine chest, into one of Duncan's glasses. Then I filled the glass with some of Gene's cheap whiskey and took it to Duncan. I even poured one for myself and joined him in a toast to truth. I waited until he drank it all. Before he passed out he told me about returning most of the original ransom money to Wahl. Even told me he had the rest of the money in the cellar. Didn't tell me about the three hundred dollars of it he had given to you, however. Got to admit, that came as an unwelcome surprise."

He was coldly admitting to murder, with neither remorse nor pity. The shock was like a whirlpool swallowing up Carrie's thoughts. She fought to clear her mind, to understand. "You got the rest of the money after you killed Duncan?"

"That night. Only real problem came when Duncan had passed out and I went to get the money. That's when the damn dog stood in my way at the trapdoor and started growling. Had to show it who was boss and kick the yapping mutt outside. By the way, there *was* exactly two thousand, eight hundred and eight dollars left. Chicken feed compared to what I'll be worth soon. I burned it."

Through a rising well of horror and disbelief, Carrie pushed her question. "Edward, how could you do it?"

He shrugged. "How could I do anything else? Do you know what would have happened to my marriage plans to Margaret if it became known that my grandfather was one of the kidnappers of the Wahl baby?"

Carrie couldn't believe her ears. "Edward, that was sixty years ago and your grandfather, not you!"

He snickered. "You're pretty damn naive. The Preston family is the nearest thing Reno has to royalty. Appearances are everything to them. How do you think I learned about my great-great-grandfather and his linkage to a baron's title? Margaret's father had my complete lineage checked out when I was first introduced to him.''

"But such ideas are archaic. In this day and age—''

"In this day and age, birth and position are just as important as they've always been. Wake up, toots. Just look at the way we Americans, who supposedly fought to overthrow the rule of privilege through birth, fawn all over Charles and Di. Do you think the Prestons would have let my engagement to their daughter continue if Duncan had made his confession?''

"But you weren't at fault.''

"Still don't get it, do you? If my grandfather had murdered a miner, that might have been forgiven. But Evan Wahl has always been prominent in this state. When his child was grabbed, all the wealthy cringed. They knew it could have happened to any one of them. Crimes against the privileged are never forgiven. Margaret's grandfather was the state senator who called for the death penalty for the perpetrators and any who aided them.''

"But to go as far as killing Duncan—'' Carrie began.

"Oh, I went a lot further than that. I pushed the old lady down the stairs when she started to get too talkative.''

"Ann Tintori? You *pushed* her?''

Edward smiled his sardonic half smile. "I was also the one who pushed Gene off that ledge. He was getting to be a blabbermouth, too. When I saw Gene following you and McKendry, I knew I'd best tag along. Of course it was a bit of an impromptu idea to push him off the ledge, but I couldn't let him go on about the kidnapping and give you any more details. As it was, his death from the fall was a lucky break, no pun intended.''

He's heartless, soulless, Carrie thought. *I must keep him talking while I think of how to get away.* She wet her dry lips.

"I don't understand, Edward. If you pushed Gene, why did Hal Sawyer run from the scene?''

"Now that was an unlucky break. He must have noticed something going on and came over to take a look. Saw me push Gene. I was armed. He wasn't. When he took off, naturally I had to follow. What McKendry didn't see because he went back to take care of you was my Corvette going after Hal Sawyer's truck. I caught up with him and forced him off the freeway at gunpoint. I knocked him unconscious and set a fuse to ignite his gas tank. He obliged me by having a full one. Just as you obliged me by agreeing to this little treasure hunt.''

Edward had leveled the gun at her chest. As though it were trying to escape, she could feel her heart pounding against her ribs. "If you shoot me, Edward, you'll be caught."

He was walking past her toward the stairs as the blood beat like a drum in her ears. "I'm not going to shoot you. You're going to get caught in the basement of your new home when it catches on fire. Just another tragic accident."

Now Carrie understood why Edward had lured her to Duncan's place. From the moment she had told him she had identified the bones of his grandfather, he had decided she, too, must die.

A furious anger licked up her spine against this heartless man who killed without conscience. It proved a useful emotion for a change. It cleared her fear and prepared her for fight. He was only a few feet away. She could tell from his smug look he wasn't expecting an attack.

With a sudden gigantic leap, Carrie pounced at Edward. As she anticipated, he was so surprised by the unexpected move that she succeeded in knocking the gun from his hand and shoving him backward onto the cellar's dirt floor. She rolled over quickly, scrambling to her feet and bolting for the stairs, her accumulated adrenaline giving her an amazing speed. She flew up the stairs and leaped onto the floor, slamming the trapdoor closed behind her.

Her eyes darted to the couch. Before she could think the thought, she was dragging the edge of the couch over and setting it on top of the trapdoor. She could hear Edward swearing loudly beneath the boards as he pounded trying to get out. Then suddenly she heard a loud explosion and a bullet whizzed by her ear. He was shooting at her from the cellar!

She jumped back just as another hole was made by a whizzing bullet right in front of her. She flew across the room to the phone, her finger jerking around the old-fashioned dial to complete the nine.

However another whizzing bullet coming through the floor right next to her left shoe caused her to cry out in alarm, drop the receiver and race for the door. He had followed the sounds of her steps to find her again.

She sprinted down the stairs and ran directly for the Jeep. She yanked open the door, but when she reached for her shoulder bag to get her keys, it wasn't there. Only then did she realize that she must have dropped it on the cellar floor when she had jumped Edward. She was stranded. Then she heard the sound of the splintering wood. She knew what it meant. Edward was breaking out of the cellar.

Desperately she looked for a place to hide. There wasn't any. She could run to the highway in hopes that someone would come by, but it wasn't well traveled. And even if a car did come along, it might not stop. Then a final option presented itself and she grabbed it. She turned toward the two-mile run to the foothills and kicked up her heels. If she could make it, she could lose Edward there.

She had always tried to keep fit, jogging and taking the stairs whenever possible. Now she was blessing every mile and stair she had logged, which was fueling the stamina to make this sprint for her life across the high desert.

Her footfalls on the parched earth matched the rhythm of the blood beating in her ears. She pressed her muscles to their limit, sucking in as much air as her lungs would take. The setting sun to her right painted a glorious purple landscape. However, she was oblivious to all but the need to press for more speed as the foothills loomed ever larger and larger.

A plane roared overhead, but it might just have been the sound of her heart. Her eyes were wide open, and yet she saw little. Or maybe she saw everything, but nothing registered in her frantic flight except the fact of that flight. Several times she fought the desire to look back. She couldn't afford to break her stride. All she could afford to do was run.

And run she did. She lost track of real time. Seconds became synonymous with the lifting of each knee, the brief touch of each foot with the ground, the manufactured breeze that soaked up the perspiration pouring off her face. She was hot, she was frightened and she was tiring.

In her mind's eye she could see Edward smashing through the wood floor, carefully checking every room in the house, gun drawn and ready. And when he did not find her, he would start looking outside. And then he would run up to the highway expecting her to have gone that way to flag down a car. Then it would come to him. The foothills. And he would head back to get his Corvette and—

From behind her came the throaty roar of a car engine shattering the thin desert air.

Pure fright spurred her the last frantic steps to the bottom of the foothills and carried her protesting leg muscles through the rocks to the enormous boulders dotting the sides of the hills. She zigzagged through them, dragging her body to the leeward side of one. She fell exhausted behind its comforting bulk, pulling her knees up as close to her body as her fading strength would allow.

Her eyes closed as her muscles melted into total collapse. For several moments, she heard nothing but the pounding of her heart in her ears and the straining wheeze of her lungs, desperately sucking up the air of which they had been deprived. Gradually the deep pain in her chest eased.

It was then she heard the footsteps on the rocks below, the shuffle of the soles scraping the rock edges, dislodging looser pebbles down the face. He was searching for her.

She lay very still as the sounds came closer. They stopped just on the other side of the rock behind where she lay. She closed her eyes in terror as she heard his heavy breaths of exertion. Then ever so slowly she listened to the light footsteps moving away. She slowly exhaled the breath that she held, not daring to move until the last echoes of his footfalls had ceased.

Then she was up on her feet and running in the other direction up the hill as quickly and silently as she could. She knew her salvation meant getting as far away from Edward and his gun as she could and eventually losing him in the canyons on the other side.

If she could make it over the top and down into the valley, she knew she would have a better chance of hiding. Thoughts of getting away and getting safe were all she entertained.

It was a steep climb. She ignored the protests of her muscles as she crawled up the rocky slope. Just as the sun stretched its last beams of the day, she made the top. She looked down the other side at the piñon pines below and felt success within her reach. Then suddenly, out of the corner of her eye, she saw the dark figure climbing, too, probably on a course parallel to hers, and now he had turned in her direction.

It was all happening too fast for Carrie to fully react, even to feel the fear. The gun was rising; her body was turning.

Before the dreadful cracking sound of the gun's discharge reached her ears, she felt the bullet burning into her thigh and knew she was falling. As her shoulder hit the hard desert floor and she began to tumble down the hillside, panic and pain both caught up with her. But it was the panic that took over when she realized she couldn't stop falling.

Desperately, she tried to wrap her arms around her head to protect herself from the blows, but the downward momentum was too strong. Her arms flailed about her as she rolled across the sharp rocks, bumped into the shrubby tree branches, tumbling, crashing against the scratchy brush. And still she fell.

As though in the center of a beaten drum, the blows kept coming. She was utterly helpless at stopping the battering of her body, the bruising and scraping of her skin, the ripping and tearing of her clothes. She couldn't even control her vocal cords to expel the scream that constricted her throat.

Toward the end, she must have blacked out, from the terror, from the pain, or maybe from a particularly sharp blow to her head. Whatever did it, the next thing she knew, she was awakening as though she had been asleep.

The first thing she noticed was that her body was still—wonderfully, gratefully, finally still. Then the pain erupted.

It was everywhere and it was horrendous. She couldn't believe she could hurt so much and still be alive to feel it. Even the uncontrolled tears that wet her cheeks stung. She choked on a sob and forced her eyes open.

Once her vision focused through the haze of pain, she realized in some awe that she was on the floor of the canyon, in a small clearing, lying slightly upright against a large boulder that must have broken the final few feet of her fall.

She tried to move, but her body only responded with more pain. The burning and throbbing of her thigh wound was excruciating. Carefully, inch by inch, she slowly rolled her neck in the direction of the canyon face she had fallen down. It had to be close to four hundred feet and somehow, miraculously, she had survived. Despite all the pain wracking her poor, beaten body, she felt a certain wonder at it all.

Then wonder, pain, everything vanished as in shock she heard the broken bush and then saw the dark figure enter the clearing. He walked till he reached its center, a cruel, half smile lifting the side of his mouth as he stopped to survey her predicament. A sinking, sick fright froze her body and mind. He had followed her down and she was helpless to escape him.

"My, my. Still alive?" Edward's mocking voice asked, as he leaned back on his heels. "You are a tough one to kill. But no matter. I am known for my thoroughness."

He was leisurely raising the gun to point at her chest again and Carrie's heart was pounding so loudly and she was trembling so badly that the ground moved beneath her. She wondered why Edward even thought he had to shoot her. She was about to shake herself to death.

But no! Suddenly she knew it wasn't just her. The pounding expanded to deafening proportions as the distinct thunder of many hoofbeats rose to fill and crack the air. And then they charged the clearing, a glorious collage of wild mustangs, with blazing eyes and glistening flanks, painted and bay, sorrel and black and leading them all, a huge mottled-gray stallion.

He swallowed the ground with fire and rage, his speed fanning his silver mane and tail like singed wings. Edward had turned at his approach, but he must have known it was already too late. His scream died stillborn as the stallion's powerful bulk knocked him to the ground, right into the path of the trampling, deadly hoofs of the runaway herd.

Carrie's breath caught in her throat as the magnificent gray stallion flashed by, mere inches from where she lay beside the rock, leading his stampede of the wild and the swift into the desert skies of sunset.

She closed her eyes then as their kicked up desert dust swirled over her body in a bountiful benediction, making her as one with the landscape, fading her into part of the rock she lay against.

Then quiet. Soft, soundless peace. And unconsciousness.

THE NEXT THING SHE KNEW something wet and rough was licking her face and she opened her eyes to see Bonanza's little white head bobbing in front of her face. His soft whine reached her ears through the freezing night breeze. She shivered, wanting to lift her hand to pat his head, or her voice to give him a greeting, but the cold and pain prohibited everything.

Then she felt warm, strong arms picking her up and a wonderful, deep familiar voice near her ear. "I'm here, darling. Hang on. I've got you. Can you hear me?" Cash asked.

Her heart answered him. It called out to him in love and longing. However, the pain wracking through her body produced only a soft moan. She could feel the unconsciousness sweeping in and she battled it, but it was too strong. Her last thought before the blackness overcame her again was that she must not die before she told him how much she loved him.

SHE WOKE to bright, blinding lights. She tried to move her arms and found them hooked up to tubes. Momentarily stripped of a familiar environment, she felt an instant fear of dreadful apprehension. Then a dull, throbbing ache in her left thigh pricked her memory and the recent events flooded through.

They all coalesced into one. Cash. Had his voice and the feel of his arms around her been imagined?

A bright and cheery nurse leaned over her bed to tell her the doctor would be along soon. Then her white uniform swished out the door. It made Carrie all the more surprised and relieved when the door opened a moment later and she saw it was Cash's face and not some impersonal doctor's. He came directly to her side, gently taking a hold of her hand. She felt its steady warmth and an unbidden tear formed in her eye.

He saw it and reached another hand to gently caress her forehead. "Are you in much pain, sweetheart?"

She sighed into a smile. "No. I'm just so happy to see you."

He sat beside her then, clasping her cool hand firmly within his warm ones, a relieved smile on his tired, unshaven face.

"How did you find me?" she asked.

"Bonanza led me to you. I'm sorry I arrived so late, but the desert house was the last place I looked. When I found your Jeep, the numerous bullet holes, the floor torn up, your shoulder bag on the cellar floor, I thought..."

He stopped and swallowed, and Carrie could see the strain and worry liquefying in the golden brown of his eyes.

"Carrie, I'm so sorry I tried to force you—"

Her free hand reached out to touch the rough stubble on his chin then moved over to rest against his lips, halting the apology that was forming on them. A lump of love expanded inside her chest, love she had feared she might never get the chance to tell him about. It ached to be out.

"I love you, Cash. I know you would never do anything to hurt me."

He sighed, his relieved smile big, warm, full-hearted. She felt it light up her life as well as the room around her. He captured her hand within both of his. "I love you, Carrie."

He had gone on to say more, but Carrie hadn't heard. A soft blanket of unconsciousness had descended over her again. Only this time she hadn't fought it because her heart was at peace. Now there was time to mend.

THE NEXT DAY CARRIE sat up as the doctor came to check her over and pronounced her battered, bruised, but already beginning to heal.

"You're very lucky," he said.

She felt very lucky when she saw Cash come through the door a moment later. Lucky and loved and very happy. He stayed with her the rest of the day and they shared their stories of Edward Van Epp and Ann Tintori. Carrie felt overwhelmed by it all.

"Cash, this is unbelievable. To find out that it was *your* mother who was kidnapped! That Evan Wahl is *your* grandfather!"

He sat near the edge of her pillow and put his arm around her. "Amazing isn't it? To think that all those records we uncovered were about my family. I'm thankful Ann won't be prosecuted. Tom and his superiors decided she had done more good than harm."

"Did you ever find out what was in that missing letter?"

"Yes. Eileen Packer finally admitted to Wahl that Duncan told her Wahl's natural daughter had not died in the kidnapping and that he had a grandson. Duncan didn't say who it was, only that he was going to tell all to Wahl. Later, when Eileen thought about the implications, she wrote Duncan offering him money to keep quiet. She thought her son's inheritance would be jeopardized. Tom found the letter at Sawyer's place."

"Did Sawyer read it?" Carrie asked.

Cash shook his head. "It was unopened. Looks like what Edward told you was true. Hal Sawyer just showed up at the wrong place and time. He paid dearly for being nosy."

Carrie looked up at Cash's face. "How do you feel about Wahl being your grandfather?"

"I'm a bit numb. I think Wahl is, too. But it feels kind of nice, Carrie. When Tom told him the true story of his baby's kidnapping, he looked at me and there were tears in his eyes. Then the gruff old son of a gun fractured my ribs in a bear hug. I like him, Carrie. I like him a lot."

She saw the moisture collecting in his eyes and put her head on his shoulder. "Me, too."

He nuzzled her neck, enjoying her special scent, the feel of her safe in his arms. "Good enough to name our first son Evan?"

She looked up, tracing her finger along his jaw and smiled her answer to the real question in his words. "As long as he's blessed with your magnificent mandible."

Cash laughed as he leaned over to kiss her gently, lovingly.

"We're going to have a great marriage. We're both the kind of people who will work hard at making it so. God, Carrie, I'm so happy I met you."

She lay back in his arms again and sighed. "Do you think Duncan ever thought about our getting together, Cash? Do you suppose that's why he arranged for us to have joint custody of Bonanza?"

Cash rocked her gently. "I wouldn't be at all surprised. He always talked about you in mysterious terms, knowing it would pique my curiosity."

"And now that there's no more mystery?" Carrie asked.

He smiled as his arms gently hugged her to him. "You're joking, of course. You grow into more of an exciting mystery every moment I know you. That's why I plan to take a lifetime to unravel all your delicious twists and turns."

As Carrie smiled happily at Cash's words, her mind wandered to shadows of other thoughts and feelings, as yet unsaid, born in that desert clearing where Edward Van Epp III had met his death and where Carrie had been delivered from hers.

Her voice sounded strange to her ears as she expressed those thoughts. "It was the wild mustang stallion that saved me, Cash. The one from Duncan's figurine."

"Yes. You told me."

She licked her lips, finding she had to give the breath of life to her thoughts by evolving them into sound and substance. "The old Indian legend said if the wild stallion raced his soul into the next world and joined with it, they would meld into one, immortal."

He held her to him more tightly. "Yes, Carrie, I know."

"Cash, do you suppose Duncan and the stallion..."

He shook his head. "Who can know for sure, darling? Logic tells us it was just coincidence that the wild herd chose that moment to pass through the clearing. And if it wasn't just coincidence, if... Well, the only thing that really matters is that you're alive and in my arms and we now have a life together. A life we'll live to the fullest."

He leaned over to kiss her then, a soft, satisfying kiss. Carrie melted into his arms, feeling more in control with the strength of his love than she had ever imagined and looking forward to a future she had once only glimpsed in the most searching of her dreams.

AND ON TOP of a high canyon ledge, above the ghost town of Contention, the wild, mottled-gray stallion rose high on its hind legs, his forelegs pawing, striking out in freedom as the wind sung its eternal song through his silver mane and tail.

HARLEQUIN
PROUDLY PRESENTS
A DAZZLING NEW CONCEPT IN ROMANCE FICTION

One small town—twelve terrific love stories

Welcome to Tyler, Wisconsin—a town full of people
you'll enjoy getting to know, memorable friends and
unforgettable lovers, and a long-buried secret that
lurks beneath its serene surface....

JOIN US FOR A YEAR IN THE LIFE OF TYLER

Each book set in Tyler is a self-contained love story;
together, the twelve novels stitch the fabric of a
community.

LOSE YOUR HEART TO TYLER!

The excitement begins in March 1992, with
WHIRLWIND, by Nancy Martin. When lively, brash
Liza Baron arrives home unexpectedly, she moves
into the old family lodge, where the silent and
mysterious Cliff Forrester has been living in seclusion
for years....

WATCH FOR ALL TWELVE BOOKS
OF THE TYLER SERIES
Available wherever Harlequin books are sold

Back by Popular Demand

Janet Dailey
Americana

A romantic tour of America through fifty favorite
Harlequin Presents, each set in a different state
researched by Janet and her husband, Bill. A journey
of a lifetime in one cherished collection.

In January, don't miss the exciting states featured in:

Title #23   **MINNESOTA**
            Giant of Mesabi

    #24   **MISSISSIPPI**
            A Tradition of Pride

Available wherever
Harlequin books are sold.

JD-JAN

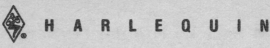